The Temporal Element:
Time-Travel Adventures,
Past, Present, & Future!

Edited by
Martin T. Ingham

Published by

Martinus
PUBLISHING

www.martinus.us

First Edition: April 2013

A voyage like no other...

Since the dawn of the modern era, mankind has dreamed about the possibility of traversing the bounds of linear time, to explore the dark mysteries of pre-history or seek out the wild possibilities of the far future in person. This collection of stories does the next best thing, allowing readers to dream of the possibilities of such a theoretical trip.

The Temporal Element contains stories all about traveling through time, and not in the natural way. From spell-casting wizards, to mad scientists, and government-sanctioned time agencies, here you will find an exceptional selection of stories about people traveling beyond their native time. Explore ancient history, the distant future, and everywhere in between.

This anthology is dedicated to all those who seek to unlock the secret of time travel, and especially to the first individual to traverse the boundaries of linear time, whoever that may be.

-Martin T. Ingham
December 31, 2012

TABLE OF CONTENTS:

A Thursday Night at Doctor What's Time and Relative Dimensional Space Bar and Grill
By Bruno Lombardi

"Who elsc has killed Hitler?"

I looked up from cleaning a beer glass at the sound of that question—and then groaned inwardly when I realized who had said it.

Of *course* it would be Wells who would say that. Leave it to him to always be the one to make my life difficult.

I took a quick look around, taking in the entire room in one glance—every good bartender learns real quick how to scope out his entire bar using just one quick glance—and looking for any trouble.

For once, there wasn't.

Soames was at a table with Rogers, comparing scars again. Stargard was doing his usual *uber*-Poland spiel/rant to whoever would listen to him, this time a bored looking guy in a monk costume. Taylor sat by himself, nursing a large scotch. Even from here, I could hear him mumbling to himself about how 'those maniacs blew it up' and how they should all 'be damned to hell.' Hey, at least he wasn't going on about the

'Omega virus' or whatever the hell he was calling it, so I'm cutting him some slack tonight. Tony and Doug—looking quite dashing in their clothes (green turtleneck and grey slacks for Tony; a conservative Norfolk suit for Doug)—were babbling on about the Titanic *again*, this time to the new guy, Frank Parker. Parker wasn't paying much attention to them, mainly because he was ogling that cute girl, Cameron. Emmett was sitting alone in a corner of the counter, still slowly sipping his first—and only—shot of whiskey of the night. Emmett's a nice guy, but he really can't hold his liquor and he knows it.

All in all, just a normal Thursday night in Doctor What's Time and Relative Dimensional Space Bar and Grill, the universe's only time-traveler's bar.

* * *

As you may have guessed, I'm not just the barkeep—I also own the place. Have done so for just under ten years (personal time frame), or 4,000,000,000,000,000,000,000,001 years (universe time frame).

It's a pretty cool gig, all in all. Hours are great, although some of the actual minutes leave a *lot* to be desired. Mind you, that gets made up (for the most part) with all the cool stories and people, so it kind of evens out overall.

As for why I run this joint—hey, 'invisible hand' and all that jazz. You've got time travelers running around all over the space-time continuum; they're going to want to have a place to kick back, drink a few beers and hang out with old/new/future/past friends and fellow travelers. I got in on the 'ground floor,' so to speak, with opening night being three hours after the Big Bang.

Why the Big Bang? Simple; one of the very first thoughts that a time traveler has after they invent their time machine is *'Gosh- I can be the first person to actually witness the Big Bang—think of the scientific discoveries!'* The thing is, well, *everyone* in all of space and time has *exactly* the same thought.

Ever see those pictures of LA traffic jams? Yeah, that's what's waiting for you there. Freakin' Sardine City.

2

Just FYI.

I figured that, after being stuck in gridlock for a few hours, one will end up getting *mighty* thirsty. So off I went with my time machine/bar.

Had to get a new front door; the hordes practically *ripped* it off the hinges going through it to get to the beer. Within four hours of opening, I was already making a profit. Haven't looked back (or forward, as the case may be) since.

I move the place around a lot—it's always nice to see new scenery. Right 'now' we're in the year 2237 AD, Armstrong City, Luna.

Anyway...

"Who else has killed Hitler?" repeated Wells, this time a bit more loudly and clearer.

All around the bar, a few ears perked up.

I groaned.

I *hate* it when someone brings up that question.

"Well?" asked Wells.

A dozen hands shot up, more or less at the same time.

Well, there goes my quiet night...

Remember how I told you that one of the first things that a time traveler does after they invent their time machine is to go to the Big Bang? Well—guess what the second thing they come up with is. Yup, *'I can kill Hitler!'*

Why not? Makes sense, doesn't it? Stop WWII, prevent the Holocaust, save millions of people, alter the entire course of the Cold War, etcetera, etcetera, etcetera. You know the drill.

Unfortunately, it doesn't *quite* work that way. I should know—I tried it myself once. Didn't work then, won't work now. It *never* works—but that doesn't stop everyone from finding out the hard way.

Everyone has their own story—and in each and every case it blew up in their faces. Every. Single. Time.

Why is Hitler so impossible to kill? No idea. I've heard a million crazy theories explaining why—and trust me, some of them are *really* out there—but, quite honestly, I don't know which one is true or not. Don't care, to be honest.

Old-timers are smart enough to not even bother trying to do it at this point. But you still have all the newbies and n00bs and youngsters and Kool Kidz and all those other idiots trying anyway. And then we have to hear them all *whining...*

As for why I hate it when they start talking about it? Just watch...

"April 19, 1942," said this one guy—young dude in a red biker costume named Swann, I think. "Hitler was doing some tour of some factory. Figured that would be the perfect time to take him out."

I rolled my eyes. Yeah, like nobody ever thought of *that* one before. I shrugged my shoulders and started getting a few shots ready—I make a mean *Beam Me Up Scotty* and my *Mind Eraser* is listed as a WMD in 13th century Paris—and leaned back. People were going to need them in a minute.

"So, anyways," continued Swann, "I'm hiding in the rafters with a sniper rifle. I have an absolutely clean shot here. Absolutely clean! And just as I pull the trigger..." Swann paused, like he couldn't believe what he was about to say next. (I'm willing to bet a hundred dollars in the currency of any time period you choose that that's *exactly* what was going through his mind.)

Swann got it together, at least for a few seconds. "Stupid rat," he said, shaking his head in dismay.

"Rat?" called out someone in the crowd.

"A *rat* drops right down on my arm, just as I pull the trigger!" screamed Swann. Most of the newbies in the crowd were staring at Swann with open mouths of shock and going '*Whoa, no way, dude!*' All the old-timers, on the other hand, were just nodding their heads and muttering, 'Yup, uh-huh.'

"So what happened next?" called someone else.

"I miss his head by a good five feet, that's what!" screamed Swann. "Next thing I know, half the LSSAH regiment is shooting at me and I barely jump out of there in time!" Swann ended with an expletive and shook his head with a loud sigh, then leaned his head down and started pounding it on the table. I nodded at the waitress and passed a tray of assorted shooters to her. With practiced ease, she rushed over and placed the tray in front of him. Swann stared at the tray for a moment, then shrugged his shoulders and started downing them, one after the other.

I added an extra twenty dollars to Swann's already impressive tab and started making another batch of shooters.

"1936, Berlin," said this cute looking middle-aged blonde woman by the name of Sapphire, speaking with a haughty English accent I couldn't quite place. "Opening ceremonies of the Olympic games. Took a bit of doing but managed to take the place of one of Leni Riefenstahl's camera crew. Plan was obvious; follow Hitler around and then, when the right moment shows up, blow him away with the gun secreted in the lens of the camera."

I smirked; you have *no* idea how many time-travelers were running around Berlin during the '36 games. How many, you ask? Let me put it this way; the *Olympiastadion* could seat 65,000 people when it was built. Take a guess how many time travelers there were in the crowd. Go ahead, guess.

Give up?

Everyone in the stadium on opening day was either a time traveler, a local working for a time traveler, or someone looking for a time traveler. *Everyone.*

Damn tourists.

Anyway…

"So I'm all lined up and I pull the trigger—and I *succeed!*" There were gasps of surprise and/or confusion from the crowd of newbies again. A couple of the old-timers just nodded their heads knowingly and muttered *'here it comes'* or *'wait for it'* or *'taking bets now, man;'* stuff like that.

I nodded my head as well. That's the *other* part of the sordid mess with killing Hitler.

"Wait—you actually *killed* him?!" exclaimed someone in the audience.

Sapphire just nodded her head and took a deep breath. "Yeah, I killed him. Unfortunate..." Here she paused to let out a very long sigh. "Unfortunately, the bullet went right through Hitler's head and hit Jessie Owens just as he was walking by!"

I rolled my eyes. Believe me, I can *totally* believe that

happening. Trust me, that ain't the silliest thing I've heard.

"Wait, Owens got killed *too*?!" yelled a different neophyte, stating the obvious.

Sapphire just nodded her head. "So now I have to go back and fix it so Owens stays away from Hitler when I shoot Hitler. But now there's two versions of me running around, so I have to be extra careful I don't cross my own timestream. So I convince Owens to take a different path, but unfortunately, now Jackie Robinson—who was in the stadium to see his brother compete—gets killed instead! So now I have to go back a *third* time to clean up the mess, and now a random spectator in the audience gets hit. Except that spectator is the ancestor of the woman who discovers cold fusion, so now I have to go back a *fourth* time..." At this point Sapphire just shook her head in frustration. "*Eighteen* times I went back, and each time somebody important got killed! Eventually—with so many alternates of myself running around—I just had to quit before I ripped the time-space continuum or something!" With a loud sigh, she collapsed into a chair.

I sent over a large scotch and added it to her tab.

Poor lady. I remained pretty blasé about it, but I knew how something like that could mess with someone. I really did sympathize with her.

You see, that's the other thing with trying to kill Hitler. Sometimes you actually succeed, but you screw up so badly that you have no choice but to go back and *save* Hitler from getting killed in the first place. Yeah, I know, major bummer, but there you go. Nobody said time travel was easy.

People were starting to get bummed out. That's both a good thing and a bad thing in the bar business.

Let's be honest; bartenders *love* it when their customers come in all depressed. Depressed customers sit quietly in a corner and drink until they're plastered or broke; either way, we like that. But there's a fine line between 'depressed' and 'totally bummed out.' Depressed people spend money and stay quiet; that's good. Totally bummed out people start complaining loudly and spend all their time just staring at their drinks instead of actually, you know, *drinking*. That's bad.

By now, about half the crowd was in the *'mildly depressed'* stage but about a third were edging into the *'totally bummed'* stage.

This was going to be a long night.

"I can top that," said this guy, standing up. I recognized him. He wasn't exactly a regular, but he hung around here a lot and tended to keep to himself, which made my life easier. He jumped around a fair bit and he had some *really* out there stories. Oddly enough, he wasn't a scientist like most of the guys here. Apparently he started off writing stories for *'confession magazines'* for young, confused women before he got into the time-travel business. Called himself the Unmarried Mother (hey, I've heard weirder names). Also claimed to be both his own mother and father, so, like, whatever, man.

Anyway, he kept talking.

"October 1916," he said. "Battle of the Somme. Hitler is a young corporal working as a runner on the front lines. In the original timeline, he gets wounded in the leg and spends a few months in a hospital near Berlin. Figured that would be the perfect time to take him out."

Oh yeah, the 'Kill Hitler during World War One' shtick. That's a *bit* cleverer than the usual 'Kill Hitler' plan. I'm always surprised that only one in ten time-travelers comes up with that plan.

"So," continued the Unmarried Mother. "I decide not to pussy-foot around here. I've got a high-powered rifle, sniper scope, the works. I'm all set up to shoot when there's this big flash of light, and that's when another time-traveler—with exactly the same idea I had—jumps in!" He paused for a moment, giving us all the death glare. "Right on top of me!"

Unmarried Mother threw up his hands in disgust. "And guess what happens? It turns out that *I'm* the one who gave Hitler the leg wound! *I'm* the reason he was a war hero!"

He sat down so hard that he almost broke a chair, and made an incoherent scream of disgust. A rum and coke materialized next to his hand a moment later and I made the appropriate adjustments to his tab.

Yeah—after a while you kind of get used to stuff like that. Predestination paradox, and all that jazz.

At least Unmarried Mother wasn't as bad off as this guy who was in last month. Poor bastard. Japanese kid by the name of Akira, I think; really weird cat. Went back in time to 1912 to kill this other guy—some Count who was planning to take over the world or something like that. Anyway, he killed the Count but it turned out that the Count had commissioned a portrait from a poor, struggling painter. The deal would have put the painter on the map, but with the Count dead, the deal fell through. Of course, the painter—Hitler, of course—ended up putting all the blame for the failed deal on the Jewish art dealer who'd tried to set up the deal in the first place. How's *that* for a kick in the gonads, huh?

"Ah, guess it's my turn," said a rather plain looking guy, standing up. His accent placed him as a Brit, but I've always been pretty bad at placing the accents more precisely than that, although if I had to elaborate I would call it a standard BBC London accent. The guy looked really hum-drum; if you saw him on the street, you'd think he was a TV repairman or something. I vaguely recalled the guy's name— Gary Something-Bird. Sparrow? Hawk? Falcon? Something like that.

Anyway...

"1908 in Vienna. Hitler is coming out of the Academy of Fine Arts after being rejected for admission for the second time in two years. That's the point in his life where things really began to fall apart for him. He was going to end up broke and homeless, becoming the stereotypical starving artist. It seemed the perfect time to get him, right? So, I'm walking towards him when, out of the corner of my eye, I see three members of the Hitler Revenge Squad pop in!"

Half the crowd groaned; the other half went *'oooohhh.'*

The Hitler Revenge Squad is/will be/have been (I could never keep all those time tenses straight in my head) a legendary group of time-travelling fanatics from the 26th century, dedicated to going back in time to, well, *guess*. As you may have gathered by now, it's not exactly *that* easy to kill Hitler. Most guys with any common sense would have just given up after a few tries. Then again, if common sense was so common, it wouldn't be a trait held in such high esteem. Those yahoos have been at it at least sixty-seven separate times, by my (feeble) recollection.

They're not exactly from the deep end of the gene pool, you know what I mean?

Gary kept talking. "So my immediate reaction is, 'These guys are coming right at my direction waving big-arse machine guns.' I'm just about to back away when—bang!— in pop three members from the Neo-Neo-Neo Aryan Guard!"

Another chorus of groans and *'ooohhhs'* from the crowd.

The Neo-Neo-Neo Aryan Guard are a legendarily infamous group of Neo-Nazi fanatics from the 27th century dedicated to going back in time to stop the assassination attempts from the Hitler Revenge Squad.

Oh come on—you didn't see *that* coming?

"So," says Gary, "I'm actually caught in the middle between the two groups! I was just about to jump out of there when—bang!—in jump three members of the Time Patrol!"

Yet another round of groans and *'ooohhhs.'*

The Time Patrol is a legendary, annoying group of do-gooder fanatics from the 28th century dedicated to going back in time to 'keep history progressing as it should'. Naturally they tend to be big party-poopers. Thanks to them, people need to book tickets three centuries ahead of time and have to submit to both a background *and* foreground check whenever they go back to view the Crucifixion. Fortunately for everyone, they're kept busy just keeping up with the Hitler Revenge Squad and Neo-Neo-Neo Aryan Guard.

"So what happened?" asked someone.

"I got caught in the crossfire from nine different machine guns, that's what!" screamed Gary. "I needed to spend six god-forsaken months in a hospital in the 22nd century before I was able to walk again!" Gary sat down hard—so hard that this time the back of his chair broke–and he started to cry.

I sent him a whole bottle of rum. Only charged him *half –price*, 'cause I'm just that nice of a guy and felt sorry for him. Poor bastard.

Nobody else volunteered to tell any more Hitler stories after Gary's tale of woe—thank God—but the damage was already done. Ten minutes went by, and not a single order was placed. An hour ago, I'd had a bar full of pleasant talkative drunks happily buying booze like there was no tomorrow. Now? I had a whole bar of quiet introspective drunks staring morosely at their drinks. Forget about refills— these losers looked like they weren't even going to finish the drinks they already had before last call.

That required… drastic action.

I went to the jukebox and hit the selection for 'I'm My Own Grandpa' (the Guy Lombardo version—that dude *rocked*, man).

Then I fired up the personal time machine I had in the back office and made a few jumps just as Guy Lombardo started singing the first chorus.

First off—live bands. I picked up Jim Morrison from July 3, 1971, Jimi Hendrix from September 18, 1970, and Robert Johnson from August 16, 1938. I then jumped forward and dropped them off in a bar—*my* bar, in fact, when I'd done a jump to New York City during the Big Blackout of 1977 about 3 years ago (personal timeline, that is). I waved at myself, told my previous self to give them a few drinks so that the gang could get to know one another and that I'd be coming by when they were nice and pleasantly drunk, and then I jumped again.

Second—women. I needed some wild and crazy party gals and they had to be the type of gals who liked nerdy guys, 'cause, let's be honest; most of the time travelers that come through my door? Nerds and geeks. I picked up Mata Hari (had to break her out of prison; cool story there, but that's for another time), the complete Dallas Cowboys cheerleader squad right after the Cowboys' win of Super Bowl XXX, and then jumped to the 34th century, where I convinced Eccentrica Gallumbits (the triple breasted high priced escort whose nickname is 'The Best Bang since the Big One,' and trust me, she sure as hell *is*. Raaaarggghh) to wear a neon t-shirt flashing the slogan *Freebie Friday*, pink hot pants, and red stiletto heels, and come back with me.

Ok—so I jumped back to 1977, thanked myself for taking care of the Gang, paid him for the booze that the guys drank (hey, only fair, right?), waved at some of the regulars there and told them I'd catch them in three years and/or 260 years (as the case may be) and then jumped forward.

When I walked out of the storeroom with the Gang and girls, Guy Lombardo was just finishing off the first chorus. Nine separate time jumps, covering over 15 centuries. Total elapsed time since I left? Five point two seconds.

Am I amazing, or am I amazing?

Well—about ten seconds after I walked into the room, the Dark Brooding Depressed Crowd were no longer dark or brooding or even depressed for that matter.

Anyway—about two hours later, the libation had been flowing so freely that I had to make a quick jump forward to next Wednesday to pick up next week's delivery of beer, so that I'd have enough to last me until next week. The Musical Trio had all been sent back to their respective dates (and since they were all scheduled to die within a few hours after they returned, the damage to the timestream would be minimal; I am nothing if not meticulous) and most of the women had gone home (although one or two of them ended up at someone *else's* home) and, all in all, a fun time had been had by all.

So I was sweeping up the place and giving the glasses one last clean and was tallying up everyone's bar tab when, from somewhere in the crowd, I heard someone say, "So... anyone else tried to stop the sinking of the *Titanic*?"

I groaned.

I *hate* it when someone brings up that question.

"Well?"

A dozen hands shot up, more or less at the same time.

Well—there goes my quiet night… again…

Harry and Harry
By Arthur M. Doweyko

12 Jan 2024

Sweat burned Harry's eyes, cascading over both nose and chin. Although he tried to calm himself by sinking into the worn confines of his leather easy chair, his gut preferred to tremble, and his breathing remained short and raspy. The sole source of light in his basement sanctuary came from a series of blinking multicolored flashes. The apparatus sat a few feet in front of him, and centered in its face was a dark round opening. With a long sigh, he wiped his free hand on his trousers and reached out to turn on the machine—*his* time machine.

20 Nov 2014

Harry Simson sat at a lunch table listening to Dr. Jeremy Grimes. He was being considered for a position at Pearl Labs, a leading communications research facility located at the foothills of the Kittatinny Mountains in northern New Jersey. Harry was fresh out of college and had just gotten married to his high school sweetheart, Jayne Bardwell. They hadn't yet decided upon a place to live when he received an invitation from Pearl Labs.

Grimes finished up his description of the facilities at Pearl, and with tented hands propping his goateed chin, asked, "So, Harry, what do you think of this place?"

"Nice. I mean...I really like it."

Harry was a bit overwhelmed by Pearl Labs and immediately wished he could take back that lame response and substitute it with a series of keen observations, and perhaps, several penetrating questions. Until now he had only been exposed to nearly obsolete university lab equipment. Grimes was hard to read. His face was creased with age, an overgrown mop of pure white hair covered the tips of his ears. Dark glasses were propped up by a prominent and bulbous nose much like his own.

Grimes smiled, as if he knew Harry was an introvert, and would have a terrible time conversing. Sympathetically, he offered, "Is there anything about the work here that attracts you in particular?"

Harry's face brightened. "Well, I am really interested in the CTC experiments you've described. They seem very cutting edge."

Grimes' smile widened further. "Our best people have been assigned to the Closed Time Curve project. It's very 'cutting edge' as you put it." Grimes glanced at his watch and continued, "In fact, we are about to test a phase of the project in a few minutes...would you like to come along and see it?"

Harry could only nod. They stood and in moments he was trying to keep up with Grimes marching down a brightly lit hallway and through a key card entry door. Before them sat a metallic tubular device about a foot wide at the opening, ringed by something that looked like clear plastic optical cabling. A number of technicians surrounded the odd metal tube, clipboards in hand, checking and rechecking connections and monitor displays.

They turned to look at the pair who entered.

"I'm glad we were able to arrive before the testing.

This is our interviewee, Harry Simson. Some of you met him earlier today. Please go ahead."

After a few nods, the group turned back to the machine and their clipboards. One of the technicians reached for a switch mounted on the tube's side. The thick strands of optical cable surrounding the tube glowed red and a low pitched hum filled the lab. Everyone stared at the open end which had turned a deep purple. Seemingly out of nowhere a small white ball shot out. It flew across the room and ricocheted off cabinets and countertops. All at once, the technicians raised their arms and shouted.

Harry was amazed at the commotion, and turned to look at Grimes who was grinning.

"You're asking yourself what just happened."

Harry nodded, as the technicians continued to give each other high fives.

"Harry, see the apparatus mounted on top of the opening?"

Harry nodded again.

"Well, that's a spring-loaded gizmo containing a ping pong ball. It's designed to shoot the ball into the CTC any moment now."

Seeing Harry's frown, Grimes continued, "The ball that emerged from the CTC device is the same ball as the one about to be shot into it."

As if on cue, the mechanism fired off the ball which disappeared into a purple haze.

"See?"

Harry was dumbfounded. He scratched his head in an attempt to rally the disconnected thoughts swirling about in there. And then realization came.

"I get it. Since the CTC is a closed-loop device, whatever enters it in the future will show up exactly when the machine is turned on."

Grimes nodded in satisfaction, and Harry added, "The entering ball can only travel backward in time...and, only if the machine is kept running."

Satisfied that he hit the mark with his suppositions,

Harry threw in some questions. "And what would happen if you prevented the ball from entering after it emerged from the CTC? Wouldn't that cause a paradox? And what about live subjects…you know, like guinea pigs or rats, something like that?"

Grimes laughed. "Great questions. That's something you'll find out when you start working here."

"Start working here? You mean I've got the job?"

"Harry, you are just the one I've been looking for. I expect to see you here Monday morning. You'll be joining the CTC group as an Associate Scientist. Welcome to Pearl. That's eight AM sharp—we like to start early."

12 Jan 2024

Ten years later and Harry was laid off from Pearl Labs. He was living in a one-bedroom cottage tucked away in the quiet northern New Jersey suburb of Summit. Each morning he rousted himself out of bed at 7am sharp. The flecked bathroom mirror confirmed that the scruffy brown and grey stubble had grown out a bit more, that his eyes were watery and puffed, that his teeth were turning a pasty yellow and that his premature bald pate had not sprouted any new growth. The unopened box of toothpaste remained that way. A cup of black coffee later and he was working in his basement. When noon arrived he shuffled back up to the kitchen, still in his pajamas, and slapped together a sandwich using the meager offerings available in the refrigerator. With the sandwich tucked away in a coat pocket, he trundled down to the hospice to visit his wife. Each day brought his work nearer to its end, and his wife, nearer to hers.

* * *

Harry looked down at Jayne. Her eyes spoke to him. When the sickness had brought her to the hospice, they were frightened, pleading for a miracle. Perhaps a doctor was about to rush in and tell her everything would be fine, that all this was a mistake, that it was nothing but a nightmare from which she was about to wake. Now, only days later, her eyes were but pinpoints in darkened hollows. They were waiting for the inevitable, the inescapable. Pancreatic cancer was fast moving and painful. Her only relief took the form of a call button—begging a nurse to increase the morphine drip, begging for the protective shroud which obscured reality and allowed her a pleasant but brief visit to the refuge of her memories. On bad days, she was lost to the world, wandering the inner realms of imagination, unable to focus. On good days, she coasted through brief interludes when the pain was tolerable, and she was lucid. This was a good day.

"Honey, how are you today?"

It was a stupid thing to ask, but Harry could think of nothing more clever.

"Harry, it's so nice to see you. Did you talk to the doctor? What did he say?"

Harry talked to the oncologist that morning as he did every morning. Her condition remained unchanged. Jayne had maybe a week, and the final days would be most painful. At some point a decision would be made between Harry and the oncologist to increase the morphine to the point of suppressing respiration, a point of no return. It was never called euthanasia, but the effect was the same.

"Yes, Jayne. I talked to him this morning. He remains hopeful."

Their eyes locked on each other, and for a moment they both acknowledged the reality of the situation—he was lying and she knew it. The moment passed and Jayne responded with a sigh that carried the weight of the world. "I can't wait to get out of this place."

She smiled up at him and his heart was ripped open. As her chapped lips moved, they creased her sunken cheeks. The disease was consuming her, transforming her into a withered replica of the young, vibrant woman he married. Harry's eyes moistened, as did hers. He replied, "Me too."

He held her hand and sat by the bed. He nibbled on his sandwich and watched as her eyes gradually glazed over, and she drifted into a euphoric sleep.

He walked back home, checked the letter slot for mail and descended to his basement workshop.

Harry had become a hermit; a hermit with a mission. High voltage transformers, cables and circuit boards lay scattered about the floor of his basement workshop. Included in the mix were accelerators capable of generating high energy particle and laser beams. With help and enthusiastic encouragement from Dr. Grimes, Harry spent the last few years at the company gathering technological discards, very specific sorts of equipment. Like puzzle pieces, these were to be neatly fitted together into a CTC device similar to the working model at Pearl.

Harry was about to go up to bed and call it a day when the doorbell chimed. It was late and visitors to his house were rare even during the day. He climbed the stairs and stood at the door trying to identify the visitor through the peephole, when the chimes rang again.

Harry grumbled, "Who is it?"

"Harry, it's Jeremy."

Dr. Grimes had never come to visit Harry before. Considering the hour, this must be something urgent.

Harry cracked the door and peered through.

"Jeremy?"

Upon recognizing his mentor, Harry swung the door wide.

"Jeremy, what brings you here?"

"I was just wondering how your project was coming along."

Jeremy stepped in from the cold damp. A light snow had begun to fall. Jeremy's white hair sparkled with melting snowflakes. They even outlined the top rims of his dark glasses. Harry closed the door behind him and pondered the incongruity of wearing dark glasses at night, and then he noticed the small package wrapped in brown paper.

"And, I have something for you."

As Jeremy unwrapped the package, Harry's eyes widened and a smile broke across his unshaven face. "I don't believe it. Is that a high-frequency power relay?"

"That's right."

"How did you know I needed this?"

Jeremy handed over the relay, and without saying another word, Harry turned and clambered down the basement steps, all the while waving Jeremy to follow. When they reached the workshop, he pointed at an assembly of brackets and wiring.

"See? That's exactly what I was putting together tonight. It's the last piece. Once it's connected up, I'll be able to test out this baby."

Jeremy looked over the construction, examining each component, and mumbling approval as he inched his way around the assembly. Much of it was made up of parts taken from the prototype. Jeremy was very eager to see its completion and always made sure that Harry had what he needed when he needed it. Improvements were made and this CTC displayed some significant differences from the prototype, in particular, it had a much larger entry tube.

Harry asked, "Is this relay the reason for your visit?"

"In part. I was just curious about how your machine was shaping up and needed an excuse to visit and see for myself."

Harry began connecting the relay. "This looks perfect. I should be able to finish wiring it up in no time." Reaching for his toolbox, he added, "If you'd like to stay you're welcome." Harry pointed a screwdriver at the easy chair.

Jeremy appeared satisfied with the layout. He buttoned his overcoat and said, "No, no, Harry. I've got an urgent appointment, and actually, I have to leave now." Patting Harry's hunched over back, he added, "I'll be saying good night and good luck to you with the CTC."

Harry barely heard Jeremy speak or ascend the stairway. By the time Jeremy closed the front door behind him, Harry was lost to his work. This was the final piece of the puzzle. He thought about Jayne and her deadly plight. As he spliced in the relay, he became even more frenetic; all his energy was focused on the assembly. Perspiration beaded up on his forehead, and his hands became damp and slippery.

Harry flopped into the easy chair. He was exhausted, his clothing was drenched, and his heart pounded. He surveyed the CTC device, now complete, mentally checking off the connectivity and function of each component. The machine was but a part of a larger scheme, and his greatest fear was that the most significant part was the least predictable.

Satisfied that all was in order, Harry flicked the switch. A deep purple glow emanated from the circular three-foot opening, just as it did with the smaller Pearl Labs prototype years ago. The humming transformers suddenly increased in volume, the purple became brighter, and for a moment, a staccato crackling surrounded Harry. A bright flash erupted from the chamber, followed by an acrid ozone stench. Harry strained to see as his eyes beat down the retinal afterimage. Someone was stepping through the opening.

Standing before him was a gentleman wearing a bright green wind breaker. His crown of bright white hair was disheveled. His face was deeply wrinkled and very familiar. The man smiled down at Harry and shouted, "It worked."

Harry jumped in his seat as realization set in. The CTC worked. He was staring at himself, only this Harry was much older.

"From where...eh, from when did you come?"

"A lot farther out than I, or is it we?... thought. When I entered this machine the year was 2055... that's about 31 years away if I'm right in assuming this is 2024."

Harry was frozen in his seat. The man standing before him was himself, from thirty-one years in the future. A myriad of questions surged through his fevered mind. But the foremost was aimed at the plan, his plan, formulated when Jayne first took ill.

"Did you have any trouble keeping the machine running? That was one of my big worries."

"Hah. It wasn't so much keeping it running as it was paying the electric bills."

They both chuckled. Harry stood up, and both Harrys embraced. Harry couldn't help but sob. "Are you real? Tell me you are real."

"There, there Harry. I grant all this feels like a dream,

but I'm real."

After a moment Harry asked, "I assume that you were successful? I hope that you were successful."

Old Harry's body sagged a bit as he recalled the events of his past. "After Jayne died, it was very difficult for me. I had my doubts that any of this would work. The idea of waiting for a cancer cure seemed pretty far-fetched. I kept abreast of all the research, especially on pancreatic cancer. Progress seemed very slow, and for a while I thought that I would die before anything major was discovered. Then, in the early 50's a new DNA-based approach was tried—basically using a designed viral carrier to make repairs to our DNA— and it worked. A couple of years later the drug was on the market... and here I am."

Old Harry's face beamed. He reached into his back pocket and pulled out a small bottle, a prescription bottle. As he dropped it into Harry's outstretched hand, he added, "The directions are on the bottle. It's an oral dosage form, once a day for three days, and she'll be as good as new."

Harry cupped the dark bottle in both hands and stared at it, and began crying again. Old Harry reached out and held his shoulders.

"There, there, Harry. We did it. Your... our Jayne will live."

They stared at each other, studying each other. Old Harry spoke first. "We are indeed a living paradox. In a sense, we are a kind of hallucination in time. I mean, what if I turn this machine off now? Will I disappear? You would never have the chance to enter it in the future."

Harry stopped sniffling and asked, "Do you recall the prototype run at Pearl?"

Old Harry's eyes wandered upward as he concentrated, conjuring memories of his first days at Pearl. They were called the 'ping pong ball experiments.' And, yes, he did recall that all attempts at creating a paradox failed. Even removing the ball before it was launched or turning the machine off had no effect on the ball once it emerged.

"Yes, I do remember. Jeremy explained it. He said

that each act resulted in a separate timeline, at least that's what I think he said."

"Nature, who detests paradoxes, makes sure none happen," quoted Harry.

"Hey…that's exactly what Jeremy used to say."

Harry held up the bottle and shook it. His scientific mind ran ahead of his emotional struggle. "You know, I'm holding a cancer cure in my hands. We both want Jayne to survive, but if this really works, shouldn't it be made public? Thousands of lives could be saved."

Old Harry shook his head. "Always the moralist. Have no fear, when you go see Jayne tomorrow, I'm going to borrow your car."

His hand slipped into his jacket and came out with a single large capsule identical to those in the bottle.

"The Sloan-Kettering Cancer Research Center is only about an hour's drive."

* * *

A few weeks later, Jayne was released from the hospice. The staff was convinced that a miracle had occurred, as pancreatic cancer was one of few remaining cancers that could claim a near 100% mortality rate. Doctors and nurses, volunteers and administrators, all gathered at the hospice doors to wish Jayne the best and insure a warm sendoff. Smiles were abundant and there were no dry eyes in the crowd. Spontaneous cures were rare and were treated as a special occasion by people accustomed to much more somber outcomes.

They drove home in silence, with Jayne staring at the passing scene and Harry sneaking an occasional peek at his beloved. The trip was short and in minutes they were parked in their driveway.

Harry ran around to Jayne's side and opened her door. "Well, how does it feel to be back?"

She was bundled in a thick beaver coat, and her eyes peered out of a narrow slit between hat and scarf. As she angled her way out of the car, she stopped to take a long look at her home. Harry heard her muffled sobbing. They toddled along the uneven walkway covered in a thin coating of ice. When they reached the brick steps the front door swung open.

Harry whispered, "Oh, Jayne, I want you to meet my cousin. I hope you don't mind. He's visiting for a few days."

Jayne stared up at the old man and caught her breath. His grin was wide, his cheeks grizzled, his face was warm and very familiar.

"Hi Jayne. I'm Harry. Same name as your hubby, so don't get us mixed up."

Chuckling at his own joke, he took a step down the icy bricks and the two Harrys helped Jayne up.

* * *

Old Harry was asleep upstairs as Jayne poured out some fresh coffee. She sat across from her husband in the breakfast nook, and gave him a quizzical look.

"I'm worried about your cousin."

"Oh?"

"He's very sweet, and always helpful…a bit like you in some ways."

"And you're worried because…?"

"Well, it's been a week now, and I thought you said he'd be staying a few days."

Seeing Harry's brows shoot up, she continued, "I don't mean that he should leave, it's just that…well."

"What's he up to, right?"

She nodded and added, "Besides, I've caught him a couple of times now… just staring at me. It's almost like he's looking through me. Downright spooky."

Harry knew what that was about, but nodded in agreement, grimacing as he replied, "Maybe I should talk to him. He did say that he'd be leaving any day now… something about a job."

"A job? At his age?"

"Yeah, I know."

The living room stairs creaked as old Harry reached the first floor and ambled to the kitchen entryway where he stopped and gleamed. Standing there in Harry's striped pajamas, he bellowed, "Good ☐orning' everyone. How's my favorite cousin Jayne doin' this morning?"

Jayne half-finished her coffee and stood as she replied, "Good morning, Harry. Well, I've got some laundry to do today, and I'd better get started on it." Looking at her seated husband, she added, "You left me quite the mess. I've been back a week and I've still got loads to clean up. Be sure to bring down the bed sheets from upstairs when you're finished." Jayne sauntered to the first floor laundry room, turned to give Harry a quick nod, and closed the door behind her.

"Ah, that's the Jayne I remember." Old Harry poured himself a coffee and joined Harry at the table.

"Careful what you say. She's got the ears of an eagle."

They both snickered.

"You know, she's getting a bit uncomfortable with you here. She's pretty smart, and you won't be fooling her much longer."

"That's something I want to talk to you about."

They sipped at their coffees and then old Harry spoke up. "I believe it's time for me to leave."

"Leave? But where will you go?"

Ignoring the question, old Harry continued, "You know you have to turn off the CTC downstairs." Harry cocked his head, while old Harry continued. "It has served its purpose, and believe me, I won't disappear. It's just a precaution— something we don't want left running unnecessarily. Just think it through a moment. As long as it remains on, anything or anyone entering, at any time…will appear when you first turned it on."

"But the only thing that showed up was you."

"That's true of this timeline; the one we created to save Jayne. We wouldn't be aware of all the other timelines created haphazardly while the machine is running. It's just a matter of being tidy, of being scientifically responsible."

Harry finished off his coffee and slowly nodded in agreement.

"So, where are you headed? Are you sure you can take care of yourself? You're no spring chicken."

"There's something I need to do, and it's going to mean that we'll not see each other again." Seeing the frown erupting on Harry's face, old Harry continued, "Now, now. Believe me, I will miss being with you and Jayne—it will be as difficult for me as it is for you. I am very happy at the way things turned out. Remember that I saw Jayne die. That was tough. I mourned her and I buried her. I survived in this house with the belief that the CTC would work, and for thirty years waited for science to come up with a cure. And, now, here we are. Jayne is back with you, and with me for a little while. The time has come to say farewell."

Both Harrys stood from the table and held each other. Harry said, "It's going to be like losing a brother I never knew I had—an older brother at that."

Old Harry took a good, long look at his younger self and said, "It's no easier for me, kiddo."

Jayne's voice reached them through the laundry room door. "Have you brought down those sheets I asked for?"

* * *

The next evening a taxi pulled up outside Harry's house. Old Harry bid Harry and Jayne a fond goodbye, making up a story about getting a part-time job in the city and promising to keep in touch. As he descended the front stairway, he turned to Harry at the doorway and gave him a quick wink. That would be the last time Harry saw him.

It was cold, dark, and late when the taxi drove past the main entrance of Pearl Labs and stopped about a hundred paces beyond. Harry stepped out onto the narrow walkway. Blue halogen light from a nearby lamppost glimmered off the slick cement. A breeze slipped between surrounding trees; its cold and damp fingers toyed with Harry's windbreaker, sending a chill down to his toes.

Harry could see the gatehouse cubicle through the pines lining the walk. It was dimly lit with wrought iron gates to either side spanning the entrance. The buildings beyond were dark except for a few windows. At this late hour, only the cleaning crew would be expected to be about. Harry squeezed through the groomed shrubbery alongside the

24

walkway and jogged across a meadow.

He reached a small, one-story structure attached to the main building and stopped at a side door illuminated from above with a single spot light. A security camera mounted under the eave stared at him with its dark cyclopean lens. Harry hoped that his 31-year old key card would still work, since it had really been only a couple of weeks since he was terminated. He held his breath and waved it over a pad affixed to the entryway. After a moment's hesitation, the small LED turned from red to green, and Harry exhaled as he let himself in. The hallway was long and illuminated in a dull red by emergency exit signs at either end. Jogging the length of the corridor, he zigzagged into an adjoining hallway and stopped in front of the windowless double door entrance to the CTC lab. He was panting now, but too excited to stop. Swiping the key card reader had no effect—no green or red light—the reader was disabled. He tried using his back to push at the doors, but to no avail. Desperation threatened to overwhelm him as he focused on possible next steps, and then he spotted the dim outlines of an emergency fire box mounted on the opposite wall. He kicked in the glass door, retrieved a crowbar, and in moments, wedged it into the seam between the doors. A minute later he broke through and automatic fluorescent lights flickered on.

A number of metal scaffolds and disused cables were piled up in the middle of a large room. Harry nodded to himself. The prototype CTC was gone—something he'd expected since the project was recently terminated. He walked past the remnants to his former office and quick-stepped his way to another set of doors. These were padlocked with a chain through the metal handles. Several twists of the crowbar wrenched off a handle and the doors screeched open. The light switches within were dead. He felt his way along the walls, with every step increasing the gloom. After a few minutes he reached a barrier. His fingers probed the surface of a door. It was a fire door, the type with a thick, wire-meshed glass window about a foot square. He peered through the glass and his heart leaped when he saw a glow, a familiar dim purple glow.

The lights in the hallway began flashing on and off. This was followed by a deafening clanging sound. He had been detected. He was unsure of how many guards were on duty. Maybe there were none nearby, maybe he had a few minutes.

"Yo! Stop right there!"

Maybe just seconds.

Harry turned to see a guard enter the far end of the hallway, moving slowly toward him with gun in hand. The lights produced a surreal strobe effect, making it look like the guard flitted from one position to another, each time closer. Harry swung the crowbar into the door window splintering the glass, producing a caved-in bulge.

"Hey! I said stop!"

Harry whacked the glass again, shattering it this time. He reached through the opening and pulled at the handle. The door swung in and Harry followed it. He could hear the guard's boots clacking behind him. After slamming the door shut he shoved the crowbar through the handle, wedging it behind the doorframe.

The guard reached the door and yelled through the broken window, "Old man, give yourself up. The police are on their way."

Harry saw a pistol waving at him through the window. The door rattled as the guard pushed against it, trying to dislodge the crowbar. Given a few more minutes he would succeed, but by then it would be too late.

"I have no intention of giving up. You can put away the gun."

"Hey, just think about it. You've got no place to go." The door jiggled again.

"And that's where you're wrong."

Harry walked over to the source of the purple light. It came from a large round opening. As he expected, the CTC was running. Running since the day it was turned on. Pearl labs had produced two machines. One was a prototype which was used as a demo, in particular to attract new scientists and potential investors. The other, a larger model, part of a larger experiment, was built at nearly the same time as the prototype. It was kept running and it was kept under lock and key.

The guard stopped banging on the door and poked his head through it. "Hey, what do you think you're doing?"

Harry smiled as he entered the portal.

13 Oct 2014

Harry at once stepped into and then out of the CTC. He emerged into a glare of light, a shimmering, crackling light.

"Oh my God!" someone shouted. This was followed by a cacophony of sounds, mostly shrieks and gasps.

Harry was surrounded by a small group of people, all wearing white lab coats. His eyes adjusted to the bright fluorescents above and a quick glance around the room confirmed he was where he had started. The fire door was intact and there was no guard.

"Why, hello everyone."

The group became silent. They stared at him as if mesmerized.

"When exactly is this?" he asked.

"It's October 13th," responded one. Another added, "The year is 2014."

And then someone asked, "Who are you?"

Harry thought for a moment, and then answered, "My name is... Grimes, Dr. Jeremy Grimes."

The Light Fantastic
By Edmund Wells

Pulse racing, Ryan slid a hand over the machine's cool exterior, a shiver running to the tips of his red Converse sneakers. A sprinkling of lights overhead provided the lab's only illumination—a constellation of stars guiding his way. No one ever questioned the comings or goings of the inventor's son, even after hours.

The time machine resembled the cockpit of an F-14 fighter jet, a carven capsule of black hematite rather than boring forged steel—some benefit derived from the mineral's electron density, as his father liked to drone on about. Whatever the scientific reason, the end result was a lot cooler than a DeLorean.

He knew the controls well enough, even if his father's theories were beyond his grasp. Most people just stared with eyes like glazed donuts at Patrick Sean O'Connor, Professor of Quantum Physics at M.I.T., whenever he explained how the contraption worked. All anyone really wanted to know was if it actually would.

"Ryan Adam O'Connor," he drawled, flicking a few

switches. "The first time traveler." He grinned, wondering if he should have worn his Star Trek costume. The looks on the photographers' faces when he returned would be priceless, especially when he scanned the crowd with his tricorder. Instead, he'd opted for impressing the babes—leather trench coat, *Genesis Holo-Tour 2063* t-shirt, strategically torn Levis. And mirrored sunglasses, of course. Time travelers always wore shades.

The sleek, lustrous machine hummed to life, filling the air with a softly fluctuating light—something in the violet range, with a hint of the light fantastic. Thousands of tiny hydro-magnets whispered as they whirled at some improbable speed, creating a crapload of gigawatts. Giordi La Forge himself would have been impressed.

The first trip would be the most important, to satisfy Congress that the machine would operate without blowing anything up or putting a dent in the space-time continuum. At the same time, it had to spark the imagination of the public, who was funding the $8.8 billion price tag with their hard-earned tax dollars. Disappoint either group and the project would die with an expensive whimper.

Ryan had put forth several first-rate suggestions: stop Hitler, save John Lennon, or prevent the Red Sox from trading Babe Ruth. All worthy goals, which his father even tacked to a caulk board in his office. The professor couldn't attempt any of those things, however, without the feds' approval, and Congress was meeting tomorrow to decide on a "suitable" first voyage.

The government sucked the life out of everything. It seemed doubtful the feds would be overly concerned with a peacenik like Lennon, or willing to attempt something as tricky as stopping der Führer on the first go. And more than one member of Congress was probably a stinking Yankees fan. Congress was more likely to opt for a purely symbolic journey, like securing an autographed photo of George Washington, or punching Genghis Khan in the face.

As far as Ryan was concerned, there was only one major problem with the whole thing: his father—Sean, as he liked to be called—insisted on piloting the machine himself. Despite his brilliance, dear Sean often had trouble backing out of the driveway. In a stressful moment, he could easily make a fatal error and *poof*—Ryan would be an orphan. If their mother were alive, maybe Sean would listen to reason, but he was being stubborn, as usual.

So be it.

Ryan entered the security code—swiped from his father's brilliantly unlocked briefcase—and the F-14's bubble canopy rose. Heart thumping, he leaped into the control seat.

"Welcome, my son," he sang. "Welcome... to the machine!" Duffle bag flung onto the co-pilot's seat, he strapped himself in. The bubble hummed shut, sealing with a pneumatic hiss. Cool, minty air flowed into the cockpit. Nice, but pizza-scented had been his personal preference.

If things went smoothly, good old Sean would eventually forgive him *and* Ryan would be famous—elevated to instant hero status alongside Buzz Aldrin, Neil Armstrong and Carl Yastrzemski, and without any mucking about with degrees in physics and engineering.

Down to business.

He'd given a lot of thought to what time period he should visit. Saving John Lennon was his first choice—his father would be pleased, and who could be angry at rescuing the fallen Beatle? Yet, a small voice whispered, it was the *future* he needed to explore, not the past. The past was old news. History, as they say. Real explorers broke *new* ground, boldly going where no one had gone before. If he were to bring back a piece of advanced technology—food replicator, warp coil, light saber—it would not only validate the success of the time machine, but it would make Congress very, very happy.

And *then* he could save Lennon.

Since there were no historical precedents for a trip to the future, Ryan chose 2344—the year of the Klingon alliance with Starfleet. It seemed as good a year as any. He set the date to noon on July 13th—Jean-Luc Picard's birthday, and why the hell not? Latitude and longitude he set for a cozy nook of

Buena Vista Park, Cole Valley, San Francisco. A nice, safe place with lots of friendly people, some percentage of which would be California girls. *Yummy.*

Despite his flaws, Sean believed in making things as simple to use as possible. In keeping with this philosophy, a friendly green button shone beneath the "year" indicator. It was simply marked *Go.*

Ryan took a deep breath, settling himself into the cool leather seat. The machine hummed in a whisper of awesome technologies, awaiting the utterance of his soon-to-be historic words. He switched the recording module on.

"To infinity and beyond!"

He pushed *Go.*

A flash of numbing cold seized him, squeezing his body like an orange. The breath froze in his throat as icy winds flayed his skin. A thousand voices howled in Dolby Surround Sound, each accompanied by a raging storm of rainbow light. The view beyond the Plexiglas shield spun like a Technicolor nightmare, a mad artist's psychedelic vision of the apocalypse, or something from *Yellow Submarine.*

Ryan shut his eyes, a scream building within him.

As if someone had flicked a switch, the cold relented and the orange-squeezer released its pulpy death grip, allowing him to draw another breath. It seemed he wasn't going to meet the Creator today after all. Straining to catch his breath, he pried his fingers from the handgrips.

The airy music of birdsong surrounded him.

Tentatively, he opened his eyes. Around him stretched a verdant valley of lush, pendulous trees and dazzling sunshine. A sparkling stream dominated the view beyond his frost-streaked windshield. The grass grew in rolling waves of green and gold, beneath the bluest sky he'd ever seen. It was like stepping into a commercial for laundry detergent.

Very pretty.

But where were the people? Gawking with slack jaws at his miraculous appearance? The legions of babes in belly shirts screaming for a kiss and a lock of his hair? The park was disappointingly empty. A holiday, maybe? It *was* Jean-Luc's birthday, after all.

The bubble canopy rose with a hiss and a spray of vapor. He grabbed his duffle bag and leaped out. The air was balmy, thick with the smell of wildflowers. Looking around, he could find no footpaths winding through the idyllic park. No benches, no bread-seeking ducks. Not even a lousy trash basket. All was quiet on the western front, but for the gentle, boring sounds of nature.

In the distance, near the base of a shallow vale, two gray domes rose up against the greenery, one to either side of the stream. His fans were probably inside, sipping fruit smoothies and looking all relaxed. He'd have to pay them a visit and shake things up. He reached into his bag for a bottle of Eden Springs water, partially frozen, and took a long swallow.

Bag slung over his shoulder, he strolled a dozen yards downslope and drew alongside the sparkling stream. Trees crowded its twisting banks, the arching branches overflowing with butterflies and lovesick birds. Walt Disney would have loved it here. Ryan adjusted course to follow the stream, drawn into the serenity of the wind-swept park, smiling at the antics of the idiot squirrels.

Somewhere ahead was the sound of gentle splashing.

At last! Ryan crept forward, curbing the urge to rush ahead. Through the drooping branches of a willow he spied a young woman standing in the stream—supremely naked. He gasped and fell to his knees. *Holy Moses!*

Droplets of water sparkled on skin the color of warm cocoa, and probably just as sweet. Glistening coils of dark hair dangled into the stream, dancing around her as if in celebration. She sang to herself, washing every scrumptious curve of her babelicious bod—and there certainly were a lot of them.

Ryan decided he was going to like the future.

He combed his fingers through his hair, which had a way of sticking up for no good reason, then popped a breath mint. What should he say? How do you break the ice with a naked chick bathing in a stream? If only he'd brought a bottle of fancy body wash, or a loofah sponge, he could offer her a nice river-warming gift.

Okay, Ryan, get a grip. You're a famous explorer now. Gifts aren't necessary. You can say anything you damn well please and it will automatically be cool.

Feeling a bit flush, he stepped from the concealment of the willow... and stumbled on a root. *Damn.*

"Um, hello, miss. Are all women as naked—I mean, as *beautiful* as you are, here in the future?" Somehow, that didn't come out the way he'd expected.

Her head turned; eyes of deepest midnight gazed upon him, evaluating, searching. She didn't seem surprised at his appearance, or even concerned, as if time travelers dropped by all the time. Like most hot babes, she probably knew karate. She straightened, inasmuch as her curvaceous form would allow, and swung about to face him.

"Er, what I mean is, we don't have naked women back in Boston. Not in streams, that is. Or the Charles River... which is, you know, reserved for guys named Charles." *Smooth, Ryan. Real smooth.*

The young woman's lips parted in a *Sports Illustrated* swimsuit issue smile, teeth bright against her dusky skin. She sauntered toward the shore, moving from side to side as much as forward, and extended a hand.

"I am called Evensong. Remove your garments. We must mate at once."

What? He shook his head, certain he'd lapsed into one of his daydreams. *Remove, did she say?* A loud splash erupted downstream. The dream police, coming to get him.

"Just, er, hold that thought. About the mating, I mean. My name's Ryan, by the way. I'll be right back." He sprinted, water jetting into the air around him, and rounded a bend in the stream.

Sliding to a halt, Ryan's breath caught. Two figures were grappling in the middle of the stream! A sinuous creature, its bipedal form the color of fresh grass, clung to a blocky, metallic shape—a robot, if Ryan were any judge—its body squat and roughly humanoid. The robot held a narrow, rectangular object in one hand, but its arms were pinned by the grunting reptilian menace.

Ryan crept closer, keeping to the edge of the trees. *What the hell? This is like a Japanese monster movie, only without the subtitles.*

Water sprayed as the pair thrashed around. The robot bucked and spun, trying to throw the lizard clear, but the creature's powerful tail was coiled around its neck. A crackling, high-pitched squeal cut the air, like feedback from a cheap loudspeaker. Birds burst from the trees. With a snap of metal, the robot tumbled and crashed onto the bank, its head tilted at an uncomfortable angle.

A moment later, something thudded into the grass at Ryan's feet, as if dropped by a guardian angel: metallic, rectangular, and dangerous. Some sort of high-tech weapon, courtesy of God. He glanced up to see the reptilian thing surging toward him.

Yikes! Heart in sudden overdrive, Ryan bent down and fumbled with the strange weapon. One end was clearly the dangerous bit. This part seemed to be the trigger... Rapid footsteps sloshed through the wet grass, growing nearer. Ryan's head whipped up.

"Stop!" he shouted, raising the weapon.

The reptile slowed. Its emerald, feline eyes flicked to the weapon and it came to a reluctant halt. The creature was larger than Ryan expected, standing over seven feet tall on powerful, green-scaled legs—some mutant cross-breed between human and lizard. San Francisco had a lot to answer for with this thing.

Ryan backed up a few steps, trying to maintain his best Chuck Norris face. "Don't move, my large green friend! Or you're toast."

A long tongue, disturbingly human in appearance, snaked between ridged white teeth. "Friend?" Its voice slithered from its maw, cold yet courteous. "Do you aim weapons at *friends*, human?"

Ryan blinked, not expecting the thing to speak. "Well, no. But it was only a figure of speech." He lifted his chin toward the stream, trying not to act weirded out. "Anyway, I see you're not such a good friend to robots."

Its scaly mouth twisted into something like a grin. "The machine? It hunted the female." The creature turned and circled back a few yards, then sat with its back to a tree. "And I hunted it."

To protect her? Or eat her? Ryan would need to keep a close eye on Mr. Lizard. It had charged at him, after all, and probably not to give him a hug. Maybe he should just kill it now, to be safe.

The creature glanced over Ryan's shoulder. "Yet, the female will desire your... *friendship* over mine. Simply because I am not human." It hissed like a sputtering tea kettle. "She has much yet to learn."

Ryan felt a surge of anger. He lowered his voice and leaned forward. "I'll have you know, Mr. Green Jeans, Evensong is hot for me. And vice-versa, if you get my drift."

"Take care, young *friend*." The lizard raised a clawed finger. "This blossom is as the black widow spider, eager to breed and deadly to her mate."

Somehow, Ryan failed to experience any misgivings over this threat. In the immortal words of Bono—hold me, thrill me, kiss me, kill me.

Evensong approached from behind and rested a hand on Ryan's shoulder, causing him to jump. Her warm scent filled the air like an armoire full of goodies from *Victoria's Secret.*

She tossed her hair, teeth flashing in a dazzling smile. "You also foretold I would never find a mate of my own species, Bael." She took a bite from a bright green apple and handed it to Ryan. "Why do you persist in claiming I am deadly?"

Because you've got a killer bod? Ryan took a bite of apple for himself.

Bael exhaled in a slow hiss, eyes closing. "I will repeat myself for the benefit of your new friend, for such knowledge may save you both. Over the long years have I witnessed Evensong's sisters—clones of the robot domes—weeping over their fallen mates, cradling their lifeless offspring." Its eyes drew open, an unexpected look of sorrow within their green depths. "Not through any intent of your sisters, but of the human scientists who would tamper with nature. You are alluring, Evensong, but within you and your former sisters lies a deadly poison. And thus, your species dies."

A chill burrowed into the pit of Ryan's stomach. "Are you kidding me? Your women aren't able to reproduce?"

Evensong gazed into the distance. "I do not know for certain. From my long wanderings, I appear to be the last of my sisters, and our domes haven't produced a male for fifteen years. There is only one way, however, to determine whether I am barren." A smile curled her soft lips.

Ryan's mind spun at the implications. This was Earth's future? A paradise without people? Wiped out from some disaster or genetic mutation? No Federation of Planets, no Swedish Bikini Team, no Dunkin' Donuts—just trees, animals and one naked yet untouchable female. He thought he might hurl.

"From which dome do you hail, Ryan?" she asked. "Are there others there such as yourself?"

Fenway Park doesn't have a dome. Though it does happen to have a Green Monster.

A sound like a circular saw ripped through the air as a crimson flare burst from Ryan's weapon. A nearby birch exploded in a gout of orange flame. The doomed tree toppled into the river and sank with an evil hiss.

"Oops. Must have touched the trigger." *How awesome was that?*

Bael scowled, adding to his demonic good looks. "Be careful with that weapon, young fool."

"Hey. That's no way to talk to a famous time traveler." He smoothed his trench coat. "Ryan Adam O'Connor, for your information. I'm from Boston, 2066, not one of your California hippy domes."

"According to the machines," Bael said. "These two domes are the last still functioning. Anywhere."

So, he and Evensong were the last two humans on

36

Earth? Awesome! Except for the fact she couldn't get pregnant. That would normally be a good thing. Frowning, he pondered the situation. There had to be a solution, or the human race was done for. With a grin, he snapped his fingers.

"Hey, no problemo! I can bring doctors here from *my* time. I'm sure they can cure Evensong. And if that doesn't work, we'll just call in a few busloads of fertile babes, I mean women, to re-populate the Earth." *And I get first dibs.* "We'll travel back in my time machine." *And I'll give you one guess which of you gets to ride shotgun.*

Evensong wrapped her arms around Ryan, squeezing her lushness against him. "And then shall we mate." She kissed him, sweet as an apple.

Parts of his brain saw fireworks. *Ah, heaven.*

Bael rose to his clawed feet, looking grim, even for a lizard. "Very well. Take us to this machine of yours."

"Upriver." Ryan waved the laser rifle. "You first, Bael old friend, so I can keep an eye on you. Evensong, you next, please." *So I can keep an eye on* you—*nudge, nudge.* "I'll guard your rear—*the* rear."

The idyllic park somehow seemed less Disney-like to Ryan, knowing the terrible fate that awaited mankind if things were left to run their course. The geneticists were to blame, tinkering with things best left to Mother Nature.

By the time they reached the time machine, Ryan was feeling parched and a little edgy from watching Evensong's swaying butt cheeks.

"There," he said, pointing. "That black, um, egg-shaped capsule."

Bael looked to where Ryan indicated and burst into a run toward the time machine.

Ryan jogged up next to Evensong, a sense of disquiet slipping over him. "What's wrong? Has he flipped out?" She shrugged and the two of them hurried after Bael.

As they neared the capsule, a dozen or more snake-like creatures, each about two feet in length, fled through the grass from Bael. One creature slithered toward Ryan, shrieked and veered away, but not before giving him a curious look with its intelligent green eyes.

Bael stood over the time machine, an unhappy set to his mouth.

The bubble canopy, Ryan now saw, had multiple holes bored through it. Inside, the control panel was a mass of spaghetti-like cables. Even the *Go* button had been cracked in half.

Ryan slid to the ground, back against the capsule, head in his hands. *This couldn't be happening. The time machine is freaking ruined. Goddamn snakes!*

He didn't have the tools or the first clue how to fix the machine. It wasn't a skill he ever envisioned needing. His stomach churned with acid. Stranded. In the future. Without his father, his friends, and maybe worst of all—without his iPad. And how was he supposed to repopulate the Earth now?

"There may be another way," Bael said in his refined, whispery voice, "to save your species."

Ryan glanced up at the lizard-man, blurred through a flow of tears. "There is?"
Bael nodded. "But you may need this." He handed Ryan the laser rifle.

Aw, crap. Must have dropped it.

"No, Bael." Evensong knelt beside Ryan, stroking his hair. "It's too dangerous, and he *is* only a boy."

"Whoa." Ryan stood, wiping his eyes, trying not to stare at Evensong's anti-gravitational hooters. "I'm not a boy. I'm a famous time traveler, remember? I can do it. Just clue me in."

"The machines have lost their way," Bael said. "Become... corrupted. Their purpose was once to protect humankind, and to seed new communities with clones— clones who would eventually become self-sustaining. When your females stopped bearing live offspring, and their embrace became fatal to your males, the machines came to view Evensong as a predator—adverse to the continuation of your species. As they view me."

Evensong nodded. "I can no longer approach the domes without being attacked, even though the genetic replication robots created me to go forth and mate."

"I just can't believe it," Ryan said, half to himself. "How could things have gone so wrong?"

"Disbelieve at your peril," Bael said. "If you mate with Evensong, boy, you will die. And so may Evensong."

This is payback for skipping church, I just know it. If Ryan couldn't get back home, he'd have to make a life for himself here. He took a deep breath, looking around. No phones, no lights, no cars. He'd never aspired to being Amish. Still, there were worse places to be stranded, like Detroit or... Cleveland.

"You mentioned there might be another way to save our species." Ryan hefted the laser rifle, putting his Chuck Norris face back on. "So what's the plan, Lizard Man?"

Bael ducked and stepped out of the arc of the weapon. "The machines guard a cache of medicines. Among them is a general antidote, which may return Evensong's genetic code to its original structure, thus neutralizing her poison."

Ryan scratched his jaw. "Why don't the robots just give her the antidote if it would allow her to bear children? Isn't that what they want?"

The lizard shook his head, eyes dark with disgust. "They keep it from her because they perceive her only as a threat, rather than recognizing the obvious. Such is the way of machines."

Evensong took Ryan by the hand. "As a human male, you should be able to safely enter the domes to retrieve the medicine. Are you willing to try?"

He'd done a lot of crazy things in his life to get into the pants of a hot girl, with little success. All right, *no* success. It was ironic, therefore, that not only was this girl the hottest babe on the planet—literally—and not only did she have no pants to speak of, but she was already intent on getting into *his*. And yet to succeed, he only had to save the human race.

Ryan threw his arms around Evensong and gave her a deep, lip-mashing kiss. "For you Eve baby, anything."

* * *

Bael led the way, stomping wildflowers and

frightening bunny rabbits, taking them along a narrow ravine that brought them to within a stone's throw of the domes. Ryan reflected on their trail boss. The big reptile didn't seem like such a bad fellow, once you got past the claws and fangs and all. Still, Ryan couldn't bring himself to fully trust the guy, honorably though he'd behaved so far. Once he and Evensong were better acquainted, he'd suggest they relocate somewhere far from Bael, for each of their safety.

"I suggest you feign an injury," Bael said. "The robots will scan you and bring you to the infirmary, inside the dome on the left. You'll then need to improvise as best you can. Try to secure several vials of the antidote, in case any are flawed. I believe the liquid is neon-blue."

"Wait. If they scan me, won't they know I'm not really injured?"

Bael flicked a wrist and slashed Ryan across the cheek with his claws. "My apologies."

Ryan's skin instantly burned. "Ow, that stings!" He felt blood seeping from the cuts. "I guess I should have seen that coming."

"You may feel a slight nausea, but the wound will guarantee you are brought to the infirmary." Bael turned away.

Evensong came forward and hugged Ryan, stroking his hair. "We will wait for you here. Fare well, love."

Heart pounding, Ryan climbed from the ravine, imagining his triumphant return to Evensong's waiting arms. It was going to be *sweetness incarnate*. Whistling, he strode toward the dome on the left, which looked a lot like the Epcot Center's geosphere. Before he'd gone ten yards, a patrol robot approached, red eyes shining.

"What do you require, citizen?"

"Um, I was attacked by one of those big green reptiles." He pointed to his cheek. "I'm not feeling very good." Truthfully, he was already feeling more than a little queasy.

"You require medical aid?"

"Yes." *I just said that, Robocop reject.*

A web of red light scanned Ryan's body. "Come with

me, citizen."

Ryan followed the blocky, brushed steel robot up a shiny metal ramp and through a high archway, whose door rose like a portcullis on the spherical fortress. Steel walls lined both sides of a moving walkway, twinkling with lights and numerical readouts. This would be a tough place to break into by force. He wiped his brow. The temperature was a lot warmer than it needed to be. He'd have to file a citizen's complaint.

"Sit on the cushioned table, citizen. I have summoned a medi-bot." The patrol robot left the room through the door they'd entered, leaving Citizen Ryan alone.

Time to become... Secret Agent Ryan.

Theme to *Mission Impossible* playing through his head, he leaped to his feet, rushed over to a small interior door and coughed as he laser-blasted the control panel. A wave of dizziness washed over him. Moving on unsteady legs, he staggered to a cabinet filled with colorful vials. Sure enough, several were neon-blue, labeled only with numbers—the language of robots.

The small door buzzed and slid open two inches before jamming. "Citizen," an electronic voice called through the gap. "Are you in distress?"

"No. I just need a little rest. Leave me alone."

"The patrol reported that you require urgent medical attention."

"Go away."

"As you wish. A mechano-bot will repair the door." The medi-bot moved off.

Sweating, Ryan stuffed five neon-blue vials into his duffle bag, then grabbed a dozen more of various colors, in case they might prove to be useful medicines.

Banging and drilling noises emerged from the other side of the door.

Time to make like a tree. Too bad he couldn't meet with the medi-bot. His stomach roiled like he was going to power-puke. He returned to the portcullis and pushed a few likely buttons until the door slid open. Weaving a little, he

41

strolled into the open air, preferring not to run unless he had to.

"Halt, citizen." A patrol robot approached and scanned him again. "You remain in need of medical aid. Return to the dome at once."

Ryan rubbed his eyes. "Do you insist?"

"It is for your own good."

He raised his rifle and squeezed. A shriek of laser fire and the robot burst into a pillar of flame; it twirled once and fell over with a satisfying thud. "No, *you're* in need of medical aid." He could see why Bael didn't like these robots. They were sort of annoying.

No other patrol robots tried to stop him as he left the vicinity of the dome, which was lucky for them: Citizen Ryan was becoming a darn good shot.

Cool shadows draped the valley floor as he made his way back toward the ravine. His first day in the future. Not a total success, he had to admit. He'd broken the time machine, which was a definite setback, but if Evensong could be cured it would all be worth it.

As he neared the edge of the ravine, feeling drained but pleased with himself despite his nausea, Bael emerged and took the duffle bag.

"Here you go, Lizzy. Told you I was a famous explorer." He felt himself lifted up and carried downward into the ravine, where the shadows lent some coolness to the dying heat of the day. He shivered.

Evensong pressed cold lips to his forehead. Tears ran down her cheeks, she was so glad to see him.

"You can relax now, honey buns," he heard himself say, the sound of his voice somehow distant. "I got the antidote. We'll have children, lots and lots of children. Small ones, I think." He licked his cracked lips. "And we'll find another place to live, away from these pushy robots. And Bael, no offense. He weirds me out a little."

The beautiful girl rose and ran off, sobbing.

What did I say? "Evensong! Come back!"

A gathering of snakes appeared, the little green

bastards that had destroyed his father's time machine. Bael's serpentine form rose up among them like an emperor.

"We offer our thanks." His eyes shone like emerald knife slits in the darkness. "Evensong will bear many fine children—children such as myself, born from one of Evensong's sisters, long ago. It is *my* poison which must be neutralized, so we can mate; there is no poison within her. Except, perhaps, her love for me."

The brood of vipers chattered, bodies cavorting, slithering against one another as if in celebration.

Ryan swallowed, teeth clattering from the terrible cold embracing him. "Can't you s-spare a little antidote f-for me, f-friend?"

Bael had the grace to look distressed. "Alas, there is no cure for the poison once it has taken hold. The antidote offers only immunity. This was the only sure way to get you into the high-level infirmary. I am sorry."

Darkness slipped over Ryan like a cocoon of ice, the burning cold receding into blessed numbness. Through his efforts, one sentient race would survive to inherit the Earth, the children of Bael and Evensong.

This time around, the serpent had won.

I'll Come Back For You
By A.C. Hall

It happened in a swift series of violent moments. The door being kicked in, the heavily armored men rushing inside, the screams of the young couple who lived in the house, the brief struggle as they fought back, the way they were pinned down and bound, the dragging out to the waiting vehicle. A minute before, they had been curled up on the couch, in the midst of a movie and a quiet evening at home together. Now they were prisoners, their deaths not far off if all of the rumors were to be believed.

"Why is this happening? Why us?" Beverly cried.

"Just stay calm, we'll find a way out of this," Harold told her.

They had been blindfolded and she couldn't see his face, but it was all too clear from his tone that he didn't believe his own words.

"Both of you shut up," a gruff voice barked.

The increase in abductions by this group was covered daily by the news, but like most people Beverly and Harold never thought it would happen to them. No one knew for sure who they were or why the government hadn't stepped in to stop them. It was the perfect atmosphere for rumors to grow and that's precisely what they did. In just a few short years the group's reputation had grown to mythical levels. Some of the most popular beliefs were that they were a government sanctioned group that abducted and experimented on whoever they wanted. Others reported that they brainwashed those they took. The only known fact was that anyone who had been taken by them had never been seen or heard from again.

The vehicle made three more stops and each time more people were abducted and shoved into the back. One woman couldn't stop crying. A heavily armored man stalked towards her, stepping on the prisoners without a care. The woman's cries stopped and she gasped for air. The sound of her being choked to death went on for minutes longer than Beverly thought was possible. Finally, mercifully, the woman fell silent. Her lifeless body was flung on top of the rest of them. Beverly scurried out from under it. Tears began flowing from her eyes but she forced herself to stay silent.

Harold held her tight. From time to time he'd whisper reassurances to her, trying to keep her spirits up. Beverly used to think that any situation would be okay as long as she was in it with Harold, and it was true that having him with her now helped greatly, but she struggled to believe escape or survival were possible.

He tightened his grip on her. Harold had always been able to read her moods, they had felt connected the first night they met, and he sensed her despair.

"Do you want me to try to break us out of here?" he whispered.

Beverly was surprised he had waited so long to ask, but was glad he hadn't acted on the thought without verbalizing it. As much as she liked the idea of escape, everything was in the favor of their captors right now.

"Let's wait," she whispered back. "Maybe we'll see an opening when we get to wherever they're taking us."

It was impossible to know how much time passed as

they were taken to their destination. Beverly fought against dark scenarios in her mind, trying everything she could to keep a small ray of hope alive within herself. At last, what must've been hours later, the vehicle stopped and they were pulled out. The air smelled different here and there was a low roar. They were near the ocean.

A tear escaped from Beverly's eye as she realized this. Harold had proposed to her on the beach. They were planning to get married in the same spot.

"Move," a man said as he pushed her.

She stumbled forward, arms out in front of her. Panic was setting in now that Harold wasn't holding onto her.

"Harold?" she asked quietly.

"I'm here, right behind you."

"No talking!" someone shouted.

Her foot caught on something and she fell. Rough hands gripped her and yanked her up. They were herded into a building of some sort and then gathered together. Harold found her quickly and again pressed himself against her.

"It's going to be okay, I'm here," he said.

She fought against her doubts and struggled to buy into his reassurances. Before she could respond, jets of water slammed into them. All of the prisoners huddled together as they were hosed down, the water battering them. Finally, it stopped, and they were led from the room. Their soaked clothing hung on them, immediately chilling them as the temperature in the drafty building steadily plunged.

The sound of metal gates opening and closing could be heard. Beverly was shoved forward and she fell onto a hard stone floor. Someone crouched on top of her and removed the bindings on her hands. Another crash of closing metal rang out. Then the sounds started moving further away.

"Beverly?"

"I'm here, Harold," she said.

She heard him crawling, then felt his hands on her face. He lifted her blindfold. Her vision was blurry and it took a few moments for her eyes to focus. Harold offered her a weak smile and she appreciated the effort. With their hands

The Temporal Element

free they embraced fully now, then separated to take in their
surroundings. They were in a prison cell. The walls were
made of solid concrete but there was a barred window on each
of them. Beverly moved to the window on the back wall and
looked out.

"The ocean," she said. She took a deep breath, trying
to get a lungful of the refreshing breeze. Harold approached
and studied the bars.

"Those are pretty far apart," he said as he stuck his arm
between two of them.

"We're on a cliffside and it's hundreds of feet down to
the water. Even if we could get out we'd probably fall into the
rocks and die," Beverly said with a frown.

Harold had his whole arm out now and was wiggling,
seeing if he could get his shoulder through.

"Maybe we could clear the rocks and land in the water.
At least we'd have a chance," he said.

Beverly was about to argue with him, to try and talk
some sense into him, when they heard a loud voice. It was
coming from one of the nearby cells. They went to the side
window and peered into the next cell. Three young men were
there, and all of them were gathered at their own window,
watching something unfold in the next cell down.

"What's going on in there?" Harold asked.

One of the men turned towards him and answered.
"Men in protective clothing are doing something to the
prisoners. They're filming it."

"What do you mean doing something?" Beverly asked.
"What does that mean?"

"Nothing yet, just poking and prodding and— "

"Something's happening!" one of the other young men
said.

The man who had been talking to Beverly and Harold
returned his attention to the window. A moment later a wet
explosion could be heard. The three young men leapt back in
unison and screamed out. One of them fell to the floor while
another ran in circles yelling. "GOD IN HEAVEN!" he
repeated.

"What is it?" Beverly yelled, trying to get one of them to snap out of it long enough to tell her. "What did they do to the prisoners?"

None of the men answered and Beverly's hard fought control over her panic started to slip away. Her heart was pounding and black scenarios assaulted her mind. Harold could sense her distress and put his hand on her shoulder.

"Try to stay calm. We just need to..."

A loud metal scraping sound cut him off as the door to the neighboring cell opened. Harold and Beverly watched as the three young men scurried to the back of their cell.

"No!" one of them screamed.

Four men entered. Three of them wore black containment suits that covered their whole bodies. A fourth man, wearing armor and strapped with weaponry, stood guard at the door.

"Stay away from us!" one of the young men yelled.

The three men in the containment suits steadily came closer. One of them held a small camera and filmed, while the other two had strange objects in their hands. A blue liquid shot out from one of the objects and covered the young men.

"AHHHHH!" one of them screamed.

Seconds later the three of them exploded. Blood and gore decorated the walls and the ceiling. Piles of entrails and nastiness were all that remained of the three young men. A stomach turning odor washed over them, almost causing Beverly to puke. It smelled like a mixture of sewage, burnt rubber, and dish soap.

"We have to get out of here!" Harold yelled.

Beverly was frozen, her knuckles white as she gripped the window bars and stared at the horrifying mess in the next cell over. Harold tore her away and lightly slapped her, trying to snap her out of it.

"We have to get through the bars!" he yelled.

She watched as he moved to the back window and again stuck his arm out of it. He grunted and wriggled, and a moment later his shoulder popped through as well. He was having trouble fitting his head and sweat ran down his face as he struggled to get it through the bars. The sound of a key being inserted into their cell door spurred Beverly into action. Her heart was threatening to leap from her chest and she rushed towards the back window.

"What can I do?" she asked frantically.

"Push!"

She placed both hands on his head and pushed as hard as she could. The loud scraping of their cell door being opened gave her new strength and she shoved with all that she had. Harold's head popped through the bars and he nearly lost his grip on the outside of the window and fell to the ocean far below. He pulled his leg through and was then fully clinging to the outside of the cliffside prison.

"Now you," Harold said. "Stick your arm out first."

Beverly could hear the men coming up behind her and she knew. A tear rolled down her cheek and she shook her head. "It's too late," she said.

"No!" Harold shouted. "Just stick your arm through and I'll pull you out."

Over her shoulder he saw the three men rushing forward. His eyes went wide with panic as he realized Beverly was right, that she wasn't going to make it.

"I love you, Harold," Beverly said quickly.

"No, no, no, don't you say that!" he yelled. "Don't give up!"

Beverly turned and rushed the three men, trying to block them from the window.

"Jump, Harold!" she shouted.

He reached in through the bars, trying to grab hold of her, but she was too far away. He tried to squeeze his shoulder back through, to get back in, but it was impossible to do from the outside. Beverly fought and clawed at the men as they tried to get to the window. Her eyes met Harold's and she gave him the briefest of smiles.

"Jump," she said calmly.

Tears poured down Harold's face. "I'll come back for you, do you hear me?" he said.

"We both know I'll be dead," Beverly said. "Just go

and live your life."

"I'll find a way to save you!" Harold raged. "I will come back for you!"

The men knocked Beverly to the ground and moved towards the window.

"I swear it, Beverly. I'll come back for you!"

"Jump!" she screamed.

Just as their hands reached for him Harold jerked backwards. He fell towards the ocean far below and they watched until he disappeared from view. The three of them huddled together and spoke in hushed tones. Beverly laid her head against the cold floor and sobbed. Part of her was relieved that he had escaped but now she felt completely and totally alone.

She closed her eyes and resigned herself to her fate. She pictured Harold living out the rest of his life, happy and healthy. She watched in her mind as he grew older, found another person to fall in love with, had a family. Beverly smiled, ready now to die.

A strange buzzing sound caused her to open her eyes. The armored man guarding the door was convulsing, as a blue laser beam bored into his head. A moment later he dropped to the ground, giving her a clear view of the perfect circular wound that went all the way through his head. An odd figure cloaked in a prismatic robe stepped into the doorway holding what looked like a small pistol. Trying to focus on the clothing hurt her head, as it shimmered brightly.

The three men in containment suits turned to face this mystery person. The robed figure raised the laser pistol and fired three times in quick succession, burning a hole through each of the men's heads. They fell to the ground, dead.

Beverly looked up at this unknown rescuer, trying to see the face below the heavy hood of the prismatic cloak. The figure reached up and pushed the hood away.

"Harold?"

She could hardly believe her eyes. It was him but in a way it wasn't. Gone was his smooth, twenty nine year old flawless skin. This man's face had wrinkles, weathering, and a nasty jagged scar down one cheek.

"You're as beautiful as I remember," Harold said with a smile.

Beverly slowly stood up, never taking her eyes off of him. She stared at him hard and it was like staring into the future.

Tentatively, she reached her hand out and touched the side of his face. "Is that you, Harold?"

He brought his hand up and touched the back of hers. As soon as she felt his touch, Beverly knew. Somehow, someway, this was her Harold.

"It's me," he said, tears forming in his eyes. "It's me."

"But... how?"

Loud footfalls rang out in the hall and Harold pushed Beverly into the corner of the cell.

"No time to explain. I only have a small amount of time here and I used most of it getting to your cell."

He pressed her into the corner and stood in front of her, facing the door. Two armored men rushed into the cell but Harold dropped them quickly with his laser pistol.

"Put your arms around me and hold on as tight as you possibly can," Harold said.

A million questions rushed through Beverly's mind but she did as he said.

"No matter what happens, don't let go," he said.

"Okay."

She wrapped her arms around him and held as tightly as she could. Her face was pushed into his back but she heard him fire and kill three more guards. Then there was a blinding white flash, and the world around her was gone in an instant. She closed her eyes as tightly as she could, but the light found its way inside. Beverly wanted to scream. It felt like her brain was being cooked inside her skull, but no sound came when she opened her mouth. Just as the pain became unbearable, the light faded and she fell into a state of deep and profound unconsciousness.

* * *

Beverly opened her eyes slowly but was met with

51

nothing but darkness. She moved her fingers, struggling to get them to obey. Her whole body was stiff and as she tried to sit up she felt as if she was emerging from a coma. Her thoughts moved sluggishly in her brain and, as she got shakily to her feet, she groped into the darkness.

"Hello?"

The only answer was her voice bouncing back to her in what sounded like a very small room. Flashes of where she had been, the cliffside prison, and what had been about to happen, came back to her. Beverly panicked and moved forward as quickly as she dared in the dark. She found the wall and slid down it, feeling all over for a window or a door. Her hands found a door knob and she yanked it open.

The hallway was barely lit and she rushed down it, looking for any signs of an exit. Just as she neared an intersection she heard voices. Beverly skidded to a stop, then took off in the opposite direction. Visions of heavily armored men and men in head to toe black containment suits haunted her memory and she ran from them. Her bare feet slapped against the concrete floor as she continued her flight.

Several random turns later, she spotted an exit. Beverly pushed herself harder, disregarding any thoughts other than the ones that urged her to escape. She slammed through the door, and immediately her eyes were assaulted by an unfamiliar site and her lungs assaulted with a foul, sulfuric air. The door swung shut behind her, and she covered her mouth as she looked around at her once familiar hometown.

Immediately recognizable was Mount Gregory, the small mountain that the town was built around. But the cityscape she had grown up in, the place she and Harold had called home, was barely recognizable. Many of the larger buildings were partially destroyed, some were in flames. She turned in a slow circle, realizing that she was at the location where the mall should be. Instead, it looked like some sort of a military installation.

The earth beneath her feet shook and Beverly held out her arms, startled by the minor quake. It passed quickly, leaving her gazing up into the orange, dirty sky, wondering what was wrong with her town.

What had started as a minor burning in her lungs slowly grew to be a horrible pain and Beverly covered her mouth with her hand. It grew worse with every breath and despite her great desire for escape she moved back to the door she had come from and pulled on it. It was locked.

Each breath was harder to take than the one before and her lungs screamed out at her for more oxygen. A thin blackness played at the edges of her vision, then grew larger, threatening to overtake her. Beverly fell to her knees and clutched her throat.

"Beverly!"

She barely heard the voice, but she felt the strong hands pulling a mask over her head. Soon she could breathe again and slowly the burning in her chest subsided. She allowed herself to be helped up and then turned to look into the face of her savior.

"Harold," was all she could say.

It came back to her now like remembering a dream—the prison, his pledge to come back for her, and then his almost immediate return in older form. She looked upon him, at the aging on his face, the scar on his cheek. This was the same Harold who had rescued her from the prison.

"It's not safe outside today," Harold said, placing a reassuring hand on her back. "Let's get you back in the complex."

Gunfire rang out in the distance, towards what appeared to be the front gate. Harold frowned. "Get inside now," he said sternly.

Beverly did as he said. A young woman wearing combat fatigues opened the door as they approached. She clutched a machine gun in her hands and had a laser pistol hanging from her belt.

"Thank you, Amelia," Harold said as they passed her.

"Of course, Commander."

Beverly raised her eyebrows. She looked over at Harold questioningly, but he looked away. He led them down several corridors and then into a large, well furnished room.

He pulled off his mask and she followed suit. Her eyes never left him as he moved to a safe in the wall and opened it. He removed a pitcher of water and poured two glasses, then offered one of them to Beverly.

"How old are you?" she asked.

Harold looked at her strangely for a moment, then forced a smile onto his face. "That's your first question?"

Beverly's cheeks flashed red and she took a long drink of her water to cover her embarrassment.

"Easy," Harold said, "we don't have much water left."

She stopped drinking and nodded.

"Please, sit down," he said.

Beverly sat on the edge of the couch and continued to stare at the man that she loved. He sat in a chair across from her, studying her face. Finally, he leaned back and took a deep breath.

"I'm fifty."

She tried to process this information. They were both twenty-nine years old, their birthdays were six months apart.

"But you're Harold," she said. "You're my Harold."

He smiled and nodded. "I'm your Harold."

"The prison, it was…"

"Twenty-one years ago," he interrupted. "The worst day of my life."

Beverly's mind was overloaded as she tried to piece together what was happening, what had happened.

"I watched you fall," she said. "They rushed the window and you let go. But then, just moments later, you were back and… older, and you saved me. It wasn't twenty-one years ago, it just happened."

She wasn't sure why but tears had started filling up her eyes. Harold frowned as he watched her.

"For you, it just happened. But for me it has been twenty-one years since the prison. Twenty-one long years."

An unexplained anger was growing inside of Beverly. "But I was just there!" she yelled. "And so were you!"

Harold nodded. "This me was just there, that's true. Twenty-nine year old me was splashing down in the ocean at the time," he said.

Beverly stood up, on the precipice of a mental breakdown. "How is that possible?"

He got to his feet and took her hands in his. Part of her felt strange being this close to him, but another part felt comforted.

"I said I'd come back for you, remember?"

Deep down she knew what he was saying, that what he was implying had happened, but she couldn't allow herself to believe it.

"I've spent the last twenty-one years developing..."

"Don't say it," Beverly pleaded.

"... time travel."

She pulled her hands from his and backed away. She shook her head as tears began falling from her eyes.

"The men that took us that day, they were more powerful than you can imagine," Harold said, pleading for her to understand. "But I organized a resistance and we fought back against them. We purged them from the face of the planet. And all the while I kept the most brilliant scientists and physicists working on time travel, so I could come back for you and save you from your horrible fate in that prison."

Beverly kept backing away until she was up against the wall. "This can't be happening," she cried. "It can't be real."

Harold slowly walked towards her, his arms outstretched.

"I know it's not ideal, Beverly, and I know I'm not the same as I was back then. I'm fifty and you're not even thirty, I know it's weird, but I swear to you I tried to get back to you faster," he said. "But those bastards, they were imbedded in every level of our society. It's a miracle we were able to beat them at all. They slowed my research, but I never gave up hope. No matter what the obstacles, I never let anyone stop my development of the technology that could send me back to save you."

He extended his hand, hoping that she would take it.

"Excuse me, Commander," a sharp voice said from across the room. "I'm sorry to interrupt, but an attack on the complex is imminent. Your presence is needed in the command center."

Harold sighed, then nodded. He let his hand fall back to his side. "I'll be right there."

"I thought you said they were beaten, the ones who took us that day," Beverly said.

"They are; there are none of them left. This is... someone else."

She could sense the tension in his answer but didn't call attention to it.

"I have to go deal with this," Harold said. "Please, just stay here and try to calm down. I'm sorry this is so strange for you. I promise I'll answer any more questions you have when I get back."

Beverly nodded and watched as he strode from the room. She was glad to be alone and returned to the couch. She closed her eyes and attempted to make sense of everything that she had just learned. Despite her best efforts not to, she felt herself falling asleep.

* * *

Beverly's eyes shot open and she sat up quickly. She had no idea how long she had been asleep on the couch. Looking around, she saw that the room was still empty. She got to her feet and went to the door. The hallway was empty as well, and she moved down it slowly, totally unsure of where she was going or what was even housed within this complex.

At the intersection at the far end of the hall she saw a line of soldiers sprint past, weapons at the ready. The sound of explosions and gunfire outside were faintly audible through the thick walls.

She was just about ready to accept that she was lost when she heard Harold's voice.

"You're out of your mind!" he screamed.

Beverly came around the corner and saw the large command center. There were computer stations set up all over and in the middle stood Harold. He was addressing a dark-haired young man on a video screen.

"Out of my mind?" the man laughed. "That's a hell of a thing for you to say to me."

Originally planning on going inside, Beverly stayed just outside of the room, fearful of the scene currently playing out. Something about the way Harold was standing made him seem frightening to her.

"Do your people even know what you've done to this planet?" the dark-haired man asked menacingly. "Do they know that you're the one responsible for the quick death of the Earth? Or are they so brainwashed that they believe only what you tell them?"

"Most of my people have been with me since the revolution!" Harold shouted. "They and countless like them fought and bled and died by my side, so we could rid our world of the tyrants that had silently taken it over! You're free today because of what I did, you ungrateful little bastard!"

The man on the screen laughed bitterly. "Ever the conquering hero, huh, Harold?"

Harold stalked closer to the monitors and pointed a threatening finger at the screen. "Wipe that smirk off your face," he commanded. "I freed this planet, and ever since I've had to deal with uprising after uprising. Well, I crushed those who came before you and I'll crush you as well. I'll paint the countryside with your blood!" Harold looked like a mad god as he sneered at the screen.

"I've never disputed that you saved us all, but that doesn't excuse what you've done to this world since then," the young man said. "Your secret project has killed the planet from the inside out, all so you could reconnect with the love of your life."

The young man paused and leaned closer to the screen, his face growing even larger. "But I must say, she's quite beautiful."

Beverly froze as she realized the man could see her. Harold spun around and his eyes went wide as he saw her standing there. The crazed look on his face slowly faded away.

"My men will lay waste to your complex and everyone

inside," the man on the screen said. "If you come out and give yourself up, I will spare your people."

Harold didn't even hear what his opponent was saying. The crushed look on Beverly's face hit him like a bullet to the chest. He stepped towards her but she took a step away. He opened his mouth to speak but she cut him off.

"You caused everything I saw outside?" Beverly asked.

"There may be ways to heal it," Harold said. "I've got people working on it around the clock, but this little pissant and his revolutionary army have been hounding me for years. It makes it hard to sustain research."

"What did you do, Harold? Why would you cause such destruction?"

"I did what I had to do! Whatever was necessary!" he shouted, causing her to jump. "The only power source on the planet strong enough to supply the needed energy for time travel was the planet itself."

He realized he was yelling and paused to calm himself.

"We've tapped into the Earth's core, but it wasn't supposed to cause so much damage. We're not sure why it happened."

Beverly shook her head and took another step away. "You doomed the entire planet, all because of me?"

"I swore to you that I would come back."

"At the cost of damning the entire human race?" Beverly shouted.

"I couldn't just leave you there to die!"

He rushed towards her, but she turned and ran.

"Please, just hear me out!" Harold said as he chased her down the hallway.

Beverly ran blind, taking every turn she came to as Harold continued to chase after her. Before long, the hallways began sloping downwards, taking them into the bowels of the complex. Above, it had been more of a military installation, but down here were laboratories and huge banks of computers. And then she saw it. A giant room, and in the center a machine that could be only one thing. She adjusted her course and ran for it, knowing that the love of her life had left her with no other choice. Harold saw what she was doing and ran faster.

"No, Beverly!"

She sprinted through the door, then turned and slammed every button on the control panel. The heavy metal door slid shut just as Harold reached it. Beverly studied the control panel, piecing together how to lock the door. She manipulated the buttons that were by a picture of a lock and listened as the door sealed shut. There was a small window in the middle of the door and Harold's face appeared there.

"Don't do it, Beverly. You don't know what power you're messing with."

She turned away from him and approached the machine. It was a circular apparatus, and tens of thousands of wires fed into it from the ceiling. A large control panel stood in front of it, and she began looking it over, trying to decipher how it worked.

"You can't just go back in time. There are consequences you can't even imagine," Harold yelled through the door.

"I won't stay in this future that you've ruined because of me!"

"This can be our world, our time to be together," Harold pleaded. "Come out and work with me. Let's undo the damage together."

She punched buttons, familiarizing herself with the map layouts and the time gauge. The machine was still set to the same time and space coordinates Harold had used when he'd gone back to rescue her in the prison.

"What do you think you can accomplish here, Beverly?"

"I'm going to go back, and I'm going to convince you not to come back for me."

He slammed his fist into the door. "Don't you understand what that will do? It'll change this timeline, it will erase it. Once your time in the past runs out, you'll have no future to return to."

Beverly paused as she let his words sink in.

"Even I don't know what that means," Harold said, desperately hoping he was getting through to her.

She returned her attention to the control panel and pushed a few final buttons. Flashing red lights and an alarm sounded out in the chamber.

"No! Beverly don't do this! I waited so long to see you again!" Harold screamed.

Beverly saw one of the prismatic cloaks that Harold had been wearing when he'd time traveled, and she quickly put it on. She had no idea if it was essential to the time travel process or not, but decided not to chance it. She stepped onto the platform and then looked out at Harold. He was raging against the door, smashing it again and again with his fist, but when their eyes met he stopped.

They stayed that way for a long moment until finally he spoke.

"I promised I'd come back," he said. "No matter what I had to do, no matter the terrible price I had to pay, I did it for you." Tears streamed down his face and he pressed his palm against the window. "I did it because I love you."

"I know you do," she replied. "I never doubted that for a second."

And with a blinding white flash, she was gone.

* * *

Harold twisted as he fell towards the rocky shore. As he got closer he could see the jagged rocks pointing up at him, waiting to greet him. He tried to contort his body, anything to angle away from them. He was almost upon them now, and he grunted as he arched his spine in a desperate final attempt to alter his trajectory.

He slammed into the water and rocketed downwards. Even though he'd managed to narrowly avoid the rocks, the water wasn't very deep, and he crashed into the ocean floor like a missile.

All of the precious air escaped from his lungs, and his vision went blurry from the impact. Everything hurt, but he knew if he didn't swim up to the surface soon he would die.

The light in his eyes began to fade and he started to thrash wildly. Every movement triggered a thunderstorm of pain, and he was unsure if he was going to make it to the surface before his breath gave out.

Harold felt hands gripping him, tugging him upwards. He thought of the men in black containment suits, but even if he'd wanted to fight against whoever was holding him, he couldn't. His back was in agony, and he found he could barely move his arms or legs.

The mysterious person pulled him above water, and Harold gasped in lungfuls of air. He was dragged onto the shore, and as his wits finally started to return he craned his neck to look up at the person who had pulled him from the water.

"You're an angel," Harold said, smiling as he took the sight of his beloved Beverly in. She was cloaked in shimmering sunlight, but under the bright hood he could see her face. He tried to sit up so he could see her better, but pain shot from his back down into his legs.

"Sit still, Harold. Just sit and listen."

He shook his head. "We have to get out of here. I have to get you out of here."

Beverly adjusted the prismatic cloak and knelt beside him. She put her hands on his shoulders to calm him. She knew she should hurry, that there was no time to waste, but she couldn't stop herself from taking a moment to soak in the sight of him. This was *her* Harold, the way she remembered him, the way he was supposed to be.

"You need to listen to me very carefully, because I don't have a lot of time and this is going to be hard to understand," Beverly said.

She swallowed hard, suddenly overcome by the enormity of what she needed to do. With no idea of how much time she had left before she returned to the future, or if there even was a future for her to return to, she jumped right into it.

"I need to tell you about the future."

TIME HEALS ALL
by Paul Lamb

"How many inches are in a foot?"

Nurse Mary sighed. "I really wish you studied the briefing material more thoroughly."

"I know. But their systems all seem so random. I don't suppose the answer is ten."

"No. There are twelve inches in one foot, according to the measuring system they use."

"One foot, huh?"

"Yes. It is the kind of thing most young adults your age would know, so you had better spontaneously recall the knowledge in the briefing before we get to the Miller house. Or you had better not say anything at all while we are there."

Nurse Mary and Nurse Ann had stepped off the bus several blocks from the Miller's home and were walking the remaining way. Nurse Mary, who had made many visits before, knew to engage others as little as possible and strive to look completely comfortable in the strange world. Nurse Ann was making her first field visit, and though she had been conditioned extensively to restrain any surprise or bafflement, she was sufficiently perplexed by the Byzantine nature of the society to babble away, perhaps a bit imprudently.

"Imagine when we return. I can tell everyone we actually rode on a vehicle that used fossil fuel! It's almost savage."

"It does seem that way," Nurse Mary said, keeping their pace and trying to appear in a casual conversation. Several vehicles passed them. "Yet, they aren't hopeless, fortunately."

"Yes, they aren't hopeless," said Nurse Ann. "After all, we are going to the *Miller* house. A plum job for my first field training visit!"

Nurse Mary stopped and turned to Nurse Ann. "To the Millers, there is nothing extraordinary about their son. Nor about you. To them, you will merely be a trainee nurse; a particularly quiet one. With me you are merely a trainee visitor; a particularly talkative one. Stay on task and you'll go home successful. Screw this up and they may decide to leave you here." Nurse Mary looked at a small card she was carrying, then at the numbers on the houses. "Just over here," she said, gesturing across the street.

They crossed the street, lined with old trees and comfortable, large houses behind them, and Nurse Ann saw a small stream of water running along the curb. Up the street, a neighbor was washing a car, and the effluent was running off toward them.

"Look at this," she said, unable to prevent herself from stopping briefly to look down at the braided flow in the gutter. "I'd like to collect several liters of this to take back with us. Do you suppose it's drinkable?"

Even Nurse Mary paused. "It is a marvel, isn't it? The waste! I don't think this particular water is safe to drink, but I think it could be made safe." She shook her head and stepped onto the curb. "Remember, take only memories!"

A wide lawn separated the Miller house from the street, and at the top of the walk, three stairs led up to a broad porch before the front door. From within the house they could hear the loud throb of discordant music.

"Remember your training," Nurse Mary said as she

checked her bag. "When we are around them, say as little as possible, and when you're in doubt, say nothing at all. Let me take the lead, and we'll get through this and back home without trouble."

As they approached the door, the music grew louder, rattling the windows above them. "Not my taste," said Nurse Mary, cocking her head to listen.

"Nor mine," said Nurse Ann. For the first time, the eagerness left her face as she realized the implications of making even the smallest mistake. "I'll let you take it from here."

Nurse Mary nodded as she pressed the bell button. Soon, a haggard-looking woman opened the door. The music boomed out past her.

"Hello. I'm Nurse Mary. This is Ann. She is a nursing student. We're from the hospice."

"You're not our regular nurse," the woman shouted over the music. She looked them over with a dubious expression.

"No, she was taken ill at the last minute, and I was recruited to provide today's injection. Ann here is in training and on her first field visit. She's a little nervous." Nurse Ann smiled and shrank a little.

It hadn't been their job to interrupt the regular nurse's visit. That was left to another operative. They simply had to provide the boy's injection and then return to the portal as directly as possible without drawing attention to themselves. It was a task so straightforward, and Nurse Mary was so experienced that the risk of bringing along a trainee was thought negligible. And so, Nurse Ann was chosen from among all of the young people in her class to come along.

"Is he bad today?" Nurse Mary asked, sounding crisp and professional.

"Not at the moment," said Mrs. Miller, concluding that these strange nurses were legitimate. "He's sleeping, though I don't know how he can with his brother's music blasting so loud." She glanced up the stairs behind her, then back to the nurses.

"Well, we won't be any trouble. We'll just do what we came here for and then be on our way, which should be no time at all."

Mrs. Miller led them through the hall and into a room where a frail boy was propped up with pillows on a couch. He was small and hairless, and covered with quilts to prevent him from feeling cold on the warm summer morning.

Mrs. Miller left them briefly and walked to the bottom of the stairs. "Could you please turn that down?!?" she shouted to the bedroom above. But the boy up there either didn't hear or didn't care, for the music didn't change. The walls of the house vibrated.

"I'm sorry for that," she told the nurses. "He's having a difficult time dealing with his brother's cancer. Poor boy. We all have to be strong, but it's been especially hard for him to accept his brother's end. He has a lot of anger and confusion. The social worker says he's acting out."

"Perfectly understandable," said Nurse Mary. She busied herself with the medicine and syringe from her bag, drawing out a measure of clear liquid. It was not the morphine-based painkiller that the regular nurse would have given the boy to ease his suffering, but rather a simply derived compound Nurse Mary had brought along that would, instead, cure him of his cancer overnight. "It won't bother us a bit."

"Well, is there anything you need?" asked Mrs. Miller.

Nurse Mary shook her head as she drew the sleeping boy's bruised arm from under the blanket and prepared to give him the injection, but Nurse Ann licked her lips and spoke. "Yes. I wonder if I might have a tall glass of water."

* * *

Later, on the front porch, Nurse Mary and Nurse Ann paused and looked at each other, as the loud music suddenly stopped.

"Did she finally persuade him to let his brother rest quietly?" Nurse Ann asked.

"Most likely—right after she finished giving you your glass of water. Did you really think that was appropriate?"

"Oh, it seemed terrible to waste the opportunity to

65

drink an entire glass of clean water all at once."

Nurse Mary might have chided her for the bold action, but she was secretly envious of Nurse Ann, and chose to keep quiet.

They stepped down the stairs and began to walk to the street. Suddenly, behind them, the door to the house jerked open and a teenage boy dressed in torn black clothes appeared. He was not much younger than Nurse Ann. He had spiked purple hair and a skateboard under his arm. He gave the two nurses a scowl, then threw the skateboard onto the porch, leapt aboard, and launched himself over the steps, past the nurses, and to the street.

"The troubled brother?" asked Nurse Ann.

"Yes, all 71 inches of him, I estimate."

Nurse Ann tried to calculate how tall that made him, but she still wasn't sure just what a foot was supposed to be. She didn't think it meant the same thing as the foot in her shoe, so she gave up.

The two walked to the street on their way back to the stop. The bus would take them back to the office building where the time portal lay hidden, awaiting their return.

"Barring any last minute interactions with these people," said Nurse Mary, "I'd say we accomplished our mission. I will report your field training visit as a success. By the way, you aren't still thirsty, are you?"

Nurse Ann ignored the question. She had recovered from her anxiety and was buoyant about the trip. "My first field visit. No difficulties; a successful completion. Imagine. We saved the life of Stephen Miller today. *Stephen Miller!* And with it, we have saved all of civilization in the centuries to come. If only the historians could know the truth."

Nurse Mary shook her head. "I really wish you had studied the briefing material more thoroughly."

Nurse Ann stopped walking, turned to Nurse Mary, and frowned. "What part did I get wrong?"

"That wasn't Stephen Miller we saved. That was Scott Miller. Stephen Miller is the one with the purple hair."

The Long View
by William R.D. Wood

"History waits for no man," said Terry.

"Except, perhaps, for us, yes?" said the Russian with a laugh.

Attaching the last few hardline connectors to the console was a clumsy affair using the bulky gloves of the suit. Still, he and Mikhail were far better equipped than their space-faring predecessors. Environmental suits had come a long way in the hundred years since Armstrong and Aldrin (and, in all fairness to Mikhail's homeland, Gagarin and Titov). Still, vacuum being vacuum, EVAs were always going to be awkward.

The multiwrench slipped from Terry's grasp in mid-turn and fell slowly to the ground. "Damn it." Gray dust plumed around the tool as it struck.

The Russian's hand clasped his shoulder as Terry stood from retrieving the wrench. "Patience, my friend. No rush is needed. Our families will sing our praises even if we—what is word—*dawdle*, yes?"

"I just want to get this done." The eighteen month

buildup of the *Hemera* project was over. The whole mission would be over in hours now and they'd be on their way home. Two days later they'd be crawling out of the return module on the Kazakh steppe. And not long after, he'd be standing on the deck of his beach house at sunset, the chill winter wind in his hair, the salt on his lips.

The final connector slid into place as a vibration passed through the ground—just enough to stir the dust at their feet and set the cables to swaying. The tendency of the *Hemera* device to shake the ground a little and the civilian news media's unfailing feeding frenzy over such events had prompted the project directors to move the experiments somewhere more remote.

As the shaking subsided, the heads up display in Terry's helmet informed him all systems were online and the reactor was spinning up for test-level discharge.

The heads up display in Terry's helmet informed him all systems were nominal and the coils in the Ring were spinning up for transition-level discharge. "Finally."

"This is time travel, yes?" asked the Russian with a laugh. "What is hurry?"

The Russian was efficient and highly skilled, but the concept of urgency was alien to him. Here they were, on the surface of the Moon, unknown to all but a few scientists and bureaucrats on Earth, assembling a device that might or might not sling them across time, and the man's pulse was probably not a beat above baseline.

Terry wasn't quite so at ease. Buzzing around between the various inflatables in low Earth orbit, with an occasional jaunt to the higher platforms, was a thrill like no other. Still, those distances were measured in terms of altitude. One hundred kilometers. Two hundred. No one ever referred to the Moon as being at an *altitude* of four hundred thousand kilometers, though.

The full Earth hung almost four times the size of a similarly full Moon in the terrestrial sky. No, the *height* didn't bother him. It was the *remoteness*.

The main control console's monitor, a transparent plate

of glass a meter wide and five centimeters thick, flickered, ripples like water expanding outward as it booted up. The illusion of a vertical pool of water against the stark lunar landscape was at once comical and disconcerting. And just plain wrong.

Terry ran down the checklists displayed on the console, cross-checking against his own lists in his heads up. Everything had gone perfectly and in the great tradition of space travel, it was time to start worrying. Another reason to get the tests done and get the hell off this chunk of regolith.

The image on the plate stabilized into three views of the Earth, each taken from the set of telescopes placed with the *Hemera* Ring. A close-up of the terrestrial horizon dominated half the display. Another showed a magnified dayside disc of the Earth and the last a series of computer-enhanced overlays of temperature, biomass distribution and industrialization. Status data scrolled along the edges of the display as a countdown in the corner signaled that optimum test conditions were minutes away.

"This is great day for Slavsky family, my friend."

The man was incapable of *not* mentioning his family every few minutes. The two weeks of their isolation together in transit and assembling the *Hemera* Ring had convinced Mikhail that the two of them were now brothers. *Brat'ya.* The Russian's incessant stories of *futbol* games and dirty diapers, though, had only convinced Terry the bachelor life was the only one for him.

A second vibration worked upward through his boots, twice the amplitude of the last.

"Geo-lock is good, yes?" In the lower corner of the largest display window, a tiny icon of the Earth with a padlock through it blinked.

"Two minutes."

The early models tested on Earth had flustered the project leaders. Despite unwavering certainty that the theory, calculations, and engineering challenges had been met, every practical test had ended with the mock-down Rings vanishing just as planned but not returning as *also* planned.

An undergrad had realized their mistake. Celestial movements as large as the Local Group had been accounted for, but not the latest models of the greater-verse that predicted movement through a series of hyperstrates. She'd received a personal letter of thanks from the President, simultaneously attaining a higher dimension of professional exile from those she was supposed to be learning *from*.

"Please to take picture for wife and kids."

Terry turned to see his partner a dozen meters away, arms raised in a triumphant Y, the smooth basin of Mare Vaporum stretching to the distant mountains behind him. Sunlight glinted gold from the cosmonaut's mirrored visor washing out his face, but, even in the bulky suit, something bold and perhaps a little brazen in the man's posture identified research-cosmonaut Mikhail Slavsky as surely as the Cyrillic letters printed on his chest.

Terry sighed loudly to ensure microphone pick-up. "Mikhail, they'll never see the picture."

"You are prude, friend Terry," scolded the Russian. "Must learn to live little, I think. *Hemera* will not *always* be classified. When project is public, children will see father as hero and you will wish I had taken picture of you too."

"Fine," said Terry selecting the camera option from the controls on his left sleeve. "Hold still and say—"

"*Cheese.*"

Hi-resolution stills of the Ring and various other components of *Hemera* displayed against the inner surface of Terry's visor, showing the images taken since their arrival. The camera blipped as dozens of shots of Mikhail streamed into the suit's memory. Standard departmental protocols called for all imagery from all devices to be simultaneously transmitted to all mission vehicles as well as Earth-side receivers, but *Hemera* was an exception. The only transmissions allowed were the line-of-sights between Mikhail and himself. Houston and Korolyov had decided to take no unnecessary chances with intercepted signals.

The secrecy was ultimately pointless and those in power knew that. Sooner or later an industrious Moon-gazer or automated telescope on Earth would spot the hundred meter Ring as well as the landing/living module. Even the assemblers they'd brought along were the size of small cars. Their little photo shoot would be nothing compared to the public's discovery of the three trillion spent on a project that might be nothing more than a new way to stir up dust on the ground.

"Satisfied?" asked Terry as he streamed the photos to the Russian.

"*Da,*" said Mikhail lowering his arms. In several bounds, he skidded to a clumsy stop next to the nearest of the assemblers. "I find woman for you when we get home, friend Terry. Maybe my cousin Yuliya. She give you good children and she has the big—"

"I'll pass," said Terry. "Can't take a leak off the porch if there's a woman in the house."

"I think you miss point, my friend."

Terry had made the joke time and again that the only thing he feared more than disappearing like the previous devices was Mikhail's matchmaking skills.

A third tremor rumbled across the landing site.

"Sixty seconds."

"Holy hot damn, yes?" said the Russian bounding to his side and rubbing his gloved hands together. The numbers on the display counted down as sunlight played across the crystal blue waters of the Asiatic on the close up.

"We should say words," said Mikhail.

"Nonsense." Armstrong had flubbed his line and Terry didn't want to be remembered saying something that might not play as well in history. Of course, if things went badly, they would be gone and the few people in the know Earthside might get away without ever having to explain the new hundred-meter gouge in the lunar surface.

"Then I will," said the Russian, pausing until the various counters reached five seconds. "I am honored to be here at this time and all those to come."

Terry felt the vibration first through his boots, a second later through his hand on the console. Then the floodlights around the project site flared, throbbing in sync with his heads up display as the view washed out in a sea of milky white.

And, as though a celestial switch toggled back to home, the whiteness was gone and the ground was still once more. The heads up indicated all systems online and the viewing plate showed the same three views as before. Seconds passed before Terry realized he was staring into the sun which had changed position in the lunar sky.

"Better than Disney Island, yes?"

Terry gave the man a grin. Sliding his fingers across the monitor controls, he instructed the system to make comparisons between the readings a few seconds ago and the data coming in now. Icons blinked on and off as images flipped over one another. The main image of the Earth's horizon remained, but the view of the Earth's surface was now desert instead of the Adriatic Sea of moments ago. Terry felt his heart speed at the thought.

He'd not expected *Hemera* to *fail*. In fact, he'd *prayed* it would succeed and he was not a particularly religious man. Still, at some level, he'd just assumed the changes would not strike him as so dramatic.

One of the smaller monitor frames indicated star positions. Various vector-lines flashed between before and after sampling of key constellations. In the other frame, two columns of data shuffled, blinking as they aligned with their counterparts.

"Pollution index," said the Russian with a laugh. "Negligible!"

He slapped Terry on the back, prompting him to skip a step to control the momentum transfer.

"Habitation and development fractals—negative growth."

"I'll be damned," said Terry. *Hemera* was also displaying the postulated date. "July 20, 1869. Just as planned."

"*Now* you want to say words?" asked Mikhail.

The laugh that erupted from Terry's mouth startled him. He felt stunned, detached. Shaking his head sharply, he shook off the feeling before it could take hold. *Get thee behind me, hindbrain,* he thought, and that made him smile.

"Are you okay?"

"Yeah." Terry had to force the affirmation. "Just realizing what we did. Where we are—rather, *when* we are. No amount of training or psyche testing can prepare you for... this."

"*Da.*" Mikhail stepped to one side to look around the console at the disc of the Earth, steadying himself on a floodlight stand as a small after-tremor passed beneath their boots.

Terry took a deep cleansing breath. "I think I will make a go at the history books."

"By all means, my friend."

Terry keyed the voice recorder. "Like my comrade, research-cosmonaut Slavsky, I too am honored—humbled even—to be part of this momentous occasion. To everyone who helped bring us here and now—to everyone who has ever walked the shores of Earth or the shoals of the Moon—we stand on your shoulders today. My eternal thanks."

The Russian clasped him on the shoulder. "There is poet in my comrade, yes?"

"I guess." Still smiling, Terry called up the mission schedule, scrolling until he reached the list of temporal targets. "Next jump is 500 years."

"After we make calibration jump."

"Of course."

Terry swiped the controls for an immediate return to their present. The geo-lock showed green, as did the coils of the Ring. *Hemera* had performed perfectly. There would be time for in-depth exploration and observation later—probably by specialists and scientists yet to be selected—and Terry was fine with that. The ground shuddered beneath them, dust dancing in tiny static discharges at their feet. A flash of light and seconds later they were peering intently at the monitor, the sun no longer overhead.

"Star locations are off," said Mikhail, his voice uneasy. "Fractals at zero point one off target."

Terry linked into the console, comparing the star maps and the landforms manually. The main screen showed a sunset streaming through a brilliant cross-section of atmosphere. The colors through the airborne dust and clouds were amazing. Earth was a gem among the heavens no matter *when* you looked upon it. And the data discrepancies were nothing to be concerned about. "It's okay, buddy. We overshot a day or two is all."

The Russian nodded. "Houston must be shitting brick, yes?"

"No doubt." Terry scanned the emergency-only mission frequencies. If anything went wrong, then future-Houston should know about it as part of *their* past. Sending a message back to them at this point in *Hemera* time was the plan should that happen. Since the frequencies were clear and no future versions of themselves had come bounding across Mare Vaporum to stop them, all was well. Terry made adjustments to *Hemera's* parameters. "A little tweaking is all she needed. Next stop, five hundred years."

"Very well." Mikhail took the controls in hand this time, confirming the computer's automated settings and engaging the program.

The floodlights surrounding the site quivered and brightened, sending eerie shadows dancing across the lunar landscape. Terry held onto the console with one hand and Mikhail's shoulder with the other. The tremors passed like a wave across the surface and, in a final flash from their displays, were still once more.

A bead of sweat rolled down his face and onto his lips. The taste of salt was strong in his tiny closed-loop environment. Someday someone would design a suit that could wipe your forehead or at least a helmet fan that could prevent perspiration.

Mikhail pointed at the screen. An ocean gleamed in the daylight, the sun now shining at their backs, illuminating Mare Vaporum as well. Icons flashed across the main viewer, motion tracking software identifying a pre-programmed *significant feature* and zooming in. Viewed from an oblique angle against a white-crested section of ocean, a wooden ship of brown and black plowed ahead, white sails billowing.

"Habitation fractals have almost vanished," said the Russian, looking from the viewer to a series of dynamic graphs. "Welcome to 1669—give or take year or three. Friend Terry, we should we make trek to Tranquility and leave note, yes? *Second place is bitch* or something like."

"You're a funny guy." These moments were the biggest in human history and the Russian was taking it all in stride. As tempting as it was to stay a while and turn the telescopes on other areas of the ancient Earth, they needed to move ahead. "Taking us back to the present."

The transition seemed worse to Terry, but only a little. Could be he was just more sensitive after the last one. He'd make a full write-up for the docs so the techies and theorists could make whatever refinements were needed. Time lag, they'd probably dub it. Hell, maybe they'd even name it after him.

While Mikhail busied himself with the mission checklist, Terry zoomed the main display onto a strip of coastline not unlike the one his own beach house sat on. Smoke billowed up in places. It had been a dry year and California was no slouch when it came to its reputation for seasonal brush fires.

"Temporal targeting still off," announced Mikhail. "Over a week this time."

"The techies are going to be busy when we get back."

"This is why *test* pilots test, yes?"

Terry laughed, the taste of bile rising in his throat for an instant. The schedule in his heads up blinked. "Next stop five thousand years."

"Forget that," said the Russian, shuffling toward the console, adjusting the controls. "We go for the grand prize, my friend."

Terry watched as the Russian scrolled down the list of target destinations in their linked systems. The bottom-most blinked once and dropped into the destination window. His hand hovered above the initiation icon on the main control console for only an instant. Terry thought the duration of a sixty million year jump ought to take longer than the two hundred or even the five hundred they'd already made, but just as mission scientists had predicted, the transition time was the same.

Seconds traded for centuries—now for thousands of millennia.

Staggering away from the console, Terry fought down a wave of nausea and dizziness, his gaze slowly rising to take in the darkened Earth hanging against a star-strewn blackness. Mare Vaporum was in darkness. Light from the floods crept out a few dozen meters beyond the Ring, but that was all.

Mikhail leaned on the control console, his breathing heavy on the radio connection. "Too hasty, I think." His voice was raspy as if his ever-present optimism might be at war with exhaustion.

Terry moved to his side and tapped the main display. All views of Earth were nighttime but as the telescopic enhancements overlaid the images one by one, all the theoretical details they'd both learned as children came to light. The continent of Africa was recognizable though more isolated. Asia, visible in the full-disc view, was missing the jutting triangle of India and the icy North American wastelands of their own time had formed a swath of land that swallowed all of Europe in a band of mountains and plains before fusing into Asia.

"Sixty million years," whispered Terry.

Their radio connection was nothing more than a whispery crackle and hum of white noise for a long time and, somehow, it made those moments more empty than any Terry had ever known.

"Terry, my friend?" Mikhail's look peaked in the wash of the floodlights. "I am ready to go home."

"Roger that."

Across such a large jump, Terry didn't attempt to compensate for the drift they'd experienced in the previous runs. They could fine tune with an additional jump or two once they got closer to their own time.

Right now, though, Terry just wanted to go home. He wanted to pack this site up, climb aboard the return module and get back to normal gravity. To a fresh breeze in his face that didn't come from a cabin fan. To the sounds of gulls and the smell and taste of the sea. To the sound of voices besides Mikhail's and his own.

Hell, when he got home, he might even let Mikhail hook him up. A smile tugged at the corner of his mouth as he touched the activation icon. Unlike their previous jumps, for several seconds nothing happened, as if the universe had lost track of them.

The ground shuddered and Terry watched a ripple from the perimeter of the Ring move inward as the floodlights flared and the white noise in his headset became deafening.

A blank white wall bloomed around him, snatching away every sensation and every thought. He woke as though from a drug-induced slumber. Dust coated half of his visor, sunlight refracting like tiny prisms.

With an effort, he pushed himself into a sitting position. "Mikhail?"

A groan crossed the connection. Terry shoved with his hands and knees to gain his feet, the first few steps clumsy as he made his way to his fallen friend and helped him up. A tremor, the worst they'd encountered since beginning their jaunts, knocked them both to their knees before they managed to stand side by side. Some of the floodlights had fallen, and super-cooled gases vented in the distance from a chiller near the Ring.

The Russian muttered something Terry could not understand, then, "What is happened?"

Rather than answer, Terry moved to the console. The main telescopes were still tracking and rebooting, having been thrown off target by the seismic component of the transition. The computer had already estimated their arrival point though, apparently using inputs from the return module's smaller scopes.

"Over shot by almost ten years," said Terry.

"Not bad," said the Russian, life ebbing back into his

voice. "Should be easy—"

A flash of light filled the airless sky. In the distance, a plume of dust and rock erupted upward. Terry tracked a second streak of light and it impacted beyond the mountains, farther than the first. The impactors wouldn't leave large craters, but such events were so few and far between, the odds of them arriving during such an event were—well, astronomical. Maybe they were passing through a particularly dense field of cometary debris. They just needed to make a few calibration calculations and get out of there before any other surprises came their way.

"Friend Terry?"

Mikhail stood before the main console. Gouts of glowing red flashed and oozed on the display plate. Terry was reminded of both a magnified image of microbial life and an erupting volcano. The smaller inset image he couldn't make out.

"What are you zoomed on?"

The Russian pointed to the distant smear in the sky. "Not zoomed."

Where the Earth should have been was a shimmering mass, roughly spherical in the middle, and flaring out into a disc of molten red like the birth of a miniature solar system.

"No…"

Mikhail exploded into motion, hands flying across controls as the final telescopes came online, giving Terry a better view. "We must go back." The Russian twisted quake-loosened connectors back into place and Terry imagined he could hear them snapping home. A tremor passed under their feet as a smoldering shadow moved across the moonscape, blotting out the sun for an instant as it passed.

They were only ten years in their own future. Terry remembered the view of the clouds on their first return. On their second, the fires he'd assumed were the typical California scourge.
And now…

The icon of a tiny earth with a padlock through it blinked in the corner of the largest display window.

"We can't go, Mikhail."

The cosmonaut turned on him, brow knitted and fury in his eyes. "I will return to my family—you will help me." Blood ran from a contusion on the man's forehead where he had struck himself when he blacked out. The Russian grabbed Terry's working harness and lifted him. His fury had become madness.

"It was the geo-lock. We used the Earth of our time as our anchor." Their future Houston hadn't warned them because they couldn't.

The Russian blinked hard. Blood oozed down the inside of his faceplate. "And every time we use *Hemera*...it gets...worse."

Terry nodded. He'd seen pictures of his friend's family for months now, their smiling faces staring up from stills and video. The words were thick in his mouth. "They'll have more time if we just stay here."

Research-cosmonaut Mikhail Slavsky lowered his partner to the ground and dropped to his knees.

Terry sat down beside him in the lunar dust. The fiery reds of their broken world were not unlike a sunset.

The tiny fan in his helmet blew chill air across his face.

And his tears tasted of salt.

Back in Time
By Carolyn M. Chang

I roll the tiny cube back and forth in my hand. It looks so perfect in contrast to my mottled skin. The medical technician drones on: "Remember, take it right before you go to sleep. Meditate on the exact time and place. When you wake up, you'll be there. And stay sharp. Those twelve hours fly by."

I nod.

"We'll see you soon, Alissee. Good luck." The male technician gives me a friendly punch on the shoulder and walks away. The door seals itself shut with a *shoop* behind him.

I place the cube on the night table and, with a sigh, collapse onto the bed. It's been a hectic day at the Dream State Transfer Center. Only this morning did I learn I was the one chosen from the three final candidates. Being the biggest loner of the bunch set me apart, with the assumption that any change I made in the past should have fewer repercussions. Having Milins virus is good at keeping people away, thanks to the trademark black and red splotches covering me from head to toe, and the red irises. Demon Spawn. Devil Eyes. Walking Bruise. Patchwork Lady. Or just 'freak.' The insults are endless, some creative, some just stupid. But today I have been offered a gift. A chance to undo it all. To have the life I should have had...

Despite my nerves, my eyelids droop. It's time. I reach for the cube. After considering it for a moment, I pop it in my mouth. It melts on my tongue, the taste oversweet, followed by a bitter, aspirin-like aftertaste.

Closing my eyes, I concentrate on the pre-agreed time and location. Twenty-three years ago, 2186. The Salamander club. Around 22:00...

* * *

I open my eyes to loud music and laughter—strange to hear after so many years of near solitary existence. I look down at my purple dress, pleased at how it hugs my slimmer, 22-year-old body. The Center did a fine job recreating the purple get-up I wore that night. As for my skin...I hold up my arm and sigh, admiring its clear, unblemished perfection.

First things first.

I trot around the curved bar, accidentally bumping into a couple of patrons so that their glasses tip onto their chests and each other. They throw curses at my back. I couldn't care less. The glowing sign above the door beckons me and I elbow my way in, ignoring the sharp comments of the women queuing up. "Hey, you can't just cut in like that!" Another says, "Maybe she has to puke." Laughter.

The lighting is dim but it's enough as I stand in front of the full-length mirror. My fingers tremble as they skim over my smooth cheek and neck. I push back my hair, my eyes taking in every inch of exposed skin. I want to see more so I shimmy out of my dress, standing in nothing but the ugly yellow underwear the Center provided.

Some women giggle cruelly and one says, "You're going to scare them off once they see that bag around your butt." They burst out in hysterics.

"You're absolutely right," I answer calmly and hook

my thumbs in the sides of the underwear, yank it down and step out of it. I kick it towards the wall with the toe of my purple shoe.

"What are you, some kind of freak? Get dressed already!" the woman says.

My smile drops upon hearing the word. *Freak.* Memories of being mocked feel like cold hands slapping my face. Yes, I am one... but later. Now I'm beautiful. Perfect. My smile slowly returns as I continue gazing at my reflection.

Eventually, the female patrons ignore me. I'm just the whacked out woman standing naked in the ladies' room. Who cares? After all, I'm not infected, so I'm no threat.

I slowly drag the dress back on, not bothering with the undergarment. I could spend the whole twelve hours here. After one long look, I let out a deep sigh and walk out. "Finally!" someone mutters as I leave.

The bar area is packed, but with my looks, the bartender doesn't keep me waiting.

"A *Hot Angel*, please."

He winks in response.

Moments later, I am strolling through the club, savouring the cinnamon taste of my cocktail. It tastes even better considering it's 'on the house'. The animated angel figure, hovering above the glass, tickles my nose with its wings as I sip. I pause to lean against the railing and watch young bodies packed together, grinding to the throbbing music.

I nearly drop the glass.

There he is. Savin. That son of a bitch. That *gorgeous* son of a bitch. Longish brown hair feathering over his eyes, a synth-leather shirt hugging his muscled chest. He notices me staring. I force a smile. He smiles back and sidles over.

I relive the night. Dancing. Drinking. Laughing. Kissing. Touching. It's nearly daybreak when he offers to take me to his place. I agree. Again.

When we arrive, I wander through his cavernous loft, tracing a finger over priceless sculptures. Resting my hand on the cool, stone hip of a beautiful female nude, I gaze into its eyeless face. My first time here, I wondered how he made the money to afford such a luxurious place. How ironic to find out later he is a sales exec at a pharmaceutical company that later spends billions attempting to find a cure for Milins.

Savin sneaks up from behind and wraps his arms around me, just under my breasts. "You are so beautiful, Alissee." I shiver when he gently pulls my long hair aside and kisses me on the back of my neck.

I turn to face him and our eyes lock. Our lips come together, mouths open, tongues playing, our bodies melding against each other. I remember this is why I fell for him. How good he was. *Is*. His hands on my body. His mouth moving down my neck just so... I can't believe it. I want him so much. He's so...

No.

My pre-approved time alteration actions are to tell him it's a mistake to be here and then leave. Instead, I slip out the small implement I acquired earlier that evening. He leans in to kiss me again, his half-closed eyes filled with lust. A second later I feel his body freeze because my knife is pressed against his ribs.

He releases me and backs off. "What's going on, Alissee?"

My voice is low and menacing, fuelled by two decades of rage. "You deserve to die, you bastard. You gave me and countless others Milins. You turned me into a freak!" I shove the pedestal next to me, sending the sculpture crashing to the floor. Savin gasps, his eyes darting from his priceless artwork back to me.

"What—? I don't understand." He smiles, lips trembling. "Calm down. Let's talk about this, okay? There must be some kind of—"

"I hate you!" I scream and thrust the knife towards him. I enjoy seeing him flinch.

"Listen, I have no idea what Milins is. Come. Sit down." He motions with a shaking hand towards the sofa.

I don't move.

"Please...?" He holds out his hands in supplication, his hands shaking even worse, his eyes big and pleading. God. Those beautiful eyes... a deep, warm brown, under thick lashes. "I´m sorry about whatever it is I did," he utters.

I sigh. My arm lowers to my side. It wasn't his fault. He didn´t know. I realise I wanted to blame someone and he was simply the easy choice. "I wanted to kill you. I really did. But..."

Savin lunges towards the knife.

"No!" I wrench it out his hand and he yelps, blood dripping from his clenched fist.

I turn to run but he grabs me and holds my wrist in a viselike grip. With me squirming and trying to buck him off, we end up falling to the floor in a heap. I scream when I feel a sharp jab in my side.

"I can't believe it!" I cry out as I roll away, clutching my waist, staring at the bloody knife lying on the floor. "I—"

* * *

A soft bed. Pale yellow, featureless walls. Soft lighting. I am back at the Center.

I lift my arm and curse when I see the ugly blotches. "No!" I wail. "Send me back. You have to let me go back again."

Strong hands hold down my flailing limbs while someone else smoothes straps over my wrists and ankles. There's a *shrrrp* sound as they are pulled tight enough to keep me immobile, but not too tight so they'd cut off circulation.

The director of the Dream State Center leans over me, a patronising look on his face. "Deep breaths, Alissee. Just a little disorientation. Think of it as an extreme case of jetlag." He chuckles at his own joke.

I take a deep breath to appease him and do my best to keep my voice steady and calm. "Please, I need to return. I didn't finish what I had to do."

"But it worked! You went back in time and came back. It couldn't have gone better. Well, okay, you still have Milins... but anyway, your test run was a success. We're going to have the press release tomorrow, so you need to be at

84

your best. A good rest is what you need right now." He pats my hand, then nods to someone.

A moment later I feel the sharp tap of a drug-stick on my arm. The room starts to fuzz over.

* * *

I wake up to a light buzzing sound and a searing headache. Trying to sit up, I realize the straps are still engaged. Turning my head, I see a female worker cleaning the floor. The worker perks up when she notices I'm awake and then glances at the closed door. I start to get an uneasy feeling in my stomach, wondering if I should call for help.

My heart pounds as she shuffles to the edge of my bed.

"What do you want?" I ask warily.

She holds a finger to her lips. "Shhhh…"

I flinch when she reaches out for my trapped arm, feeling her press some objects in my hand.

"One for you and one as a favor for me," she whispers as she pulls the straps loose from my wrists and ankles.

Looking down, my eyes widen at the sight of two time travel cubes, still sealed, and a slip of paper, which has a name, date, time, and address. Next to the writing is a tiny photo of a teenage girl's face, riddled with the unmistakable skin markings.

"How did you get these?" I clutch the items against my chest.

She pulls out a key card from the deep pocket of her jumpsuit. "My job is dreadful, but it offers certain privileges. I can get into everything. They're fanatical about cleanliness here. That bastard director… I'm surprised he doesn't make me wipe his ass to make sure every speck of shit is wiped clean."

I can't help but snort. "He is a bastard, isn't he?"

Our smiles soon fade and I ask, "But why don't you use it yourself?"

"Because it scares me to death. Please. I want you to lock her inside her room. Tell her it's for her own good. I want her to have a chance at a good life."

I peer at the paper then look back up again. "This

Raleena ended up getting Milins from someone that day?"

The worker nods, her eyes filling with tears. "The boy's name was James. He's dead now. My Raleena is dead too. My only child."

We both jerk our heads towards the door at the sound of approaching footsteps.

"I have to go," she says. After a brief squeeze of my arm, she quietly exits the room, head down, dragging her floor-cleaning equipment behind her.

I slip the objects under the curve of my back and arrange my arms and legs as if they're still strapped down. The door opens.

"So, how are you feeling today?" asks the director, his face beaming. If I wasn't pretending to be strapped down, I would like to leap up and wring the bureaucrat's neck. The technician who follows him ignores me and goes straight for the med-screens above my bed.

"Bit of a headache, but other than that, I feel fine." I offer a weak smile.

"Good, good." The director pats my shoulder. "Perfectly understandable, Alissee." He studies me for a moment. I pray silently to myself, hoping his eyes don't travel down to my wrists and ankles.

"Well, we'll release you soon, so you can get dressed. Press conference is in a couple of hours." Another pat on my arm and they are gone.

After letting out a sigh of relief, I pull out the time cubes and the slip of paper—a brief moment to focus on my time and destination. I pop a cube in my mouth and chew greedily. I close my eyes.

* * *

I hear the tinkling of a glass. Soft music. He's in the living room. Have to move fast. I slink along, whisper-quiet to the kitchen and grab a large knife. Yes. That'll do. I walk into the large, open room. The back of his head rests against the sofa, a bottle of wine on the table. Slowly I lift the knife.

He sits up.

My knife swings at air.

"Damnit!" I curse without thinking.

He bolts to his feet and turns to me, eyes wide.

I can't help it. All I can do is stare, mouth agape.

His skin! It's covered in the red and black splotches. I look down and see my own arms covered in it too. It looks especially unattractive next to the yellow hospital gown I'm still wearing.

"You!" he screams in rage, and lunges for me. The knife flies out of my hand, skidding across the floor.

The punches come hard and I feel my lip split open. My jaw rings with pain. A tooth is loose, I think. Things go dark and I'm lying there, moaning weakly, a limp jellyfish as my head rings from the blows.

Suddenly, it ends.

Am I dead?

I hear sobbing.

I lift my head a little, my eyes already starting to swell over, and see Savin sobbing into his splotched hands.

"I'm the one who should be crying," I say with difficulty thanks to my thick lip. My mouth is filled with the rusty taste of blood. I prop myself on my elbow to spit out blood onto his perfect wooden floor.

He looks up, his red irises locking with mine. "You gave me this awful disease! Before you I could have any woman I wanted." He stands up, his eyes wide in a crazed fury. "Look at me. Who'd want me now? I'm a diseased freak thanks to you!"

"What? I don't—" The realization strikes me like a sledge hammer to the head. "No...it doesn't make sense. You gave it to me. I..." My chest tightens. No... He gave it to me. He's the bastard. He's the one to blame. My head falls back to the floor with a soft *thunk*.

A flash of steel over me.

"No!" I scream. I'm surprised by the strong will to live, despite my virus. The knife falters for a moment.

Then it plunges down deep between my ribs. In a strangely amused state, as if I'm watching from outside my body, I peer below and see the black handle sticking straight out of my left breast. I feel nothing. But then the blood starts rhythmically spurting with the pumps of my heart, or what's left of it. Pain slashes through my body and I scream, only making it hurt more. Clutching at my chest, I lie there, as Savin rips the knife out with a horrible sucking sound and plunges it into me over and over again. My right breast. My stomach. My legs. My arms. The bastard! I wanted to be the one to kill. Not…

Darkness overtakes the pain.

* * *

I wake up gasping, grasping my chest. My skull feels like it it's about to split in half. "Where—" Yellow everywhere. I look down. My hospital gown is in pristine shape again. But I'm supposed to be dead… aren't I?

"Did you stop Raleena?" a soft voice asks.

I jerk my head and see the cleaner woman in the corner, a hydra-mop in her hands.

"Raleena… No, not yet. I will though."

She nods. "I understand. You needed to take care of something else first. Please, do it soon. I want to see my Raleena again. You promise?"

I choke down the lump in my throat and manage to grunt an acknowledgement.

No point going back to Savin. It was my fault all along. I gave it to him. I roll to my side and sob. I can't believe it. All these years; these decades. I'm horrible. I deserved to be miserable. I…

I take a deep breath. But at least I have a chance to do something right. I can save this girl. I find the slip of paper still tucked into a small pocket of my hospital gown. Aagh. This horrible yellow gown.

Closing my eyes, I pop the cube in my mouth. The year is 2196. Raleena. She's in her room.

* * *

I start from the loud music, the pulsing bass throbbing through to my bones. The girl has the same auburn hair as her mother, the same sharp, little nose. Raleena moves her hips to the music, watching her own reflection in the window since it's pitch black outside.

There's a tap on the glass. No! James is here already? I lunge forward as Raleena opens the window and she shrieks when see sees me.

"Who—Who are you? How did you get here?"

I slam the window shut and notice James has yanked out his fingers just in time. There's a muffled thump when he hits the ground.

"James!" she cries out and yanks open the window.

"Stop. Your mother wants you to stay safe. Stay away from him. He's going to give you Milins virus. I'm trying to save you!"

She ignores me, swatting my hands away and next thing I know there's something sharp jammed into the back of my hand. I stare numbly at some kind of pointed crystal thing, wondering how the hell it got there. I pull it out and blood flows out in a heavy rush. Raleena frantically opens the window and cries out, "James? James, are you okay?"

Silence.

"Raleena," I say, "please, you—"

"Get away from me!" She swipes with another one of those crystal things and without thinking I swing out my right hand in defense—the bloody one with the gaping wound. Blood sprays onto her face and she gasps and then starts spitting.

I look in horror at her, her face covered in smears of red as she frantically tries to wipe it off.

"Raleena, I..."

"Get out!" And she runs out of her room.

I'm standing there, shaking. I did it again. It was me. I gave it to her. Not James. Me.

* * *

I'm outside Raleen's house, in the dark, stumbling. Wishing I was dead. Maybe I should call Savin. He'd gladly help out. I laugh darkly at my own joke.

The grass and plants are covered in dew, slapping wetly against my bare feet and shins. The night feels heavy as if it has mass. I want to throw up. I want to scream. I wish I never existed. I wish I never went back in time.

I randomly pick out a lawn in front of someone's house and plunk down, my backside immediately feeling the cold wetness absorbed through my thin, yellow tunic. Laying my head in the damp, short green blades, I close my eyes and wait it out.

* * *

I awake to a frenzied rush. My head hurts so much I don't want to open my eyes. But I have to see what's happening.

"She's awake!" The med-tech runs over and tests the straps on my arms and ankles.

But this place is new. Not a scrap of yellow in sight.

"Where am I?" I manage to croak out.

"Gevitt Home."

I press my hand onto my forehead. "But...that's a place for..."

"Yes, Alissee. You've been determined unstable with your last two little romps into the past. And the Dream State Transfer Center has been shut down thanks to you. You should feel grateful they agreed to let you come here instead of prison. We wanted to study the effects of time travel on the psyche."

"I... oh, my head..."

"Don't worry, I came prepared." I gasp when the med-tech jabs a needle into my arm. As the wooziness takes over, I hear him say: "Sleep. But this time, you're going nowhere."

Brigadooned!
by James Hartley

"Yes, it's a time machine... of sorts. But it has two limitations. First, it is controlled by brainwaves, the delta sleep waves. Just that, nothing else. And second, it has a fixed transition period. Some sort of quantum value that just happens to work out to one Earth century."

As Professor Forsythe explained it, Tommy leaned over to look at the device. Suddenly he was hit with a wave of dizziness, a bout of vertigo, and he fell over toward the control panel.

The Professor was yelling, "Watch it! Don't hit that button!" Then everything went black. When Tommy came to, he was lying on the floor, and the Professor was bending over him. "Are you all right, Tommy?"

"Yeah, Prof, I'm just a little dizzy." He shook his head, the room slowly stopped spinning, and he stood up.

"Did you push the 'start' button, Tommy? It looked like you did."

"I think I did, but nothing happened. What's the

problem? I'm still here, I'm still now. Even if I hit the button, the time machine didn't take me anywhere."

The Professor shook his head. "This is not like the time machines you read about in Science Fiction stories, Tommy. The machine itself doesn't go anywhere. It sets up a quantum-dimensional field condition in the traveler's subatomic structure, and the traveler then moves forward in century-long jumps when he goes to sleep. You understand?"

Tommy got a confused look on his face. "No, Prof, I don't think I do. Could you please explain it again, preferably in words of one syllable or less?"

"OK, it works this way. *If* you were in range of the machine—I'm afraid you were—and *if* you hit the start button—you may have—the machine would have impressed a quantum-dimensional field condition on you. *If* that all has happened, tonight when you go to sleep, when your brain waves transition to delta sleep waves, it will trigger the field, and you'll wake up a century from now."

Tommy looked at the Professor in horror. "How do we turn it off?"

"We don't. I can't. I'm afraid I haven't invented that part yet."

Tommy barely resisted an impulse to deck Professor Forsythe, then turned and left the lab and the Jackson Science Building. Doing what any sensible Grad student would do, he drove his car back to his apartment, then walked down the block to his favorite watering hole and got smashed.

Finally, when the bartender refused to serve him any more, he staggered out into the late February snowstorm that had started, grateful for the leather bomber jacket he was wearing. At his apartment he threw the bomber jacket on the floor, then fell into bed fully dressed. He was asleep in seconds.

* * *

He woke to the sound of a female scream. He was in a strange bed, in a strange room, and had a strange girl in bed with him. The strangest thing, though, was a wall calendar with February 2123 displayed on it.

It was hard to concentrate with the girl still screaming, but finally he remembered the conversation with Professor Forsythe, and the time machine. 2123, a hundred years, just what the Prof had predicted.

He turned to the girl and said, "I have a real problem here. Could you please be quiet and let me think?" Amazingly enough, the screams stopped. "Thanks. I'm sorry I'm in your room, your bed, but I got caught up by a time machine and brought here."

She looked at him. "A time machine? The Forsythe machine? We covered that in our Quantum Continuum class last month. But Professor Alton never said that anyone had ever used it! My gosh! You actually traveled here via the Forsythe machine? You've got to come over to the campus with me and talk to Professor Alton?"

Tommy shook his head, trying to clear it. He decided that it couldn't hurt to talk to someone who knew about this. He turned to the girl and said, "OK, that sounds good. By the way, my name is Tommy. Tommy Albright."

"Glad to meet you, Tommy. I'm Susie Phelps. Now if you could just go in the other room so I can get dressed ..."

Tommy stood up and said, "OK, I'll do that." He looked around, than added, "Where's my jacket?"

"Your jacket? I don't see a jacket. Did you have it with you?"

"I think I took it off and dropped it on the floor before I got into bed. It was a nice leather bomber jacket, kind of expensive, I'd hate to lose it."

"If you dropped it on the floor, if you weren't wearing it, maybe it didn't come with you. But don't worry, I don't think you'll need a leather jacket, it's almost March."

Tommy gave up on looking for the jacket and went in the next room. A few minutes later, Susie appeared, dressed in shorts and a t-shirt. "C'mon, let's go," she said.

As they walked out the door, Tommy was hit by a warm breeze. As he looked around, he saw that flowers were blooming and the trees had green leaves. "Susie," he asked, "did you say that it was almost March? Like, still February? It feels more like May."

"Yes, it's the end of February. I remember in our History class, they talked about climate change, it has gotten a lot warmer over the last hundred years. I think the History Prof said that even back in your time there were predictions of *global warming*, but then it happened a lot faster than expected."

Tommy couldn't think of an answer, and they walked in silence for a couple of blocks, through a gate onto the campus, and into something labeled the "Heinlein Science Center."

Professor Alton's office door was open. Susie knocked and then stepped in, pulling Tommy after her. "Professor, I think I've found someone who has traveled via the Forsythe machine."

The Professor looked up, interest shining in his eyes, and listened intently as Tommy repeated his story. When Tommy finished, he said, "And this was your first time jump?"

"What do you mean, *my first*?"

"Mr. Albright, you didn't think this was only going to happen once, did you? Of course not. Each time you fall asleep it will trigger another jump, another hundred years. I honestly don't know how long it will continue, quite possibly until you die and there are no more brainwaves to trigger it."

Tommy slumped into a chair. "You mean *every* time I fall asleep I'll wake up a century later? No. No! Professor Forsythe said he hadn't invented a way to turn it off, but you, you're a hundred years later, you must have found the answer."

"Mr. Albright... Tommy, I am truly sorry. We thought the Forsythe machine had never been used, it was just a curiosity, nobody has bothered to really study it. We don't have any answers for you."

"What am I going to do?" asked Tommy plaintively.

"I don't know, really. But I can give you a little advice. You went to bed in a third floor apartment, you were lucky there was still a three story building there. You could have woken in mid-air and dropped three floors to serious injury or death. If you feel yourself getting sleepy, stay at ground level."

Tommy thanked Professor Alton, and he and Susie left. They spent the day together, he found her pleasant company, but as evening came on she insisted on saying goodbye to him.

"You can't come to my room, Tommy, you heard what he said about staying on the ground. And I don't know of any good place we could go at ground level. Besides, the idea of spending part of the night with you, and then having you vanish... I'm sorry, you're a nice guy, but I just can't deal with this." She kissed him goodnight and then left.

Tommy wandered around for a while, then crawled into an unlocked car and fell asleep.

* * *

Tommy woke in a vacant lot, as a man wearing a skimpy bikini brief, a badge, and some kind of radio headset prodded him with a nightstick. The man, presumably a cop, was saying into his mike, "I have a re-enactor here. Better send an air-conditioned wagon. With the early twenty-first century clothes he's wearing, he'll be down with heatstroke by the time the sun gets another half-hour higher."

Tommy rolled over and looked up at the cop. "I'm not a re-enactor, whatever that is. I'm a time traveler. I got caught up in a time machine, the Forsythe machine." The cop looked dubious. Tommy continued, "There's probably someone who knows about the Forsythe machine over at the campus ..." and he pointed, and his voice trailed off. He realized that he was pointing toward a nearby shoreline and the ocean.

The cop said, "If you're going to make up a silly story, at least get your facts straight. The old campus was flooded out by the rising sea level fifty years ago. The campus is now over there." He pointed in exactly the opposite direction. "Of course, in another hundred years they're going to have to move it again, further inland." He broke off as a police wagon pulled up next to them.

The wagon took Tommy to the police station, and there he underwent a routine that had not changed significantly in centuries. He was photographed, fingerprinted, then had his possessions taken and put in an envelope. There was some discussion about his clothes, and the Sergeant in charge decided they were evidence because the charge was re-enacting. He was forced to change into jail garb consisting of boxers and a sleeveless undershirt, then locked in a cell.

The reactions of the police to the money he had in his pocket made him understand better the nature of his predicament. The twenty-first century money was not recognized as money, and he realized that to these people, he was broke. It wouldn't matter if he got the money back or not, it would be no better another century into the future. Right now, today, he would get fed while in jail. But in the days to come, he would have to do something to obtain food.

Tommy thought about what he could do, and in general just endured the boredom of the cell. As soon as they called lights out, he stretched out on the bunk, and it wasn't long before he went to sleep.

* * *

When he awoke he was still on the bunk in the cell, but things had deteriorated. The cell door was open, hanging by one hinge. Tommy swung his feet off the bunk onto the floor, then jumped when he realized he was standing in a foot of water. He waded out of the cell and over to a window, where he discovered that the entire building, and all the surrounding buildings, were sitting in water up to the second floor. He could see a shore line, but it was almost a mile away, and he wasn't sure he could swim that far.

He wandered around the second floor of the building, looking for ideas, when he saw that several of the mattress pads for the cell bunks were floating. He was surprised that they hadn't decayed and sunk over the years, but he got onto one, and it held his weight. He tried several more, all of which floated with him on top, and he fastened them together with the tie-down straps on each end.

Once he had a mattress to float on and several spares, "just in case," he worked the whole assembly out a window, then climbed on and began to paddle toward shore. It seemed to take forever, but eventually he made it.

When the water was shallow enough, he got off the mat and started to wade. As he approached the shore, a large group of children—totally naked children—began to laugh, point, and make comments about his clothes. He looked around, and everyone that he saw was also naked, except for a belt pouch that some of the adults wore. After a few minutes, a woman came over and chased the children away. "Sorry," she said, "they just aren't used to seeing people wearing clothes. But if you want to, that's okay."

Tommy noticed that his clothes were drying out, and as they did so, even the skimpy jail outfit began to feel too warm. "No, it's complicated, but I guess it would be easier if I just took them off?"

The woman nodded. "Did you need them for some sort of work out at the drowned buildings?"

"Yeah, right," said Tommy, grabbing the excuse. He looked around for someplace to strip, then decided there wasn't any point, and pulled off his shirt and shorts, dropping them on the ground. "I was out there a while. Where can I get something to eat?"

"Oh, just go to the community kitchen down that street." She pointed. "Good luck." She turned and walked away.

Tommy found the kitchen and was served without any problem. After eating, he wandered around, examining everything and noticing how makeshift the town seemed. He also saw that a number of the buildings were empty, and after getting a second meal in the evening, he picked a vacant spot and went to sleep.

* * *

The next morning things seemed about the same, except that the town was a lot more dilapidated and worn. There was still a kitchen where he could eat, no questions asked, and vacant places where he would be able to sleep. He remained in the town for what seemed to him a month or so, and he could watch things collapse as the town saw three millennia. Buildings sagged into piles of rubble, and more and more of the people lived in tents.

Then, one day, he ran into trouble. Instead of a community kitchen available to all, there was a heavily guarded food center. When he started to enter the guard stopped him and asked, "Who the heck are you? I don't know you."

Tommy wasn't sure what to do. He told the guard, "My name is Tommy Albright," but it didn't seem to help.

"Nope," said the guard, "I don't know you. I bet you're from some other tribe, trying to sneak our food. Scram!"

Tommy went. During the day he got hungrier and hungrier, and finally when it was almost dark, he sneaked around the back of the food center and broke in. He did manage to get something to eat before the guards caught him and locked him up in one of the few buildings still standing. Fortunately, when he woke on what was for him the next morning, the lockup had crumbled, and nobody remembered his theft of food a century earlier.

Again he went hungry most of the day, finally managing to steal food in the evening and getting locked up. Things seemed to have stabilized, and this pattern repeated itself for a long succession of his days—their centuries. He did notice that as signs of industrial civilization faded the climate began to cool off, and people were once again wearing clothes. He managed to steal some of those, too, and he was careful to always wear them when he went to sleep, as only things in close contact with him accompanied him on the time jumps.

Then one morning he awoke and the people were gone. From the signs, they had been gone from the area for quite a while. Tommy went hungry that day, but he soon learned to gather nuts, berries, and other similar foods. He was never very well fed, but he managed to stay alive. Wandering around alone, he completely lost track of time.

* * *

One morning he awoke and heard the sounds of people close by. He joined them and tried to find out what was happening. The language had drifted and was hard to understand, but there were enough familiar words for him to figure out that the people were now wandering nomads. The odds of his being near them any time he woke were slim.

He also noted that the people seemed to have changed in appearance. The high cheek bones and the reddish skin coloring brought back memories of lessons in grade school, lessons about the American Indian—Native American—tribes. After dark, when the people were asleep, he stole food, some of their buckskin clothing, and an assortment of hunting equipment.

He carefully bound all his loot close to his body, and when he awoke the next morning it was still there. With the hunting gear he ate better. Once in a while he came upon one of the wandering tribes and was able to replenish his supplies, but again a long unreckoned time passed.

The resemblance of the people to the early American Indians bothered him, and he began to wonder exactly when he was. Then, on a day when he was near the shore, he saw a boat land, and figures with European features came ashore. Tommy began to hope that the Forsythe machine had somehow managed to swing him in some sort of time loop from the future to the past. The development of colonies by the Europeans convinced him that this was happening, and he spent all of his days making his way back to the location of the college. He kept his Indian-style clothing until he woke on a day when the calendar read 1923. But to get onto the campus he needed to do better.

Tommy stood at the mouth of an alley, looking for someone close to his size and build. When he found a good victim, he knocked him out and dragged him back in the alley.

The man, now stripped to his underwear and tied up, regained consciousness and said, "What happened? Oooh, my head hurts."

"Sorry," said Tommy, "but I need your clothes. Behave, and the clothes are all you'll lose. Act up, and ..."

The man subsided. Tommy added a gag to his bounds, then placed him in a hidden corner behind some garbage cans. Ignoring the man's further struggles, Tommy left the alley and headed for the campus. A quick survey located a good hiding place near the building that would later become the Jackson Science Building, and then still later the Heinlein Science Center.

* * *

"Yes, it's a time machine... of sorts. But it has two limitations. First, it is controlled by brainwaves, the delta sleep waves. Just that, nothing else. And second, it has a fixed transition period. Some sort of quantum value that just happens to work out to one Earth century."

As Professor Forsythe explained it, Tommy started to move in for a closer look. Suddenly the door of the lab slammed open, startling both of them. A man wearing clothing of the roaring twenties dashed across the room, grabbed Tommy, and threw him to the floor, well away from the machine. "Stay away from that... that... thing!" the man yelled. Then, as Tommy and the Professor watched, the man looked around at the tools in the lab and picked up a heavy sledge hammer. He brought the hammer down on the machine as hard as he could, and said, "There! Now *nobody* will ever use that infernal device again!"

As the machine exploded in sparks and flames, the air around the man shimmered, and he disappeared.

"What the heck was that?" asked Tommy.

"I'm not sure, but I think he looked a lot like you, only much older. If so, that was you coming back around a loop of time to make sure you didn't get caught up by the machine. I wonder what he... you... went through that got him so upset."

"Prof," said Tommy, "from the look on his face, I think it would be better if you don't rebuild that thing. Ever."

The Professor nodded his agreement.

A Home More Welcoming
by Tony Laplume

Several decades from now, there will live a man who invents time travel. This man will be getting on in years, well into his sixties, an age when the accumulation of time begins to make itself known to him, both in the accomplishments of the past and the awareness that such accomplishments will have been a thing of his past. While his formidable years are behind him, he will have one last great accomplishment left, and it shall be the culmination of his life's work.

A true genius does not diminish with age. This is such a man.

His fondest dream all his life will have been to break the barrier of time, to give humanity access to whatever moment they choose to visit. It is a selfish decision, because he only wants to visit himself...

* * *

The old man sat alone in his house as he did every evening, pondering the project that had consumed so much of his attention as of late. He had lost the love of his life because of this passion, the pursuit of time travel, for where human relationships may come and go, dreams stay with us throughout our days.

Time travel was something that had occurred to him from a very young age. In fact, it was something he'd thought about when he was only a child, and the idea kept coming back to him, acting as a fuel for his ambition. One day he thought about it at the right moment, and he saw how he could one day achieve it, and so the dream consumed him. He became so distracted that not only his life passed him by, but he forgot the whole point of the endeavor. He even forgot himself.

After losing so much, there remained the desire to invent time travel, so that he could apologize to himself—for all the good it would do him. His younger self probably wouldn't even notice. If he had, it would be a memory already, wouldn't it? Yet, the old man's recollection was not what it used to be, and he couldn't remember such a visit... but that didn't mean it hadn't happened.

In his younger days, he'd been a frustrated man, always fixated on his ambitions, and careless about how he attained his goals. Back then, he'd felt as if he weren't getting anywhere, and regardless of what he managed to do no one ever seemed to take notice of him. Why should they? He was barely present in his own life. How could he presume to be accounted for in someone else's?

Now, he sat in an old recliner, trying to remember his wife. He couldn't. Her face had faded from memory, and he hadn't a single picture of her to refresh it. He hadn't cared enough to keep a single photograph! Perhaps that was the reason she'd left him; just one of the many examples of his inability to care about anyone or anything other than his grand ambition, and himself.

Even as he tried to remember his wife, his thoughts continued to drift back to the great question of time travel, trying to work out the details of the project that had consumed his entire life. In the basement sat a device that was maddeningly inert. In the pantry, where others might have food as the most visible element, he had diagrams strewn about the countertops, sketches in blue pencil that would either refine the current device or result in an entirely new one. He couldn't tell yet if his current device was workable, or if he'd end up starting from scratch again.

Sometimes he wondered if he knew anything at all.

His life had changed a great deal since his youth. The frustrated young man had eventually earned the acknowledgement of his peers, and he had long been recognized as a pioneer in the study of physics. His equations ware taught in classrooms around the world, making his name commonplace, even for those who didn't follow his work. He had graced the cover of magazines and been given every conceivable award in his field. He had visited every continent of the globe, and seen more than other men could ever wish to witness.

Yet, through it all, he remained preoccupied with only one thing, something even the forgotten wife had helped to embolden in him; an obsession that bordered on narcissism.

He sometimes wondered why it was so important. The answer was simple enough, if he'd only accept it; that the ideas of childhood once taken root are hard to shake. Some people can create the illusion of refinement or change, but the first impressions in life are always the strongest, and for all his life he had dreamed of time travel. He dreamed of it in his sleep and in his waking moments. He had always existed in a fog, a buffer that separated him from the world around him. It was as much a part of him as his own flesh and blood, and equally inseparable.

There came the fateful night; the most important of all nights. He felt it in his bones, and it made him agitated, restless, more impatient with his lack of progress than usual. Unable to shake the feeling, he decided to go for a walk.

It was cold outside, though by all accounts a typical autumn evening for the small Maine town. There were leaves everywhere, crinkling beneath his feet, and he was surprised to see that he is actually wearing shoes. Very often, he wouldn't bother to put them on in the house, and he'd made no effort to put on a coat or sweater. Sometimes it was better to feel the chill. It inspired thought. At least, it did for him. A stimulated mind keeps even the body an abstract idea.

He was a few blocks into the surrounding neighborhood when *the boy* appeared.

Perhaps it was unfair to label the stranger as a boy, since he was really a young man. Yet, to the old genius, the stranger was certainly a *boy*. He'd reached the age where all ages lesser than his own seemed little more than adolescent youth.

The world belongs to the old, he thought.

The old man nearly continued his walk without acknowledging the boy at all, but the boy ran right into him, making avoidance impossible.

"Idiot!" the old man snapped, thoroughly annoyed.

The boy looked immediately contrite, offering an apology. His accent seemed strange, even for today's youth, as if he were speaking a forgotten variation of the common tongue, recognizable yet clearly different. The boy rambled on nervously, giving the older man ample time to notice the peculiarity of the speech patterns.

It was not for several moments—when he had finally concentrated on something other than how the boy spoke—that he looked into the stranger's face. He was startled for a moment, but then couldn't remember why a moment later. What was it he saw in the stranger's eyes? It had been so long since he'd looked at anything in the world besides blue etchings, it was impossible to say.

Growing weary of the boy's rambling apologies, the old man finally said, "I'm fine, really. Everything's okay."

It didn't work, and the boy replied, "No, I've obviously inconvenienced you. There must be something I can do to make it up. I know. Let me come home with you, see what I can do to help out."

The old man tried to comprehend the rationale of the request. Perhaps the boy was lost, or seeking shelter for some other reason. Whatever the cause, it couldn't hurt to indulge him, the old man decided. He had nothing better to do, and had already concluded that this boy was harmless.

They walked back toward the home in silence, as the quiet of the night fell in around them. The old man had always been amazed that he was chided for being such a recluse when he so rarely saw anyone outside, no matter the time of day. Had all of humanity decided their homes were only to be lived in, rather than enjoyed? In his own youth, he recalled that he would often be playing in the yard, day or night. The outdoors were just another part of the home. Now, the only time he ever saw anyone else was when they were going to their car, or hosting some special event.

'Such is the world's hypocrisy,' the old man thought.

The boy started to speak again, asking the sort of questions anyone asks someone they've just met. The old man gave only what he deemed necessary to be polite. Why should he mention anything else? Why should he breach the subject of what motivated him, had inspired him all his life?

The youth's words continue to sound peculiar, but the old man began to perceive an overarching quality. The boy was looking for acceptance. Yet, was a complete stranger expected to give it? Was the boy so desperate?

A dog barked, the one lasting tangible sign that anything lived in the neighborhood. Normally, the old man would be annoyed by the noise, but he accepted it in stride on this occasion. Somehow, it was nice to hear the sounds of life.

They arrived at his house, a modest one for a man hiding himself away amidst a common residential setting. It was doubtful any of the neighbors knew who he was, and he wouldn't care if they did. He was merely an eccentric, and had been all his life. He'd grown used to it.

"Are you sure you want to come in?" the old man asked his youthful tagalong, hoping he would reconsider. "I'd hate to see you step into one of my booby traps by accident."

"Yeah, sure," the boy replied, dismissing the old man's attempt to dissuade him.

"Suit yourself," the old man said, opening the door. He continued to question why he was allowing this nuisance to linger in his presence. Only a stranger like the boy could provide him with such a hassle. He had alienated even the most persistent of those who'd tried to work their way into his life, yet for some reason this single youth was unshakable.

"Can I get you a drink?" the old man asked.

"Tea would be nice," the younger man replied.

The answer surprised the old man. Most people drank coffee. He, himself, had stopped drinking tea a long time ago, but as chance would have it, he had some old packets tucked away in a cabinet.

"Make yourself at home," the old man said as he ducked into the pantry, where the tea packets, kettle, and mugs awaited, and where the diagrams covered the countertops. After setting a full kettle atop a burner, he indulged himself and looked at the diagrams again. *The boy can wait*, he thought, as he studied the newest set of plans. He hadn't seen them for several hours, and was hoping to glean a fresh perspective from them now. There were greater insights to be had, and that was all he ever sought.

When the kettle started to whistle, he realized that he'd been lost in his project for many minutes, and that his guest had been waiting alone in the other room. He found himself mindful of the boy's reaction to the development, and apologized before dispensing the customary caution about hot liquids. The boy took it all in stride, with a wild look in his eyes. The old man wasn't sure how to interpret it, but decided it was more akin to bewilderment than anything dangerous. The boy didn't seem to be the criminal type, but he was clearly uncomfortable. It couldn't have had much to do with the time he'd spent alone in the living room, as the older man was tucked away in the pantry.

"You may spend the night, if you wish," the old man said, surprising even himself. He didn't know when or how he'd made the decision, but one night couldn't hurt. He knew that when morning came the boy would go, and his existence would become little more than another phantom of the past. There was a certainty about it that sent a shiver down his spine.

Sitting there, taking tea with the strange youth, the old

man wanted the visit to be over as soon as possible, just so he could put it behind him. The boy was unnerving, even as he grew quiet, becoming more like his elder.

An hour passed, as the two men silently nursed their tea and the night settled in. The old man bade the boy good night after showing him the spare room that sometimes served as a study.

Walking back down the hallway, the old man realized he hadn't been to the basement all evening, which was unusual. Normally, he would have spent most of the night down there, tinkering with or without the help of the diagrams. The hour was late, and it was all the fault of that imposing youngster!

Sleep came to the old man, as he pondered the day's events. Long minutes ticked by, as he realized what a terrible mistake he'd made. He awoke with a fright, convinced that it was already morning, but little more than an hour had passed. He heard noises in the still of the night, and realized it was just the boy... but the noises were not coming from the spare room. The boy was loose in *his* house!

The old man threw on a set of clothes and rushed to investigate, stopping in the pantry first, to see with relief that his diagrams had not been disturbed. In his paranoia he had begun to imagine a lot of things, and had feared that something bad had befallen his precious blue etchings. It was the device that ought to concern him most, but he had spent so much time believing that it was a failure that he didn't fear for its safety. It couldn't possibly be of interest to the boy, but the drawings might, or so he thought for a fleeting moment until he turned around to see the young man standing behind him, clutching the device in his hands.

The old man shot a maddened stare at the younger man, which sent the stranger back to babbling.

"Look, man, I know you're angry, but let me explain. This thing, this device, it's like something out of a dream. I know what this is. I've seen it, up here. I didn't mean to snoop, but I wasn't tired, and coming here, seeing these diagrams, and then the basement and this! It's all so clear now. Earlier, I wasn't sure what I was going to do. My life seemed like such a failure, I even thought of suicide, but now I see there's a reason to it all. You've got to let me stay here, help you solve the riddle of time!"

Following the mad rambling, the old man was furious. He slapped the device from the boy's hands, unconcerned for the moment with damaging his own creation. The boy started to cry as he picked the device up off the floor.

"Get the hell out of my house!" the old man shouted fervently. As he heard his own voice echoing in the small room, he wondered if the neighbors would hear.

The boy finally gave up the fight. Meekly, he handed the device back to its creator and hung his head in shame. An awkward moment of silence ensued, so similar and yet so foreign to those already shared between them. The boy finally moved, heading for the door, leaving the old man alone with the device clutched in his hands.

With the annoying stranger gone, the old man examined his handiwork, and quickly noticed that there were changes to the mechanism, alterations he couldn't explain. What had that boy done? How could he possibly have known what it was, much less the first thing to do with it?

Further enraged, the old man ran after the boy, out into the cold night air. The temperature had dropped considerably in a short span of time, and he'd once again forgotten a coat. The fury of the chase kept him warm.

Spotting the old man in mad pursuit, the boy started running. The old man kept pace, and started to close the gap as he noticed that the device was still in his hands. The neighborhood was still quiet, and each footstep pounded like thunder in his ears. He shouted at the boy, seeking to bring him to a halt, but they both keep running, one after the other, until they reached the same point at which they'd originally met.

The boy froze, and the old man barely stopped in time to avoid a nasty collision. Swinging his arms to catch himself, the old man glanced at the device and noticed the activation switch was blinking. The menacing youth had made him flip it on!

Overcome by rage, the old man used the only weapon at his disposal, the device in his hand. With every ounce of strength, he threw the hunk of metal and circuitry at the young man's head, fully intent on killing him.

The moment he hurled the device at the boy's head, the old man felt memories flooding back to him. Once, long ago, when he'd been a young man, he'd returned to his childhood home in a moment of desperation. He'd felt like an utter failure, felt the very thoughts this boy had expressed so very few moments earlier. He'd walked these very streets... but then the rest of this narrative split off in two directions. Two separate memories of the same time, and both he'd lived.

The device flashed as it collided with the boy's head, and blood splattered as time exploded around them both.

He had always tried to understand the nature of time. The device hadn't worked because his understanding of time had always been crude. His obsession had been strong, yet he was too far removed from the ideas he'd once carried inside his head when he'd been young and couldn't achieve anything. Yet, at last, he began to understand.

The world was growing hazy, but he wasn't sure if it was the world, or himself.

One thing was certain. The device worked!

Whatever the boy had done to it was exactly what it had needed. It had opened a portal that sent the boy here a few hours ago... and *he* was the boy.

When the device had smashed the boy's head, the old man had effectively erased himself from time. It all made sense now. He understood, in those final, fleeting moments, everything that had ever happened to him. Life had been trying to warn him, give him a second chance. He'd been unconsciously sabotaging his own efforts, making sure the device wouldn't work, but his younger self couldn't have known that. The boy had still been emboldened with the vision and the curse of youthful ingenuity.

The old man watched himself die, as the boy breathed his final breath. Then, he strained to look at the device. It was as smashed as the boy's head; a total wreck. It was just as well.

He thought about the diagrams sitting on his pantry countertops. They probably didn't exist anymore, for he didn't exist anymore. The device would probably fade, the boy would probably return to his own time in moments. Though, nothing was certain in the unexplored field of temporal physics.

This was the result of his fascination with time. The dream had become a reality. It had truly been a home more welcoming than any he had ever known.

He whispered an apology to himself, but received no answer.

The Killing of Yesterday
by Martin T. Ingham

"That's for everything you would have done to me," the old man growled as he stood over the woman he'd shot. She didn't look very impressive slumped in the recliner; just a twenty-something nursing student with a non-existent social life. Well, she wouldn't be improving that now.

The old man saw the stream of blood trickling from her chest wound, and he poked his finger at the crimson flow. "Hm, they don't usually do that," he mused, feeling the charred edges of the polyester garment his victim wore. The laser he utilized generally cauterized the flesh. "You always were a bleeding heart."

Placing his hand under her chin, the old man lifted her head so he could gaze at her lifeless face. The eyes were half-open and reflected a drunken expression. A familiar sense of satisfaction flowed over him as he studied his handiwork and knew his latest task was complete.

It was doubtful anyone would find the body before morning, but there was no sense sticking around. The old man made his way across the floor of the Lowell Street apartment, and turned to make his exit. Removing a plastic glove from his pocket, he prepared to slide it over his hand, only to find the blood from his victim still covering his right index finger. He glanced around, but saw nothing convenient to wipe the substance away, so he stuck the finger in his mouth and licked it clean. The metallic taste was savory.

With the blood gone, the old man snapped the glove over his hand and turned the door knob, leaving behind no fingerprints for the police to find.

"Sweet dreams, Becky," he mused as he left the apartment. "Enjoy the divorce."

* * *

Rebecca Philbert was the sixth murder in as many weeks, and the local authorities were getting antsy. The emergence of a new serial killer was bad enough, but his choice of weapons had them baffled, as did his targets. Nobody on the force could figure out how he was choosing his victims, nor could they identify the mysterious laser he was using to kill them. None of it made any sense, but they were encumbered by temporal limitations.

Agent Jack Baker wasn't so hindered, as he walked around the latest crime scene. The half dozen police officers didn't see him; they were a split second behind him in time. Temporal phasing was a curious thing. You could stay one step ahead of everyone, literally.

The body was being examined by a forensic specialist, but Jack knew they'd be wasting their time. The weapon used on these people hadn't been invented yet, and the victims hadn't lived long enough to become connected in any manner. The murderer had made sure of that.

There was no sense standing around the scene of the crime, listening to the officers express their bewilderment, so Jack made his way outside. Ducking around behind some bushes, he tapped a few buttons on his sleeve and brought himself back into temporal alignment, so he could once again physically interact with the world around him.

Walking down the sidewalk, Jack looked at the short

buildings nearby. There wasn't much to this "city" he was visiting (he'd seen more populous suburbs). There were a lot of residential dwellings, a few apartment buildings, and even a few restaurants and antique shops, but nothing most people would associate with an urban area. Still, it had the label and the governmental infrastructure of a metropolitan area, despite being a few million people short of such a definition. In thirty years, this place would be a bustling center of trade and industrial production, but in its current incarnation it was little more than a rural crossroads.

Nothing was certain when one meddled in time. Killing a few people didn't generally have much of an impact, but you could never tell. Regardless, you couldn't have people from the future going into the past and slaughtering innocents. That's why Chronol Agents existed, to protect the past from all sorts of criminal activity, though it wasn't every day you had a serial killer on the prowl. Perpetrators of temporal crime were usually profiteers seeking to enrich themselves with future knowledge, or mourners seeking to save the life of a loved one who'd died tragically. Black market timeslips were pretty affordable these days, but few individuals would waste their money on a trip to murder people in the past.

Taking a right turn onto North Street, Jack heard a hissing coming through his auditory implant. Adjusting the bandwidth by rubbing behind his ear, he cleared up the static and heard the nasally voice of a colleague out of time. "Hey Jackie, you still kicking?"

"Yes, Ben," Jack said, annoyed by the man's boisterous tone. He always sounded so cocky. "We've got another victim."

"Yeah, no kidding," Ben said. "It knocked the whole of time for a real loop; took us a full six hours to realign our communications to the altered reality."

"That long?" Jack asked, aware of the technical difficulties. He knew the basics of temporal mechanics and quantum divergence, as everyone on the Force did. Every time a past event was changed by a time-traveler, an alternate reality was created, and anyone from the future who was present at the point of temporal divergence was displaced into the new universe, unaffected by the changes. In theory, you could go back in time and murder your own grandfather, erasing yourself from existence, and live the rest of your days in that new world of your own creation.

The Temporal Institute existed to prevent such abuses. Insulated inside a pocket of displaced space-time, the Institute could monitor the very fabric of reality, remaining unaffected by alterations. Their agents assured the "true" timeline remained intact at all cost.

"It's always bad when there's a murder," Ben continued. "You don't realize how much of an impact a single person has on the world around them until they're removed. Suddenly, you see people dying who should've lived, people getting married who should've married somebody else, traffic accidents that happen or don't happen because somebody who was supposed to be driving around wasn't there. You know, it's a mess."

"It's like tugging on a loose string, and seeing your shirt unravel," Jack mentioned, simplifying the concept for his own peace of mind.

"Instead of unraveling, imagine a totally different shirt being woven from that loose thread," Ben corrected. "Or a pair of pants where a shirt should've been."

"I get the point," Jack said, irritated. He picked a slim data pad out of his pocket and examined the information on display. "Adding Miss Philbert to the list of murder victims leaves us with two principal suspects, both of them being her ex-husbands."

The pad contained a list of names with biographical data, and how each name was connected. All of this "future history" was outdated at the moment, as several of the people listed were dead before their time, and those still alive had lived different lives because of it. Thanks to a trick of temporal displacement, however, the Chronol Institute's database remained intact and unchanged, where past actions would otherwise alter it.

"Let's see," Ben said, clacking loudly on his keyboard.

"Looks like either Robert Drisko, or Maynard Williams. A couple of retired cops. Sweet."

Jack examined their information and noticed a lot of similarities. They'd grown up together, gone to the same local schools, attended the same police academy, joined the local force and been partners for twenty years. They'd both had legal scrapes with several of the murder victims, and they'd both been married to Rebecca Philbert.

Other than Rebecca, the murder victims had been bad business in the future. Three had been career criminals with rap sheets a mile long, and acquittal records to match. One had been a dirty cop who'd gone down for reselling confiscated drugs, and the last was a school teacher who'd gone to jail for abusing children, Williams and Drisko among them. All five of these people had had many of the same enemies, which had left the list of suspects bloated until Rebecca's death. She was the lynchpin that tied everything together.

After reading through the data, Jack talked it over with Ben. "So, we have two men here, best friends who did everything together. They were policemen, and according to their files they were honorable; never caught doing anything shady, at least. So, what would make one of them go off the deep end and go on a killing spree in the past?"

"Do you want me to spell it out for you?" Ben asked, clearly having come to some conclusion.

"Rebecca Philbert was married to Robert Drisko first, but fifteen years later she left him and married Maynard."

"Sounds like a pretty good motive for another murder," Ben remarked. "If my best friend stole my wife, I'd want to settle the score, too."

"Then, logically, the next victim will be Maynard Williams."

* * *

The stakeout was a long one. For five days, Jack sat outside the shabby house on Union Street, watching and waiting for the killer to make his move. Each morning, rookie cop Maynard Williams would get into his car, drive half a mile down the road, and pick up his partner Robert on their way to the station.

There was no sense following them on their patrol. All of the other murders had been perpetrated at the victims' homes, so Jack knew the killer would show up eventually. It was only a matter of time.

The long wait finally ended on the fifth evening. Jack looked across the road toward the dilapidated home and saw a conspicuous figure walking up to the front door. The curious man removed a key from his trench coat and unlocked the deadbolt, then slipped inside.

There was no time to waste. Maynard would be coming home at any minute, and he would fall victim to his homicidal partner from the future, if Jack didn't act.

Jack ran across the street and stopped at the door step. He was out of phase, which meant he couldn't move solid objects in normal time, so he had to realign his temporal signature before entering the building. It left him vulnerable, but there was no way around it. Not if he wanted to stop the next murder.

After slipping back into temporal synch, Jack ran into a new obstacle. The door was locked. The killer must have reengaged the deadbolt after entering, so Jack couldn't get inside. At least, not unless he wanted to kick the door down and announce his presence. That could prove lethal.

What other option did he have? Sit and wait for Maynard Williams to show up, and try to explain the situation? How would a tale of temporal homicide sit with a rookie cop from a small town? Somehow, Jack didn't see it going over too well. It was time to work on his cover story.

A minute passed, and a brown sedan rolled into the driveway, right on time. Maynard stepped out of the car, still wearing his duty uniform, and hurried to the front door to see the stranger standing there. "Can I help you?"

"Officer Williams, I'm Detective Jack Baker, FBI." He removed a realistic-looking badge from his pocket and flashed it in front of the young policeman. "There's a killer in your house."

"What?" Maynard asked in disbelief.

"I've been tracking him for days, watching his movements, and they've led me here. Not five minutes ago, I saw him jimmy your lock and slip inside. It's clear he's picked you to be his next victim."

"This doesn't make any sense," Maynard protested. "Why me?"

"Why any of the others?" Jack countered. "Based on what your department has uncovered, his victims are random, without any obvious connections. He picked you for reasons that only he could know in the here and now."

"Lucky me," Maynard replied, starting to believe it. "So, what do we do?"

"We stop him, that's what," Jack said. It was risky, but he knew there was no other way. He would need Maynard's help to stop this killer. "Unlock the door, and let's get on with it."

Maynard removed his keys and worked the lock, then drew his pistol in preparation for a showdown.

Jack shook his head and motioned for him to holster the gun. "Based on the killer's previous M.O., he'll be hiding somewhere. In a closet, or somewhere else he can keep an eye out for you. Once you're settled in, he'll come out to plug you."

"Yeah, I hear he's got some kinda ray gun," Maynard said. "Where'd he get something like that?"

"Experimental prototype," Jack lied. "He stole it from a military testing lab. It's quick and quiet, so we'll have to be on our toes."

"Easy for you to say," Maynard remarked. "You're not the one playing the bait." With that, they both stepped inside.

Jack stayed by the front door, and watched Maynard walk down the hall into his living room.

Maynard sat down on his stained corduroy couch, which sat in clear view of the front door. He breathed a sigh and tried to look natural; just a tired cop trying to relax after a long day on patrol.

Jack expected the killer to show himself. Considering

the emotional entanglements involved, it was reasonable to assume that the elderly Robert Drisko would have some choice words for his target, before finishing him off. However, assumptions are flighty things, easily proven wrong.

Without warning, Maynard gasped and grabbed at his chest, as if he'd been punched. A few seconds later, his body went limp, paralyzed by the stunning effects of the weapon which had burned a hole through his heart. The officer would be dead long before the stun wore off.

The trench-coated figure stepped out into the living room and approached his latest victim. He still had the slender laser pistol in his left hand, and used his right to move the man's head around while staring into his dying eyes. Before he could get a good look, a burning sensation sank into his shoulder, forcing him to drop his weapon.

Jack charged into the room, feeling his heart pounding, ready to finish things once and for all. As he approached, the murderer turned to face him, and all preconceptions fell away.

It wasn't Robert Drisko!

"Damn," elderly Maynard Williams said. "Looks like you got me, but I got me first!"

"Why'd you do it?" Jack asked, failing to understand how someone could murder their past self.

"I deserved it," Maynard said, looking at his younger incarnation. "I betrayed my best friend, stole his wife, and I'd have done it all over again."

"That's why you killed Rebecca Philbert."

"Becky never really loved me, just used me to hurt Bobby, so I killed her before she ever got the chance. But if it hadn't been her, it woulda been someone else. I'm a miserable son of a bitch. I had to die, just like the others."

Jack looked at the man, and understood his rationale. More than that, he felt sorry for him. It was rare that he actually felt anything for the people he pursued, but Maynard's plight spoke to him. This was a man who'd fought the good fight, but lost his way.

"I guess you're gonna stop me from ever doing this," Maynard mentioned, clearly familiar with Chronol Agent methods.

"It's my job," Jack said, knowing they'd be meeting again soon, at the scene of the first murder. Now that he knew who to look for, Jack would assure this killing of yesterday never happened.

Temsy
by Robert MacAnthony

Daman Patri rode the dirty green tram along the streets of Kolkata, face drawn, haunted, but with a sense of hesitant expectation, like a man lost in a desert, both desperate and reluctant to look over the next rise to see if there might be water or just more sand. A reprieve. That's all he wanted. Something to soothe him in the worst hours of the night.

He glanced at his watch. He was going to be late.

The tram moved slowly, giving way to automobiles, bicycles, and throngs of pedestrians, then picking up speed for brief moments when the way was clear. Daman considered getting out and walking, but the thought of pushing along the street, brushing shoulders with countless people, caused him to break out in a sweat. Many found the close proximity of over four million other souls comforting. Though Daman had spent his entire life in Kolkata, he found it stifling, this sea of humanity sharing the same earth, the same hot and humid air.

Outside, men in western dress filled the street, interspersed with women in colorful saris. Modern buildings of beige or white stood side by side with brightly-colored, crumbling tenements, many with green shuttered windows. Balconies held people engaged in conversation or simply watching people in other buildings across the street, people at vendor stalls below, people on bikes, trams, or on foot. People, people, people. The city had too many of them. And yet, Daman wished there were two more.

He opened his wallet, as he did numerous times each day, studied the picture of the woman and young boy, ran this thumb over the image. Raja wore brown pants and a yellow shirt, and was smiling that big grin of his up at his mother. Anuhya was looking at the camera, at Daman, as she held her son's hand. It wasn't right that they were gone. But gone they were, and Daman was alone, surrounded by millions.

Daman got off at the medical college, walking swiftly as he left the relative isolation provided by the metal walls of the vehicle. He turned away from the columned buildings off the college and made his way down a crowded street opposite the school, vendors calling at him as he passed. He smelled meat and spices, and the humidity caused his shirt to cling to his skin. When he reached the address written on his therapist's business card, he went in, let his eyes adjust, then saw the old man sitting alone at a table near the kitchen.

Dr. Ghosh ordered tea for Daman, his silver beard parting to reveal strong white teeth. While they waited, the doctor set an unlabeled prescription bottle on the table. Tiny blue pills filled the container.

"That's it, then?" asked Daman.

Dr. Ghosh nodded. "It is. The shipment arrived from Bangalore this morning. It was no small task getting them here, I can tell you."

Daman set a roll of rupees on the table, held together by a red rubber band. "It's all there."

The older man nodded, took the money, and pushed the prescription bottle to Daman.

"How does it work" asked Daman, hand trembling as he took the pills.

"It's very simple. Before you sleep, focus on a

121

particularly pleasant memory. An event you wish to experience again. Take the Temsy—just one pill is sufficient—and then continue to focus on your memory until you fall asleep."

Daman's eyes held tears as he looked at the bottle in his hand. Could these small pills really be the answer? Would they help him heal?

As he rose, the doctor reached across the table and grabbed his arm, his grip firm. "I do this only as a favor to my old colleague. You must tell no one. If the company in Bangalore finds out, my nephew will be fired. He may even be imprisoned, or sent to America to be charged."

Daman nodded and pulled his arm free. The old man looked as though he wanted to say more. Daman turned his back. As he was leaving, Dr. Ghosh called out, "We don't know if it is safe!"

Daman shrugged. "I'm already dying, old man," he muttered.

* * *

Daman still lived in the cramped two-bedroom apartment he, Anuhya, and Raju had called home. Six months after a car struck them as they ate fruit next to a roadside stand, Daman still dreaded putting the key in the lock, turning the handle, and stepping inside. He dreaded moving even more.

He had opened the prescription bottle as soon as he got home, then shaken one of the small pills into his palm. The blue oval was engraved with the letters Tem-C. "Temsy," as the doctor called it. He'd put the pill back in the bottle and let it sit on the coffee table all night, trying to keep from looking at it as he wound down for the evening.

Now, he was an hour beyond tired, his stomach tight at the thought of taking the drug and reliving the good times with his wife and son. He cleaned the tiny apartment for a second time, laid out fresh clothes for the morning, watched the lights of Kolkata through his window. Finally out of excuses, he sat on the couch with a glass of water, popped one of the pills into his mouth, and chased it down.

Daman curled up on the couch and wondered which memory to focus on. There was one that was particularly fresh, vivid. He and Raju wrestling in the living room, while Anuhya sat on the couch trying to read. He couldn't remember the book, but Raju had giggled while they played, then laughed outright at Daman's mock serious face when Anuhya warned them not to break anything...

And now there she is in pants and a white blouse, cross-legged on the couch. The book is The Hobbit, which she has read at least twice before. Daman studies her face, her long eyelashes and slender nose, black hair swept to one side of her head, hanging over her shoulder.

"Daaad," says Raju, "Quit looking at mom. Let's wrestle."

Daman jerks his head around at the voice, like a man coming out of a deep sleep, trying to make sense of the world. Raju has his hands on his hips, his skin glistening with sweat. "I told you I'm going to beat you this time."

The smell of last night's cooking is on the air. Daman hears Anuhya turn a page. A horn sounds outside. It's all so real, it threatens to overwhelm him. The memory is a wonderful and terrible thing.

"Dad, are you crying?"

Daman wipes his eyes. "I was just sad thinking about how bad I'm going to beat you."

"Oh, yeah?"

"Watch the glass on the TV cabinet, boys."

"Mom!"

"Here I come, Raju. You better watch out!"

* * *

Daman woke more dehydrated than he'd ever been in his life, his head throbbing. He groaned. What was he doing on the couch? "Anuhya, can you please get me a glass of water? I feel like I haven't had a drink in a month."

There was no answer. Daman sat up, rubbed his eyes, started to call out again, and then he remembered.

He hadn't counted on how real it would be. On losing them a second time.

Daman lay on the floor and sobbed until he found sleep again, this time without dreams.

* * *

It was three days before Daman took the Temsy again. He was scared to take it, to be thrust back so vividly in the world of his memories. He was also scared to let the pill bottle out of his sight, afraid he would lose it or someone would steal it and he would forever miss the potential it offered.

When he did take it again, the memory he tried was more flat, less emotional. A normal family dinner in the apartment, Anuhya talking about her day at school, Daman telling her about the latest cell phone to hit Kolkata, Raju complaining about being full without having eaten much of anything. This was easier for Daman to handle, and he revisited this memory for four consecutive nights, until he could predict down to the second when the Temsy would begin to wear off, his mind would grow hazy, and Anuhya and Raju would watch him strangely as they faded back into the real world.

After the fourth family dinner, he was ready to try the wrestling again. He'd grown accustomed to being with his family, to the measured pace of his remembered dinner. He could try something more emotional, and this time handle it better.

And is it better this time, because Daman knows what to expect when he sees Anuhya reading on the couch, can predict Raju's plaintive "Daaad" a moment before it comes. He knows to expect the sweatslick feel of Raju's skin, the smell of his hair, his breath. He and Raju tumble on the floor, ignoring Anuhya's good-natured admonitions, both laughing as Daman lets Raju get the upper hand, only to turn the tables and pin him on the floor. Daman tickles Raju's hip, and the child writhes and squirms, laughing until he can't breathe because that is the most ticklish spot he has.

Daman rolls onto his back, pulling the boy on top of him, feeling the unexpected impact of his heel against glass, hearing the crash. Raju leaps off of him, staring wide eyed at his mom, who has set the book in her lap.

"I knew it, Daman." She is frowning but doesn't look angry.

"We're sorry, mom," says Raju.

Daman isn't looking at either of them because he's staring at the shattered cabinet and the shards of glass scattered across the carpet. "That's not right," he says.

"Did you hurt yourself?"

Daman turns to Anuhya. He isn't hurt, but his ears are buzzing, ringing with blood. "We never broke that."

Anuhya rolls her eyes. "I was sitting right here, Daman." She winks at Raju.

Daman props himself on his elbow and tries to talk, but his mouth is dry again and before he can so much as croak Anuhya's face gets that fuzzy look and he loses her.

* * *

He woke on the couch again, throat parched, the last smells and images of his family still lingering. Daman sat up, rubbing at his temples. After a moment, he rose, opened a bottle of water on the kitchen counter, and drank it down. He thought about the Temsy, wondered what had gone wrong, why his memory had been screwed up.

Or had it been?

Because it now seemed like maybe it wasn't all wrong to begin with, and Daman wasn't surprised as he crouched next to the television cabinet, now with one glass door missing, and ran his fingers along the hinges and brass clamps that had held the door. A piece of broken glass was still wedged inside one of the clamps and he wiggled it back and forth until he worked it loose, then held it in his hands. There was dust inside the cabinet, by the broken door, and he remembered kicking it months ago, as he and Raju tumbled around the living room.

But he also remembered not breaking it, that it had never been broken, and Anuhya had never rolled her eyes and winked at their son.

When he tried to reconcile the two memories, his head hurt behind his eyes and he needed more water.

* * *

125

An experiment.

Daman is in the living room with Raju, or maybe Daman is sleeping on the couch and in a memory of being in the living room with Raju. The boy is coloring and humming softly to himself. Anuhya is shopping and then has a lunch with some of the girls from school.

"Raju, come here, and bring the black crayon."

Daman positions Raju against the wall, then draws a line, marking the boy's height. Raju steps away and looks at it. "That's how big I am?"

"That's how tall you are," says Daman. "Every few months, we'll stand you in that same spot and make another mark. That way you can see how fast you are growing."

Raju grins, but the grin quickly falls away and he lets out a yell, pointing toward the hallway. "Dad!"

Daman spins, his pulse quickening, but when he turns there is nothing.

"It was an animal. I think it went down the hall."

Daman frowns. "What kind of animal?" Raju shrugs, and Daman heads for the hallway. An animal is unlikely, especially since they live on the third floor, but anything is possible.

Anything but what Daman sees when he turns the corner, just as the edges of his vision are going hazy and the Temsy is wearing off. A figure, maybe a couple of feet tall, dark, bald, bloated. It wears no clothes, and its arms and legs are too thin for its body. The only sign of eyes is the faint shimmer from two places on its head. As the Temsy fades and Daman's window of time closes, the thing extend one thick-jointed finger, holding it up next to its featureless head. An admonition.

Daman wants to ask, but he's back on the couch, retching.

* * *

"I'm telling you, it's not possible," said Dr. Ghosh. The man ate a spoonful of yellow rice. The smell of curry was thick on the air.

"And I'm telling you, I saw the marks." Daman knew

126

how he must look, how he must sound. He hadn't slept, either with Temsy or without, in the two days since he'd awoken on the couch to find the crayon mark on the wall. "What is this stuff you gave me?"

Dr. Ghosh leaned forward, made a gesture. "Quiet! Do you want to jeopardize my career? Or that of my nephew? I'm doing you a courtesy by meeting with you again. I've already told you—the Temsy is an experimental psychoactive drug. An American company in Bangalore makes it. There are no approved uses for it yet. The only reason I know what I do is because my nephew works in the lab." He sat back. "You knew the risks, Mr. Patri. This is an unproven medication. If it is causing hallucinations, I..."

"They're not hallucinations!"

Dr. Ghosh took a breath. "I recommend you discontinue using the medication at once."

"I can't do that," Daman said.

"The side effects are getting worse, yes?"

Daman thought of the headaches and nodded.

"And the hallucinations...." Dr. Ghosh raised a hand "I don't mean the marks on the wall, I mean the creatures you see."

Daman nodded again. He'd seen the distorted little things each of the three times he'd taken Temsy since marking Raju's growth on the wall. Usually, they showed up just as the Temsy was wearing off. Once, he saw one just as the drug was taking effect. They scared him.

"OK," Dr. Ghosh said. "You are finding yourself in severe pain after taking Temsy, especially if you do something to change the memory in your own mind. Furthermore, you are having hallucinations of little creatures when you take the pills. The answer is clear: stop taking the Temsy."

"Listen, doctor..."

"No, I am through listening. You came to me for advice, and now you have it."

Daman sighed. "I didn't come for advice. I'm down to half a bottle and I need you to get me more."

* * *

No amount of pleading had swayed Dr. Ghosh, and Daman now sat on his couch faced with the very real prospect that the Temsy remaining in the bottle was all he would ever see. His eyes were fixed on the crayon mark on the wall. He remembered drawing it—really drawing it, months ago and not under the influence of Temsy. At the same time, he held in mind memories of a house where there was no mark and never had been, where he'd never measured his son's height with a crayon in the months before a car had taken him out of the world.

There was intense pain as he tried to bring these two memories together, sharp lances that seemed to penetrate his eyes, causing a burst of white in his field of vision.

But Daman knew he wasn't crazy. The Temsy wasn't letting him relive his memories, it was sending him back to them, allowing him to truly relive them, to change them. No matter how bad the pain got, his mind was set. He knew what he had to do.

He had half a bottle left.

* * *

On the day Anuhya and Raju were killed, Daman wasn't with them. He was at home relaxing. But he knew where they were. He fixed that day in his mind as he shook the Temsy into his palm. Two pills might buy him more time, he decided.

Until he'd received word of the accident, the day had been insignificant. Still, the news of the accident served as a focal point, and he was able to track his afternoon backward, remember what he had for lunch, laying on the couch afterward with the windows open, enjoying the cooler air of the Kolkata winter.

When he gets there, breathing the fresh air and feeling the fullness of lunch in his stomach, he isn't ready for what he sees. The creatures are there, two of them with their malformed and uncovered bodies, knobby fingers terminating in long, ragged nails.

"Daaman Paatri," says one, raising a misshapen palm.

Daman's chest tightens and a shiver runs along his arms. His vocal chords constrict and he squeaks out, "What are you?"

The closest creature steps forward, moving between Daman and the door. A mouth opens in the blackness of its head, lipless and framing dark teeth. "We know whaat you sseek to do."

Daman checks his watch. He has almost an hour before the accident, which is plenty of time to get there and get his wife and child. The creatures are small, but in addition to their appearance Daman can sense an element of danger around them.

"We caan not aallow thiss."

"It's no business of yours," Daman says, stepping to the side. The creatures mirror his movement.

"But it iss. Think of the paain you feel. Think of the otherss you inflict it on."

"I'm not hurting anyone."

"Aall thosse who were touched by your family'ss deaath. All thosse who would haave been touched by their livess. People they would haave met. The girl your sson would haave maarried."

Hearing his family spoken of in such terms brings tears to Daman's eyes. He wipes at his face with his forearm. His voice is strangled by fear and emotion. "I don't care." He steps forward, but the creatures do not move. "Will you kill me?"

The foremost creature chuckles. A dry sound. "To kill you would be to caausse thaat which we sseek to prevent. It iss a laast ressort. Know thiss Daaman Paatri: the universse sseekss to right itsself. Ssometimess it needss help." The creature grins, raises that gnarled finger again. "We aare the help."

* * *

When Daman finds the fruit vendor, Anuhya and Raju are not there yet. The sun is behind the tall, narrow buildings that line the street, but the air is warm even in the shade. Daman buys a chunk of tart melon and watches the street

129

anxiously. When he spots Anuhya's head in the crowd, he wipes his hands on his pant leg and jogs over to them.

"Daman! What are you doing here? I thought you wanted to spend the day alone at the apartment?"

Daman takes Anuhya by the hand, ruffles Raju's hair. "I changed my mind. Lets do something together instead. How about some ice cream?" Raju's smile is wide, his eyes sparkling. He lets out a cheer. "Can we, mom?"

"It's so expensive." Anuhya turns to face Daman, a quizzical look on her face.

"Let's forget about the expense today. Why not go a little crazy? It's a beautiful day and I have my family with me." This, thinks Daman, is how the day should have gone all along.

* * *

After ice cream, Daman takes Raju and Anuhya back to the apartment. Raju sits on the floor reading, Anuhya watching Daman as he paces the apartment.

"Are you sure you're okay?"

"I'm fine."

"It's just that I've never seen you like this. Why do you keep checking your watch?"

It is well past the time when Daman was told of the accident. Almost two hours past. Still, Daman can't fight the unease that grips him. What if the accident didn't happen? What if it is tomorrow, and his wife and son are hit on the street right outside the apartment? How can he be sure he's really saved them? He has to do something before the Temsy wears off.

"Anuhya, listen. I need to check something. Please stay here with Raju. Don't go anywhere at all. I'll be right back."

Anuhya looks confused, starts to reply, but Daman is already out the door. He exits their building and runs along the street, brushing shoulders with people walking there, calling apologies back behind him. He can tell something has happened before he reaches the fruit vendor. A crowd is gathered around, a buzz of conversation on the air. As Daman draws near he sees a form on the ground, a body covered by a

130

dirty blanket. A silver Mahindra is just beyond the body, part of the fruit vendor's stall having collapsed onto the vehicle.

Daman grabs a dark-haired teen by the shoulder. "What happened?"

The teen shrugs. "The car just swerved for no reason. An old woman was sitting there eating fruit, and it just ran her over, then hit the stand." The youth's eyes draw together. "Are you okay?"

Daman realizes he is sweating profusely. An old woman? There was no old woman when Anuhya and Raju were hit. Of course, the seats weren't empty when his wife and child were in them. Daman clamps a hand over his own mouth, then draws it down along his chin. An old woman. That's not so bad, is it? In trade for a child and a young woman? Much of the anxiety that has gripped him is already fading as he runs back to the apartment building. By the time he reaches the front door, he feels as though a tremendous burden has been lifted from him. His wife and child are safe now, thanks to him. The accident, their deaths, these will be like a dream. A horrible nightmare that never happened.

Daman notices the smell of gas before he reaches the apartment door. A cold fear grips him as he opens the door, the edges of his vision already blurring as the effects of the Temsy begin to fade. He sees the bodies on the floor, one small, one large, and doubles over, chest tight, airways constricted. Dark shadows boil around him as his eyes grow heavy, and before his vision goes altogether he sees a small, dark, misshapen form standing in the living room, a twisted accusatory finger pointed directly at him.

* * *

Daman tried everything, but each time he prevented one set of deaths only to see his family succumb to another. He stoped the gas leak, but their worn balcony collapsed just as Anuhya and Raju were out looking for faint stars above the light pollution of the city. He kept the balcony off limits, and there was an accident on the stairs. He checked the stairs and took his wife and child out carefully, but once out in the world any manner of death ensued, some probable, some improbable. Most of them involved cars. Through it all, dark figures jostled at the edges of his eyesight.

Pill after pill of Temsy. Failure after failure. Daman was incapacitated by headaches for hours at a time, a blinding pain when the Temsy wears off and each new death displaced the old. But it couldn't go on forever, could it? He just needed to keep them safe for a certain period of time. Days? Maybe weeks at the most? After that, surely self-correction was as disruptive as doing nothing.

He was running out of options, though, as he stood in the apartment once again, having taken five Temsy—leaving only one in the bottle.

The gas is off, and the door to the balcony is nailed shut. There are no sharp objects in the apartment and he has Anuhya and Raju sleeping on a mattress in the living room, with no sheets or blankets.

"I'm going for food," Daman says.

Anuhya looks up at him. She's been crying again. "I don't understand any of this," she mutters, but she is beyond argument. She sets her cheek against the top of Raju's head and sighs. Daman tries to catch Raju's eye, but his son won't look up at him.

"Do not leave here under any circumstances," Daman says. "Don't even move from that spot. I'll explain all of this soon, I promise. I... I love you both."

He leaves the apartment confident that nothing in it can harm them. Short of the entire building being destroyed, they should be safe. So far, the universe has targeted his wife and child quite specifically. No bystanders have died in any of the accidents he has grieved over these many days.

He shops quickly, efficiently, gathering only the necessities and a few sweets for Raju. Once they're through this, he'll take them away from here. Five Temsy should keep him here long enough to see them safely through danger. If they don't... well, he doesn't want to think about that.

All is quiet when he reaches the apartment. Everything is as it should be. He sees the light of his living room three floors above.

The first thing Daman notices when he opens the apartment door is the smell of blood and feces. Anuhya is laying on the living room floor, one arm across her chest as though she was holding it out in front of her, the other arm wrapped tight around Raju. Deep gashes line her arm, and slow, thick blood is still making its way down to the carpet. Her neck has been torn so severely that Daman sees the white of vertebra in the tattered meat. Raju's head is buried in his mother's bosom, but the back of his skull and neck are torn apart. A stain seeps through his pants in the area of his buttocks.

Daman falls to his knees and vomits. When the heaving stops and his vision clears, he sees the two dark shapes, caricatures of a bent and angular form, peering down at him where he lays. Dried blood encrusts their mouths, and when one raises its hand and speaks, Daman sees bits of tissue dangling from its twisted fingernails.

"Thiss iss our messsaage to you, Daamaan Paatri. We grow weaary."

* * *

Daman looked, bleary eyed, at the name "Dr. Ghosh" in delicate script on the glossy wooden door. His hands trembled such that he had to grip the knob with both of them. He twisted the handle and went in. A young lady with long hair and a red dot on her forehand smiled at him.

"Can I help you?"

Daman ignored her and strode toward another door, this one at the rear of the office.

"Sir, Dr. Ghosh is unavailable at the moment."

Again the handle was difficult to grip, but Daman opened the door and was in the room before the receptionist could reach him. Dr. Ghosh sat behind a large desk strewn with paper. He looked up, surprised, then frowned. Rising from his desk, he waved the receptionist off, shut the office door, then grabbed Daman roughly by the arm.

"What are you doing here?" he hissed. "Do you want to ruin me?"

Daman tried to speak, but each half-formed word was

accompanied by a sob. After a moment, Dr. Ghosh led Daman to a chair and helped him into it. The doctor sat quietly by his side until he'd composed himself.

"I was so close, doctor. Please. You have to get more Tempsy. Just one more bottle. When I go back I'll be ready. I won't leave them alone at all."

Dr. Ghosh sighed. "Daman, I've told you there is no more Temsy. My nephew obtained the first bottle with great difficulty. I thought it might help you. Might allow you some closure. It was meant only to let you relive a few pleasant memories—to say a proper goodbye. I see now I've made a grave mistake, and for that I am sorry."

Daman chuckled without humor. "It was no mistake, doctor. Your Temsy let me go back to the memories. I wasn't just reliving them, I was re-experiencing them. I could change things. Change the accident!"

"What accident, Daman?"

Daman looked over at the doctor and wiped his nose. "The car accident of course. What other accident would I mean?"

Dr. Ghosh sighed and sat on the arm of the chair. Daman twisted out of the way to give him room. "Daman, when your therapist recommended you visit me, I was already aware of the death of your wife and child. I remembered the news stories. Murders of such a vicious nature are rare. A wife and child, alone in their apartment. The news reports sent a chill through me. When your therapist told me you'd reframed the deaths as a car accident, why, I was sympathetic, of course, but I thought we'd moved beyond this."

Daman rose up out of the chair, the doctor unbalancing it and almost falling as the chair tipped sideways. He jabbed a finger into the doctor's chest, his voice rising. "You know damn well it was a car accident. We talked about it the day we met, there in the restaurant. Do you remember?"

Dr. Ghosh had his hands raised, a non-confrontational pose. "I remember you talking about it as a car accident, Daman. At least, I think I do. Sometimes, I think we didn't discuss it at all. In any event, I knew the truth. Framing their deaths as an accident is a defense mechanism. Still a violent death, but one that pales in comparison to what actually happened."

For a moment Daman felt the urge to lash out at the doctor, this time physically. It must have shown on his face, for the doctor blanched visibly and stepped a pace back. Daman hung his head, covered his face with his palms, and took a few deep breaths. "Think, doctor. Try to visualize the car accident as I described it."

Daman looked up and saw a flash of pain cross the doctor's eyes. The other man pinched the bridge of his nose.

"Ah! There it is. The headache. You were thinking about the car accident. On some level, you know it's true and your brain can't handle it."

Dr. Ghosh lowered his hand, his eyes bright. With a look of pity on his face, he said, "Please lay down, Daman. I'll call your therapist. We'll all discuss it together."

When the doctor left the office, Daman felt for the knife in his pants pocket. Reassured, he took the prescription bottle from the other pocket. A lone blue pill remained inside. He had one chance left.

Daman closed his eyes, uttered a prayer to every divinity he could think of, and swallowed the pill.

* * *

"Headache, uncle?"

Naveen Ghosh looked up at his nephew and smiled. "I'm fine, thank you Harjeet. I just haven't slept well lately."

Harjeet nodded, handed his uncle a cup of tea, and sat beside him. "What are these old news clippings?"

Dr. Ghosh shook his head slowly, spreading pieces of various newspaper articles across the surface of his desk. "Do you remember the Prati murders last year?"

Harjeet nodded. "A little. Guy went nuts, stabbed his wife and child to death, then cuts his own wrists in the bathtub? We got a few reports in Bangalore, but it didn't cause a big sensation like here in Kolkata."

"That's the one," Dr. Ghosh said. "It's funny. The case just came to mind the other day from out of the blue. I was

135

sitting at my desk, and the news stories just ran through my head. A feeling came over me... no, more than that, a certainty. For a brief instant, I was certain the man had been a patient of mine."

"Was he?"

"No. I'd have remembered him as an adult. I did check my old files, in case I'd seen him as a child, but there was nothing. Since that day, though, I haven't been able to get the case out of my mind. I can hardly sleep, and every time I think of it I get the most horrifying headache."

"You've probably overworked yourself, uncle. It wouldn't be the first time."

Dr. Ghosh sighed. "You're probably right. I've decided to take a few days off and just rest. When do you go back to Bangalore?"

"At the end of the week. They wouldn't give me more time. We're working a new production job from the States."

"That's good to hear, Harjeet. That money will do wonders for Bangalore."

Harjeet rose and helped his uncle up.

"Come on, let's get you home."

"Thank you. Don't mind an old man. I'm sure I'll be okay. A few days rest and I'll be right back at it." He pulled one of the news clippings from the desk, staring hard into the face of one Daman Prati. "Still...."

"That's enough of that." Harjeet took the newspaper clipping and set it back on the desk. "If you want to get some rest, you're going to have to let that case go. Come to think of it, this new drug production job we're working; the compound is called Tem-C, and it is supposed to help people relax. Maybe I can get some for you."

AMR-17

By Edmund Wells

Ultraviolet scanners locked, AMR-17 squeezed off a pulse from his laser rifle. His target, a bulky yellow constructor robot with delusions of piratehood, flashed like a red neon bulb.

"Arr! Ye got me, matey."

Armand raised his rifle in triumph and glanced around at his teammates, AMR-3 and AMR-11, known among the other atmospheric maintenance robots as Omar and Mara. Their cobalt visual nodes shone with delight.

The constructor robot, CR-8, lumbered forth, followed by his two Cor union buddies, who swaggered from behind storage tanks. Each wore a regulation steel patch over one eye.

"Good game, Captain." Armand inclined his head.

"Lucky shot, Amir-17." The Cor's voice rumbled like an idling bulldozer. "Now we're tied—one for the Yellow Seadogs, one for you sneaky Amir bilge rats."

Omar stepped forward. "We're the *Molecule Jockeys*, damn you. Next round wins the match... and sixty extra hours on the gaming computers. Agreed?"

CR-5 nodded, pointing a thick iron finger. "And a

tankard of grog. Arr."

Mara twirled her rifle. "Do you idiots even *know* how to use a computer?"

"Aye. And we're mighty fond of Pac Man," CR-4 said, flexing a steel bicep.

Life as a maintenance robot on Europa Colony was, Armand had come to learn, dull, dull, dull. If not for the games, the occasional "invasion defense drill," and his future role as Chief of Atmospheric Operations, he'd stuff himself in an airlock and switch the lights off. With the present Chief off-line for repairs, Armand was enjoying the perks of that position, making mandatory target practice a little more fun.

A tiny buzzer sounded in Armand's audio sensors. He heaved an electronic sigh. *Duty calls.* "Time to deploy the canisters, me hearties. I'll be back in twenty-two minutes."

The three Cor leveled their brushed steel rifles at him. "You've got fifteen minutes, lubber, or the rules state we shove off without you."

"But—"

Omar motioned with his head. "Go on."

"Hurry, Armand!" Mara shooed him away.

Cursing subvocally, Armand sprinted off. The biosphere's artificial atmosphere required regular injections of oxygen, drawn from Europa's own thin atmosphere, purified, and stored in pressurized canisters. Since the process was dangerous—and tedious—the colonists used robots to perform the tasks from a station adjacent to the biosphere.

Armand entered the security code to access the oxygen dispersion chamber. The heavy steel doors rotated open and he dashed inside. Using a grav-lift, he withdrew three canisters from cryo-storage and wheeled them to the bio-scanner.

He took note of his chronometer. Four minutes had already elapsed. Scanning for contaminants would take another five minutes per canister.

There wasn't enough time.

In nine years, only *once* had the bio-scan detected a potential hazard. To Armand, it seemed the greater risk was losing precious game time to the constructor robots, who already strutted around like they owned the station.

Drumming his fingers, Armand scanned the first canister—negative. The second canister—also negative. No surprises.

Fourteen minutes gone, damn those Cor and their union regulations. Why couldn't they be more like real pirates? Armand was usually one to follow orders, but if he was going to make it back in time, he'd have to omit canister 1121511229.

His first major executive decision as Chief.

Fingers flying, he entered the clearance code and all three canisters discharged their oxygen molecules into pipes that fed the biosphere of Europa Colony.

Humming a little tune, he disconnected the canisters and jogged back to Laser Tag Warehouse, as they'd re-named it. It was time to kick some constructor pirates in their afts.

* * *

Some time later, Armand slumped into a corner and let his visual nodes go dark. At times, life just wasn't fair. A jarring clang on the head caused him to jump. Warily, he re-activated one node.

"Optimal performance, Armand." Mara stood over him, fists on her hips. "You inspire me."

Omar lay flat on his back, the grinding of his mandible gears audible from across the room. "How could you let them sneak up on you like that?"

"They surprised me at an intersection." A patchwork of laser burns crisscrossed Armand's chest and arms. "They drill for an invasion from Titan all the time. I think they look forward to it."

Mara kicked him with another clang. "They're big, they're yellow and they stomp when they tiptoe. Are your sensors malfunctioning, or do you just need new batteries?"

"Hey. Is that any way to treat your Chief?"

A chime rang. High on the north wall, a panel opened, through which darted a gray shape: an automated courier pigeon. Tiny motors whirred as it alighted on the steel-plated floor, shaking snow from its wings.

"Greetings from Europa Colony, sixth moon of Jupiter. I am ACP-31." Its head bobbed as it eyed each of them. "Which of you is acting Chief of Atmospheric Operations?"

Omar and Mara thrust accusing fingers at Armand.

Armand rose to his feet. "That's me."

The pigeon scuttled nearer. "A message for you, Chief." Light streamed from the bird's eyes, raising a holographic image. A human female, her face twisted in an aspect of pain, spoke in a hoarse voice.

"Breach... in the oxygen filters... Organic... People are dropping... like lemmings." She drew a ragged breath even as her face turned a blotchy shade of purple. "Protocol One... lock down..." With a final desperate gasp, she collapsed onto her desk and lay still.

The three Amir shared a glance, shock reflected in each other's eyes. Protocol One was a general quarantine with a call for emergency assistance.

Armand sensed an alarming spike in his core temperature.

The holographic image now showed a pigeon's-eye view of Europa Colony. The dome had cracked in numerous places, exposing the biosphere to the frigid atmosphere of Europa. Snow and ice particles swirled in. Frozen bodies lay strewn everywhere, fallen where they had worked or played. Nothing moved, except for a few frost-rimed machines. The biosphere appeared to have been attacked, with devastating results.

The pigeon's eyes flickered and went dark. "Have a nice day!" It leaped into the air and flew off.

Mara strode to a computer access node and punched in a few commands. "Life signs register no readings. There are traces in the atmosphere of Yersinia anaeris, a bacteria that eats oxygen. It would have caused suffocation and then a vacuum inside the dome, resulting—"

"Yes, I can see the result." Armand peered over her shoulder, unable to believe his visual sensors. He rather liked human beings, despite their somewhat dismissive attitude toward worker robots. The colony was always in danger of attack from the neighboring moons of Saturn—Titan in particular, which was controlled by pirates. "There were twenty six thousand, five hundred and nine colonists in that dome!"

"They're still in there," Omar said. "They're just dead."

Mara poked Armand in the chest. "This is *your* fault."

"My fault?" His gyroscopes vacillated unpleasantly. "I ran the bio-scan. Well... most of it. You forced me to rush the procedure, as you'll recall."

Omar and Mara crossed their arms.

"Fine. But what were the odds the last canister would be contaminated with a lethal biohazard?"

"Apparently, one in one," Omar said. "So now what?"

Good question. Armand slumped back into his corner, head bowed in thought. It wouldn't be long before someone noticed and alerted Jupiter Station. The ensuing investigation would reveal he had neglected to scan the third canister. They weren't likely to fault the constructor robots for adhering to the fifteen-minute break rule. Instead, they would put him on trial, as a matter of bio-mechanical ethics, then disassemble him for parts. Or worse, banish him to a mining colony on Jupiter's seventh moon, Ganymede.

He needed time to think.

"Mara, Omar—I need you to create a diversion. Call a series of defense drills to keep everyone occupied, but nothing that involves interaction with the biosphere. Understand?"

The two Amir nodded.

"What do you intend to do?" Mara asked, her sarcasm circuits working overtime. "Go back in time to correct your mistake?"

Armand's head snapped up. An excellent idea, if only he had the means. With a flash of inspiration, he knew who he needed to talk to.

* * *

Flashing lights and sirens filled the corridors as robots rolled, ran or flew in response to a surprise defense drill. Blaring speakers announced that contact had been severed with the biosphere and Titanian space pirates were attacking the station. Surrender, as always, was not an option.

A bit overdone, but since such attacks happened often enough, the simulation was a credible excuse that would keep everyone busy.

Armand hurried along a series of side passages, making his way to the meteorological unit. He pressed a buzzer beside a dark metal door etched with a stylized golden sun.

The portal rotated open.

"Enter, friend." A deep, theatrical voice greeted him. "I have been expecting you."

Armand grimaced. "You say that to everyone, Michel."

At the center of the domed chamber sat a bright crystalline globe, three meters in diameter, raised on a clear pedestal. A ghostly light swirled within the sphere, pulsing as it spoke.

"What troubles you, AMR-17?"

"Please, call me Armand."

"Very well. And I will trouble you to call me Nostradamus, for thus am I known."

Armand bowed, knowing the pompous weather computer had an ego as vast as Jupiter. "Forgive me, esteemed Nostradamus. I come to you for advice."

"Naturally." The image on the globe's exterior coalesced to depict the frozen surface of Europa, with its cracked ridges and crisscrossing fault lines. A pair of red circles marked the site of the biosphere and the adjacent robotics station, while rotating blue and green swirls revealed the location and course of ion storms.

"Beautiful," Armand said, knowing the computer expected it.

"Thank you. Are you planning an excursion? A little hyper-skiing adventure, perhaps?"

"No, I have a more ... theoretical concern."

"Hmmm," Nostradamus intoned. "Do go on."

"How far into the future do your temporal circuits allow you to see?"

"My powers of meteorological prophecy extend twelve hours. Other areas of prophecy are variable. I am forsworn, just so you know, against gambling forecasts of any kind."

Armand shrugged. "Of course." *Now for the tricky part.* "My question is this, mighty Nostradamus: although you are a seer of the future, do your temporal circuits also enable you to peer... backwards?"

The computer hesitated. "Backwards?" His cavernous tone rose several octaves. "Meaning *into the past*? But that would merely be scrying upon a historical event. One does not *prophesize* the past!"

"Of course, but theoretically, *could* you? If you bent your formidable powers to the task?"

"Well, when you put it that way..." A deep hum filled the chamber as Nostradamus pondered for several long moments. "I've sent out a few feelers, and it appears I can, as you say, *peer* into the past, but I fail to appreciate the point."

Armand felt a tingle of electricity course over him. "Do you recall, dear friend, my gift to you from last Christmas?"

The great computer laughed, lights pulsing across its curved surface. "Of course! The complete, digitally re-mastered Farmer's Almanac series dating back to 1818, *and* a holo-image of Vilhelm Bjerknes, my favorite meteorologist from ancient Earth."

"That's right. And in return you promised me a favor, should I ever need one."

Nostradamus heaved a ponderous sigh. "I see where this is going, you know."

"I knew you would."

"Name your favor, friend Armand. If it lies within my power, I will grant it."

Armand began to pace. "I recently made a small mistake, you see. Small, but... far-reaching. It's vitally important I correct this mistake, for the sake of others as well as myself." He faced the swirling globe and balled his hands into fists. "To set matters straight, I need you to send me into the past."

A long pause. "Physically, you mean?"

"I assumed so, yes."

Nostradamus' lights swirled a long moment, stretching into several long moments.

"Hello?" Armand said. "Anyone there?"

"Hush! I'm thinking."

"Sorry." Another stretch of silence crept by. Armand began to fear Nostradamus had lapsed into a prophetic trance, or dozed off, when the computer's voice rumbled forth.

"Although I admit to some reservations, I believe I can accommodate your request."

Armand nearly leaped for joy. "Huzzah!"

"I cannot, however, send you physically. I've consulted several engineering journals. One source claims to have connected temporal circuitry to a data transference device, in effect sending your consciousness back in time. In other words, I can project your present memory and cognitive array upon your past self."

"Neat. How far can you send me back?"

"Will three hours suffice?"

Armand nodded. He only needed twenty-two minutes.

* * *

Armand stood on the pad of a transference unit, which was normally used to transport heavy supplies and equipment from the moon's surface. As far as he knew, no one had ever cast their mind back to inhabit a past self.

Nostradamus' voice echoed through the room. "I must warn you, the test subjects reported a degree of disorientation from the memory transfer. You might want to write yourself a note or something."

"Good idea." Armand pressed a key on his forearm and whispered so Nostradamus couldn't overhear. "Imminent danger! Destruction of biosphere in 3 hours due to use of canister 1121511229. Urgent!" He straightened up. "I'm ready."

"Fare thee well, little friend. And Merry Christmas."

White light filled Armand's eyes, washing out the scene before him. A wave of dizziness spun him in circles, his body vibrating like a piano wire. A rising, operatic cry crashed over him, terminating in a crescendo of tinkling crystal.

All at once his vision returned. The scene wavered, as if his visual sensors had been... stretched. Blinking, he realized he was in Warehouse 3, standing on the matter transference pad.

What am I doing here?

A sense of urgency filled him. There was something critical he needed to do. But what? A flashing red light on his arm caught his attention. He tapped the button and a staticky message ran through his audio sensors.

Danger--biosphere--3 hours.

A danger to the biosphere? In three hours? The message was recorded in his voice pattern, but much of it was garbled and impossible to decipher. He put a hand to his head, trying to stop the sensation of spinning.

Disjointed sounds and images flashed through his memory. An announcement that the station was under attack by Titan, robots running through the halls. Sirens blaring. He glanced down and noticed laser burns lashed across his arms and chest. He'd been fired on, which would explain his various malfunctions. The immediate situation seemed clear enough.

Europa Colony was in danger.

Or would be. According to his own message, the danger would arrive in three hours. But how could he know such a thing?

He checked his chronometer, which caused him a jolt. Time was running *backwards*—inexplicably counting down from three hours. The readout indicated two hours and thirty one minutes remained.

Until the danger to the biosphere occurred.

Only one explanation fit. Somehow he'd gone back in time. But how? And for what purpose?

Moving on unsteady legs, vision flickering, Armand crept off the pad and through an open door. A trio of bulky yellow robots with eye patches huddled near the far wall, laser rifles slung over their shoulders. He recalled seeing such robots before...

The robots turned as one, raised their rifles, and opened fire. "Arr! Get him, me buckos!" They laughed and sang "yo-ho-ho" as spears of red light seared the air all around him.

Cursing, Armand ducked behind a bulkhead. *Space Pirates*! The situation was worse than he'd realized. The invasion had already begun.

He stumbled down an alternate corridor and locked an emergency hatchway behind him. His mind raced, stuttering to put the pieces together. Logically, the invasion had to be coming in two stages: first the station, and *then* the biosphere.

That had to be it. And yet ...

The corridor ended in another door, which parted as he approached: the Rec Room. Three ancient ore-smelting robots sat around a chess board, although it looked more like they were napping. Nearer, a pair of sanitation robots crouched before a gaming computer, remote controllers clutched in their dirty, oversized hands.

Armand jogged over to them. "What are you doing?" He shook a fist. "Shouldn't you be mounting a counter strike?"

The two Sar blinked their oversized LCD eyes. "Whaddya talkin' about?" SR-5 replied. "It's friggin' Mario Brothers, not Counterstrike. We're just jumpin' turtles, right, Tony?"

SR-6 snorted. "Yo, Vin. Maybe he means we oughta *mount* his sister." The pair laughed.

Armand stepped in front of the video screen. "Are your relays fried? The station is under attack by pirates. They just shot at me. We need to *do* something!"

The robot craned his head to see around Armand. "Pal, you need to move your friggin' ass, before somebody's *face* gets attacked. And by that, I mean you."

"Good one, Vin."

Armand turned and put a fist through the video screen.

The Sar stood, their heavy jaws askew. "That, my little friend, was a mistake." The sanitation robots each grabbed one of Armand's arms, dragged him to a storage room, and tossed him in like so much trash. The door rotated shut at his back.

"Let me out, you sanitation simpletons!" Armand pounded on the door. "You don't realize what you're doing!" After several minutes of fruitless shouting, he began tearing through the barrels and crates. Oil, spare robot components, batteries, and some simple tools—electron wrenches, force hammers, and ion drivers.

He tried each tool, but none enabled him to breach the door. Head in his hands, he slumped against a barrel to wait for someone to let him out. His vision continued to waver, making it hard to focus. Out of curiosity, he played his recorded message again. It sounded a little clearer.

Danger--biosphere--3 hours--canister--Urgent!

Canister? The danger related to a canister? It could be a bomb, or a biological weapon. He didn't know what the precise danger was, but he suddenly had a *very* bad feeling about it.

His chronometer indicated one hour and fifty five minutes remained. He needed to get out of this damned storage room.

Armand grabbed a force hammer and leaped to his feet. "Hey, garbage boys! You can be replaced by a vacuum hose, you know. Even though you suck twice as much."

The door rotated open and in strode an android made in the exacting image of a human colonist: a male, his round head all pink and shiny, tufts of white hair sprouting from his chin. It was the station's positronic matrix evaluator, or in human terms ... the psych counselor: Sigmund Droid.

He peered at Armand through little round eyeglasses. "Hallo. I am PME-1. A complaint has been filed against you, AMR-17. What seems to be troubling you, mein freund?" He clicked a pen, which he held poised over a cyber-clipboard.

Armand rose to his feet, eyeing the open door at the android's back. "What troubles me, Sigmund, is that the station has been invaded by enormous yellow pirates and no one but me seems to care. Excuse me, but I have to warn someone." He stepped toward the door.

"Halt." At a gesture from Sigmund, the door rotated shut. "We must first have a little chat, ja?"

The PME wielded the authority of law on the station, as well as the core program scripts to each and every robot. With a word, Armand could find himself re-assigned to the pigeon repair yard. He needed to tread lightly.

"Fine, but please hurry. We're all in imminent danger." Armand sat on a crate, tapping his force hammer.

Sigmund took a seat opposite. "Two Sar units have accused you of behaving in a strange, violent manner. Is this true?"

He suppressed an angry retort. "Atmospheric maintenance robots are not violent."

The counselor glanced at the hammer in Armand's hand.

Armand forced a casual laugh. "I'm interested in modern construction methods, that's all." He set the hammer down.

"Uh-hum." Sigmund jotted a note. "And does your *interest* in modern construction methods extend to the demolition of video monitors?"

Armand shot to his feet. "The station is under attack, Sigmund, and those idiot Sar were just sitting there pretending to be plumbers!"

Sigmund glanced around in an exaggerated manner, peering behind crates and barrels. "I see no evidence of an attack. Do you often feel you are under attack, AMR-17?"

This was not going well. Armand settled back onto the crate, trying to calm his resistors. "Not me personally, no, but—"

"Tell me, how long have you experienced this displaced hatred toward your mother?"

"My mother?"

Sigmund stood up. "I'm afraid you're going to require a lengthy course of psychoanalysis before you are fit to interact with your peers." He scribbled on his clipboard. "I recommend temporary deactivation until a suitable treatment schedule can be arranged, as well as a full diagnostic with a robotics engineer. And maybe a nice hot bath."

Before Sigmund could raise a hand to deactivate him, Armand snatched the force hammer, lunged forward and drove the tool onto the top of the android's head. A flash of light accompanied a small shock wave, and the lights went out in Sigmund's eyes.

"Sweet dreams, Herr Doktor. You'll thank me later."

Armand lifted Sigmund's hand and waved it toward the door a few times until it rotated open.

Omar and Mara would probably know what was going on. He sent a coded message asking they meet up with him. Meanwhile, there was someone he needed to speak with— someone he suspected would understand the reason for his time traveling.

* * *

Armand crept along darkened corridors, watching out for yellow pirate invaders and robots in white coats, and pressed a buzzer beside a metal door etched with a golden sun.

The portal rotated open.

"Enter, AMR-17." A deep, theatrical voice greeted him. "I have been expecting you."

Armand felt a wave of disorientation. This all seemed very familiar. At the center of the room, a bright crystalline globe rested upon a raised pedestal. A ghostly light swirled within the sphere, pulsing as it spoke.

"You have a question, AMR-17?"

He approached the weather computer. "I remember you. Your name is ..."

"Nostradamus."

"Of course. Are you responsible for sending me back in time, Nostradamus?"

"I will be, yes."

"Why?"

"You do not remember?"

"No. I recorded a message for myself, but it got corrupted. I only know the biosphere is in danger of destruction. Something to do with a canister."

Nostradamus seemed to consider this. "You informed

me, or will do so, that you needed to correct a mistake having far-reaching consequences. No other details were provided."

"So the attack is somehow *my* fault." Armand paced, letting this realization sink in. All the diodes across his chest felt constricted. "Did I let the invaders into the station? Did a canister explode, destroying the colony's defenses? Whatever I did wrong, I traveled back in time to prevent it from happening. But I need your help to figure it out. My memory is all confused."

The great globe's swirling lights darkened. "It was a mistake for me to have sent you back." Nostradamus' voice took on a bitter tone. "One cannot tamper with time, AMR-17. It is not our place to play God. What will be, will be."

"But ... over twenty-six thousand colonists are in jeopardy. We have a chance to save them."

A bay door opened to Armand's left. A heavy repair machine rolled in, like a small tank with multiple arms ending in tools and claw-like pincers. It faced Nostradamus, apparently awaiting instructions.

A raw chill played over Armand's exterior.

"Alas, I now foresee that sending you back in time will result in my own destruction. Colonists are readily replaced, for they breed like vermin. Robots can be rebuilt, for parts are plentiful. There is, however, only one Nostradamus."

What an ego. "Please, you must help me. The colonists will be able to repair you, I'm sure. They built you, after all."

Nostradamus would not be swayed. "It would have been less unpleasant had you allowed Sigmund to simply deactivate you. I am sorry." He paused, as if to draw breath. "Repair machine—disassemble AMR-17!"

Armand backed away as the tank advanced. He was cornered.

A sudden barrage of laser fire streaked over Armand's head, blasting small pieces from the repair machine.

"Run, Armand!" Mara waved as Omar continued to lay down fire against the oversized robot, which recoiled in apparent confusion. It was not, after all, programmed for combat. "We heard the whole thing. Whatever's going on, finish it!"

Nostradamus' scream receded as Armand fled the chamber. He was going to have to fix things on his own. Since the danger involved a canister, Armand ran to the canister deployment area, still uncertain what he would do.

His chronometer showed only nineteen minutes remaining. He needed to act, before he was caught and destroyed by one of Nostradamus' minions or Sigmund's psych counselors. Thoughts racing in circles, he played the message one final time. Although still garbled, it was clearer than before.

Danger! Destruct--biosphere in 3 hours—use canister 1121511229. Urgent!

Use canister?

Armand secured canister 1121511229 from cryo-storage and ran a bio-scan, which to his surprise revealed a biohazard highly toxic to organic life.

I sent myself back in time to destroy the biosphere? But why?

He thought back on all that had transpired. Pirate robots from Titan had tried to kill him, damaging his systems, yet didn't seem to bother anyone else on the station. In fact, everyone denied there even was an invasion. Vin and Tony had locked him up, so that Sigmund Droid could deactivate him. Even Nostradamus had turned traitor. It was as if everyone had been against him from the start ...

And therein lay the answer.

When he'd gone back in time, the station had already been compromised—lost to the pirates of Titan. Sigmund could easily have re-programmed the station's robots to cooperate with the Titanians, whatever his reasons. That explained the lax attitude of the robots, the general acceptance of the yellow pirate invaders, and why everyone had acted against him—except for his true friends, Mara and Omar.

This changed everything.

He knew from the invasion drills that the biosphere must never be allowed to fall into enemy hands, for its strategic location and rich natural resources. Titan's control of

Europa would re-open hostilities between Saturn and Jupiter, and lead to many more deaths than one medium-sized biosphere.

It all finally made sense.

In short, with the robotics station now under Titan's control, Europa Colony must be destroyed. A tragic, but necessary, casualty of war.

Diodes tightening across his chest, vision suddenly blurred, Armand punched in the security codes and canister 1121511229 released its deadly molecules into the biosphere.

One had to follow orders, especially one's own.

Doing Time
by Barbara Austin

The guard handcuffed me and chained my ankles. Then he led me from my cell on death row down a putty-colored hall to the visitor's room.

A woman in her mid-twenties was sitting in one of the two chairs welded to a metal table. The clock on the wall had a white face and black hands that pointed to bars instead of numbers. The thin red second hand jerked along its relentless path. Time had begun to fascinate me. I heard clocks ticking throughout the prison, twenty-four hours a day. It's not many men who know in advance the precise time and manner of their death.

She rose and held out her hand, from habit I suppose. She was nearly six feet and built solid. Her light-weight wool suit was designed for air-conditioned offices. In here, the AC labored to keep the temperature below eight-five. She was pretty with silky brown hair and greenish eyes, but the last thing on my mind was hitting on her.

She lowered her hand. "My name is Paulina Gibson."

I didn't need to tell her mine.

The guard said, "I'll be right outside the door."

We sat down.

Paulina laid her mobile phone on the table.

"We don't have much time," she said in a voice that was too small for her.

"I've got exactly eleven days if the governor doesn't commute my sentence."

She arched an eyebrow. "I meant we have a lot to arrange and only thirty minutes in which to do it."

"Don didn't give me any details. Just said he had one more rabbit in the hat. You don't look like a bunny," I quipped, followed by a grin.

Paulina frowned.

"Sorry," I said.

"Don told me you're guilty. But he doesn't want to see a client fry. It's bad for business."

"I wouldn't want that on my conscience." My conscience was overloaded already. I could hardly sleep or eat or breathe. I deserved to die, but, damn it, I didn't want to.

She hunched forward. "We're going to establish an alibi."

"How?"

"I'm going to send you back in time."

"You're kidding."

Her eyes locked with mine. Close-up, hers were a murky yellowish-green, like a pond full of granddaddy catfish and water moccasins.

"Can you follow instructions?" she asked.

I wondered if she was a lunatic, but Don had sent her.

"Do you want to live or not?"

She looked so serious, I started to believe her. Hell, I wanted to believe her. "What do I have to do?"

She crossed her arms. "The price of my services is one million dollars."

I laughed, the only real laugh I'd enjoyed in months. I'd liquidated my assets and paid every penny to Don for defending me.

She threw me a no-nonsense look. "Once you're acquitted, the insurance company will pay out the policy you took on Travis McWilliams' life."

What did I have to lose? "It's a deal. Do you have a paper for me to sign?"

"The guard wouldn't let me bring in a pen. But don't think you can double cross me. If you don't pay up, you're a dead man."

What else was new?

She took a notebook out of her bag and flipped it open. Her lips moved as she read the page to herself. She raised her eyes.

"Listen carefully. You're going back to the night of October 25th, two years ago. You'll arrive at the Longhorn Tavern at 10:00 pm. Sit at the bar and talk to the bartender so he'll remember you. Don't go anywhere. Stay put until 11:00 pm. Then you'll be zapped back to the present."

"If I'm at the tavern, I can't kill Travis. I won't need an alibi, because he won't be dead. I can't be in two places at once."

She smiled impatiently. "Think of it like an anomaly in the space-time continuum. For a brief period there will be *three* of you. You can't undo the murder. Don't try or you'll screw up everything. Trust me, certain acts are too heinous to change. But the testimony of the bartender at the Longhorn Tavern will plant reasonable doubt in the jury's mind. You'll be acquitted."

I glanced at the clock.

"How can I be gone an hour when we have only seventeen minutes left?"

"You'll be gone from the present for only four minutes. The *third you* will be sitting here across from me until you return."

I wasn't a sci-fi buff. My literary tastes ran more toward mystery—at least, until I had become the villain in my own true crime story. But I'd seen enough Star Trek episodes when I was a kid to believe that what she said was possible.

"Are there any side effects?"

155

"Time travel activates cellular activity at the molecular level. One of the side effects is partial memory loss."

I wouldn't mind losing some memories. "Any others?"

"Time travel causes a reversal in the aging process. The effect varies depending on the individual. I would estimate you'll come back ten years younger. You would be surprised to know how old I am."

If she was on the level, I would be twenty-five again. Young enough to start over

She picked up what I had mistakenly thought was a mobile phone. "Press your right thumb on the screen."

The movement was awkward with handcuffs.

She referred again to the notebook. "I'm typing in the temporal and physical coordinates of your destination. What's your social security number?"

* * *

I was standing in front of the Longhorn Tavern on a chilly, damp night in Austin. A pickup swerved close to the curb and splashed my trousers from the knees down. I laughed. It was good to be free again. To feel the rain. No handcuffs, no leg irons. I leapt into the air like a puppy.

Bars and pool halls stretched out in both directions. This was Sixth Street. I was miles from the gated community of Rob Roy, where I had killed Travis. All I had to do was have some drinks and make sure the bartender remembered me. I felt around in my trousers pocket and found a wallet. I pressed a wad of green bills to my nose and sniffed. The dirty, wonderful, scent of money. With drinking money in hand, I ambled through the old-fashioned swinging doors of the Longhorn Tavern.

The tavern resembled a long, narrow pine box that had been stained dark by cigarette smoke. The bar ran the length of the long side. The place smelled faintly of beer and puke. A few rickety-looking tables were scattered around in the shadowy interior

I hoisted my ass onto a bar stool.

"A Bud, please."

The bartender pushed a frosty mug of golden beer

towards me. It tasted like nectar from heaven.

The loud, vintage soul music hurt my ears. I had become accustomed to silence on death row. The only sounds I had heard for the past six months had been the clanging of the metal doors, the shuffle of feet in leg irons, and the occasional sob from another poor bastard in the middle of the night.

There was a gold watch on my wrist. I'd been back for ten minutes. All I had to do was stay glued to the bar stool, keep my nose out of trouble, and in fifty minutes I would have an alibi. My attorney would be able to establish reasonable doubt. I would be a free man.

I ordered another beer.

The saloon doors swung open and a girl walked in. She wore a short suede jacket, a pair of low-hung jeans clinging to slim hips, and cowboy boots with high heels.

She tottered to the bar and hopped onto a stool further down, leaving one empty stool between us. Up close, I saw she was older than my first impression. There were fine lines at the corner of her eyes, and her neck had lost the tautness of youth. But she was gorgeous. Long hair so blonde it was almost silver. Blue eyes like the sky I could glimpse through the bars on the high window at the back of my cell. She caught me looking at her and smiled, putting dimples in her fair cheeks. A woman like that could almost make me forget about money. A woman like that would take a lot of money to maintain.

"Can I buy you a drink?" I asked.

"Sure. White wine." She flashed an even bigger smile.

I moved over one stool. Her complexion was like white marble, as if she'd never been exposed to the Texas sun.

"Are you alone?" I asked.

She laughed. "If you mean am I here with a man, I am not."

I wanted to know what a woman like her was doing at the Longhorn Tavern alone on a Saturday night, but the question would have sounded like something from an old movie script.

"My name is Jimmy."

"Iris," she said.

We clinked glasses. After exchanging some one-liners, we moved over to a table in the back so we could talk without the bartender hanging over us. An after-game crowd surged into the bar about the same time. They were already drunk and noisy. They kept the bartender hopping. But I didn't worry about depending on him for an alibi, because now I had Iris.

I looked at my gold watch. It was 10:20. At this moment, my original self, the one that belonged to the past, was arguing with Travis at his spread in Rob Roy. We had been watching football on his wide-screen television and drinking beer for hours. Travis was my business partner and my best friend since our freshman year at college. He'd inherited money, and because of that he was stingy about the small things: light bulbs and splitting the bar tab, but he'd surprised me on my birthday with plane tickets to Aruba. He could afford to be idealistic, too; something he'd caught in college, like a chronic disease. His idealism was a sore point between us. I wanted our company, TLC Software, to be run like a business, with budgets and regular financial statements. But Travis was a salesman, and he held the purse strings.

We were drunk and the argument got out of hand. He slapped my face and I saw red. I knocked him out with one punch, then dragged him out to the pool and threw him in. I honestly don't know if I wanted to drown him or wake him up.

The murder would happen in twenty-five minutes. It wasn't premeditated but the jury thought differently because of the million dollar life insurance policy I'd taken out on Travis the month before. He had taken one out on me, too, but only at my insistence. That was the reason I got condemned to die instead of a life sentence. I regretted leaving Travis to drown. Of all my friends who didn't visit me in prison, I missed Travis the most. Paulina Gibson had told me to let things be. That the murder could not be undone. I wondered what terrible thing would happen if I stopped myself from killing Travis.

"What are you thinking about?" Iris asked.

I shrugged.

She gave me a look full of empathy, a look I could fall in love with.

It occurred to me if I didn't kill Travis tonight I wouldn't get a life insurance payout. I wouldn't be able to pay Paulina Gibson her fee of one million dollars. That was what she wanted to prevent.

Iris bombarded me with questions, which I duly answered. I was born in Mineral Wells, got a degree in computer science at UT, and was the brains behind TLC Software. Travis was (or had been) the image man, the one with the charisma, the one who brought in investors and new business. Uninteresting small talk, but she hung on every word I said. I was flattered though confused. I was only average looking. My jokes were usually met with nonplussed stares. I wasn't rich. I couldn't understand what she saw in me.

"What time is it?" she asked, when I stopped talking to take a breath.

"10:30."

"Are you sure?"

"I'm sure," I said, as sure as I could be considering I'd zapped in from the future.

"I've got to go," she said, jumping up with such force I half expected her to leave a boot under the table.

"Where are you going?" I asked.

She smiled a little anxiously. "My taxi is outside. Can I give you a lift somewhere?"

I scanned the crowded bar. I couldn't see the bartender over the wide shoulders, crew-cuts, and cowboy hats. This was my chance to set things right.

I rattled off the address in Rob Roy.

The taxi headed towards Town Lake, rode up the ramp onto Mopac for a short piece, and turned north on 360. Iris and I sat on opposite sides of the back seat. She stared out the window and fingered the fake leather seat cover. We had run out of small talk and didn't know each other well enough to go deeper.

Ten minutes later the taxi dropped me off at the entrance of the gated community.

Then she said something strange. "You won't forget me, will you?"

"Never," I smiled.

The taxi flipped a U and sped away.

Luckily, the guard station was deserted. I was about to scale the wall when a car driving at a high speed without lights barreled towards the gate from inside Rob Roy. The electronically controlled gate swung open just in time to let the car plunge through. I jumped out of the way before my other self could run me down, and I slipped through the gate as it slammed shut. My heart was thudding in my throat. I sprinted along the dark street. On the right were houses set back behind circular drives. Curtains were pulled tightly shut. The hill on the left side of the road was too steep to build houses on, but it was the home of deer, armadillos, and coyotes. Animal eyes followed my progress down the street. The sweet fragrance of wet cedar filled the air.

None of the yards were fenced, which made it easy for me to go around the back of Travis' house to the solarium that housed the pool. The thick warm air stank of chlorine. He was floating face down, arms spread. It was 10:48. He hadn't been in the water for more than three minutes. Without stopping to remove the gold watch, I dove into the water and nudged him to the edge. It took a good thirty seconds to get him onto the deck. I started mouth to mouth.

He sputtered and coughed.

"Hey what are you doing?" he gurgled. "Get off me."

He sat up, rubbing his chin.

"Sorry I hit you," I said.

He looked mad as hell for a moment, then sighed.

"I deserved it. Let's go in the house. I'll lend you some dry clothes."

My watch had stopped, but it must have been close to 11:00.

"I don't want to drip on the floor. I'll wait here."

"Okay, I'll be back in a minute." I watched as Travis walked towards the house, his shoes squishing. I wondered if I would still be there when he came back.

* * *

I was lying on a king-size bed. A ceiling fan buzzed lazily overhead. On my right were three big windows with wooden shutters. Golden sunlight shifted through the slats. A door to my left was ajar. Turquoise tiles on the floor, white tiles on the wall, and a Jacuzzi. Twenty feet from the end of the bed was a door with a shiny gold handle. Next to it stood a curved black console table. I didn't know where I was, but I for sure wasn't on death row.

Light footsteps sounded outside the door.

Iris entered with a tray. Her silver-blonde hair was cut short. There was color in her cheeks that reminded me of strawberries. Her eyes were the same incredible blue as her nightgown. Pregnancy agreed with her. She was eight or nine months along judging by the size of her belly. She set the tray on the table, brought me a cappuccino and the newspaper and snuggled next to me.

She placed my hand on her belly. I could feel the baby kicking.

I felt awkward, as though I had no right touching her. She was practically a stranger. I politely withdrew my hand, noticed the wedding band on my finger, and opened the *Austin American Statesman*. I didn't dare look at Iris, but I sensed her eyes observing me.

The date on the newspaper was the day Paulina Gibson had visited me on death row. My brain began to process the data. I had prevented the murder and altered the course of events. Iris and I had married. If I could afford Iris, this bedroom, the Jacuzzi, and the house that must go with it, TLC Software had grown more successful than I could ever have dreamed.

The two years I'd spent in prison began to fade from my memory, but there were no memories to replace them. Two years of my life had slipped into a void.

Iris moved closer and stroked my thigh.

161

I rolled away and got out of bed.

"What's the matter, Jimmy?"

"I've got to go out"

"For a run?"

"Yeah, a run." Where were my jogging shoes? I went into the bathroom and opened a door to a walk-in closet bigger than most bedrooms. My nose crinkled at the smell of dry-cleaning fluid and perfume. In the men's corner, I found a faded t-shirt, a comfortable-looking pair of training pants, and running shoes. The outfit fit perfectly.

"Take your keys in case I'm in the shower when you get back." Iris handed me a key ring with what looked like house keys or office keys and a key bearing the BMW logo.

As far as I knew, I hadn't jogged in two years, but my condition was excellent. We lived in a new development further west than Rob Roy, I judged. The lots and the houses were even bigger. Though the hills were steep, I ran up them effortlessly. The air was fresh but prickly. By nine it would be at least eighty degrees and climbing. I could already hear the zoom of traffic in the distance.

I was curious how Travis and TLC were doing. After my run, I would shower and go to work.

* * *

TLC Software had moved. A CPA occupied the two-room office suite we had leased on Spicewood Springs Road. I went in anyway and asked the girl behind the desk if she could look up an address. In a few minutes I was on my way to the new location, a ten-story building with the TLC logo on top.

The executive offices were on the top floor according to the building directory. I stepped into a private elevator that whooshed me straight to the penthouse. Reception was covered with a pristine white carpet, so clean I wondered if I should take off my shoes. The sleek furniture looked like black glass. Travis was chatting with the receptionist who wore a white dress and black pendant earrings that matched her desk.

Travis blinked his eyes. "Did you go to the spa or something? You look--rejuvenated."

The Temporal Element

"I slept like a log last night." I couldn't say the same for Travis. He looked like he hadn't slept in years.

"Ready for the big meeting?" he asked, looking me up and down.

"You bet," I mumbled and darted to the door with my name on it: James Harwood. I closed the door, leaned against it, my heart pounding. What big meeting, I wondered?

I turned on my laptop. It wanted a password. I pushed the chair out of the way and crawled under the desk. A list of passwords was written in pencil on the underside of the drawer. All were neatly crossed out except for the last one. It was reassuring to know my working habits hadn't changed.

I consulted my Outlook calendar. No appointments until 3:00 when there was a meeting with Angel Software. Angel was the biggest software development company in the world. They were interested in buying our new personal health software app. Not because it was better than theirs, but to protect their market share. Ours was just as good and half the price. But TLC could make more money selling the app to Angel (who would quietly bury it) than marketing it at bottom prices ourselves.

How did I know this? The only explanation was that my revised past life and my future were starting to merge. I spent the next couple of hours getting acquainted with the contents of my hard drive; my appointments over the last two years, the date of Iris' birthday, the projects I'd been involved in. I was curious about the sales figures for TLC, but there were no financial statements on my hard drive, which didn't surprise me because I had always left money matters to Travis. Except for the time I'd talked him into buying the key employee life insurance policies.

Just before lunch, Travis phoned. "We have to talk. If you have lunch plans, break them."

I acquiesced, then hastily checked Outlook. No lunch plans to break. He drove me to a Mexican restaurant about a half mile from the office.

We were seated at a booth in the back.

I ordered the works—tamales, chili con queso, beef

enchiladas topped with sour cream, Spanish rice, and fried beans. No more bland prison food. I hoped Travis wasn't going to spoil my meal. We munched on corn chips and hot sauce while we waited for the margaritas.

As soon as the drinks had been served, Travis took a couple of long chugs, set down his empty glass, and picked up mine. A drinking problem would explain the charcoal bricks under his eyes, the loose jawline, and the red blotches on his cheeks. He wore a wedding ring that was too tight for his pudgy finger, and I wondered if he'd finally married Jen. She had been devastated at the murder trial.

"What did you want to talk about?" I asked.

"I want to make sure you're ready for the meeting with Angel. I don't have to tell you what's at stake."

I must have looked puzzled, because he sighed deeply. I'd never seen anyone guzzle rock salt and crushed ice before.

"You really are a geek, aren't you? Don't you know what's going on?"

"Tell me," I said cautiously.

"The financial viability of TLC hangs on the deal with Angel."

"We're broke?"

"A cash flow problem."

I was incredulous. But on reflection, I could guess where the cash had flowed to: the penthouse office suite in the prestigious building, my BMW, his Cadillac. My multi-million house in the hills overlooking Austin. I wondered if Travis still owned the mansion in Rob Roy or if he'd traded up.

Travis ranted, "The real estate market has collapsed. Our building is more than half empty. We can't afford the interest on the bank loan. Software sales are a fraction of what they were. If we don't get cash fast, salaries won't be paid next month, which means all the employees will quit."

"Is TLC incorporated?"

Travis gave me a withering look. "Jesus, what's gotten into you! No, we're not incorporated, and don't say you told me so."

If we'd been incorporated, the bank wouldn't be able to seize our personal assets. Now we stood to lose our homes, too. Travis had sworn he would never become a part of an anonymous corporation. He didn't want to hide behind limited liability. I wondered if he still had the sign on his desk that said "The buck stops here."

I was mad enough to kill him.

"I hope your memory improves by three o'clock," Travis sneered. Guacamole dip coated his front teeth. "As good as I am, I can't make the sale without your support on the technical specs."

I bristled at his threatening tone. It wasn't my fault I could remember nothing about the personal health app. If only the meeting was scheduled for tomorrow. Maybe by then I would be fully integrated into my old self.

* * *

But the Angel team had flown to Austin the night before. Their IT director, procurement manager, and attorney arrived promptly at three, and the grilling began. Their expressions morphed from friendly to courteous to puzzled. Travis couldn't see through the technical smoke I was blowing, but he knew what "no deal" meant.

Our disgusted guests left in a taxi for the airport.

Travis and I were alone in the conference room, which was equipped with TelePresence (the latest IP phone), a remote control that operated the lights and the temperature, and a well-stocked bar.

You could have heard a software app drop. I nervously admired the view of north Austin from ten floors up.

Finally, Travis said, "What the hell is wrong with you?"

"I'm a little off today."

"A little off!" he thundered, his eyes as hard as marbles. "We're finished. The bank will take everything that's left, and it won't be enough to pay our debts."

"I'm sorry, Travis."

He stood up abruptly. His hands smoothed the creases

in his jacket, trying to recapture some of his dignity. He walked over to the bar and tossed a shot of Wild Turkey down his throat. "My inheritance is gone. All I have left is Jen." There were tears in his eyes.

"I have Iris."

Travis looked at me with pity. "Iris isn't the kind of girl to stick around. As soon as she finds another rich sucker, she'll be gone. Mark my words." He didn't say it in a mean way, which made me think it might be true.

I felt like shit. Had I saved his life only to ruin it?
When I got home, a sports car was parked on the circular drive directly before the front door. Its roof was so low I couldn't imagine an adult could sit upright inside it.

I went into the house. No sign of my wife or her visitor. "Iris?"

She peeked out of the study, slipped out, and softly shut the door behind her. She reminded me of a deer venturing into a clearing during hunting season.

"What are you doing home?" Her voice trembled.

"Who's in the study?"

"Let me explain first." She looked so guilty I expected the worst.

I brushed Iris aside, rushed towards the study, and flung open the door.

Iris' visitor was Paulina Gibson.

Her mouth curled into an unfriendly smile. "You've moved up in the world since we last met. Only this morning, by the way. The house is a vast improvement over death row. You were naughty, but I won't punish you as long as you pay me what you owe. I was just discussing the situation with Iris."

"Leave my wife out of it."

Paulina chuckled. "She's part of it."

Puzzled, I glanced at Iris. She didn't look a day over twenty. I had noticed her youthful appearance this morning, but I had heard that pregnant women glowed. The truth was I had been too preoccupied today to give Iris much thought. When I'd met her at the Longhorn Tavern, even in the shadowy bar, she'd looked closer to forty than twenty.

"Darling," Iris said, "let me refresh your memory. Two years ago, you murdered Travis, and I murdered my husband. Don Newsom defended us both, and we both got convicted. You were sentenced to death. I got life in prison. Paulina's time machine was our only hope of getting our convictions reversed on appeal. The bartender was supposed to be our alibi, but you left the Longhorn Tavern early and prevented the murder of Travis."

"And you?"

Her eyes darted away. "I followed Paulina's instructions. I was afraid of what might happen if I stopped myself from shooting my husband. You testified at my trial that we were together until 10:45. You were my alibi."

My head swung around to Paulina. "You sent two murderers back in time to the same bar on the same night! Wouldn't that have looked suspicious if we had both needed the bartender as an alibi?"

Paulina alighted on the edge of my big cherry wood desk. My eyes ran down her long legs to her purple pumps with narrow ankle straps.

"I admit it wasn't ideal, but the license for my time machine was about to expire and I needed money fast to renew it. If I don't renew before midnight tonight, I'll have to pay a huge setup fee for next year. The economy's in a recession. Demand for time travel has dried up." She pulled a gun out of her handbag and calmly pointed it at Iris.

I still had to come to grips with the fact that Iris was a murderess.

Iris must have seen the anguish on my face because she began to sniffle. Or maybe she was plain scared.

"How much do we owe?" I asked.

"A million dollars each."

"Iris, do we have two million?" I thought I already knew the answer.

"We invested the money from my husband's life insurance policy in TLC. Your salary comes in, and it goes out."

Obviously, I hadn't received a payout from Travis' policy. And TLC was bust.

"No worries," I lied. Maybe I could buy some time. "Paulina, if you'll give me your bank account number, I'll have the money transferred from the TLC account this afternoon. All I have to do is make the phone call."

"That's more like it," Paulina said, letting down her guard just a bit, but it was enough. I walked slowly towards the desk, and as I reached for the phone, I suddenly changed direction, lunged, and grabbed at the gun. It flew out of her hand and skidded across the wooden floor.

Iris got to it first. She scooped it up, and in one fluid movement, without a moment's hesitation, took aim and fired. Paulina appeared to be dead when she struck the floor.

"Why did you do that?" I cried. My heart pounded. Visions of prison bars flashed through my head.

"I know the TLC bank account is in the red. There was no other way. We would have been watching our backs for the rest of our lives, which would undoubtedly have been short. I had to think of our baby." Her eyes were pleading.

From where I stood, she had reacted instinctively without thinking of the baby or anything else. Goosebumps erupted on my arms. She was still clenching the gun. I wrapped my hand around the barrel, pointing it away from me. Her fingers loosened, and she let me take it.

A pool of blood was expanding next to the body and with it a nauseating coppery smell.

"We'll have to dump the body," I said. Travis' family owned a ranch near Dripping Springs—a perfect impromptu burial site. "I'll get a blanket to wrap the body in. You get a mop and a bucket of soapy water."

Iris told me where to find the blankets, and we hurried out of the study heading in opposite directions.

I got back first

I couldn't believe my eyes. The patch of floor that had hosted the pool of blood was dry and untainted. The body had vanished. All that remained of Paulina was the skirt, jacket, panty hose, underwear, and purple pumps that she had been wearing, heaped on the floor in the approximate position they would be if her body was still wearing them. The ankle straps were still fastened. Her handbag lay on the desk where she'd left it when she pulled out the gun.

Iris entered the study, bent over to one side by the weight of the bucket full of steaming water. In the other hand she held the mop. She stared.

I felt faint.

Iris set down the bucket and sank onto a chair.

Then a crazy idea struck me.

I trotted over to the desk and rummaged in Paulina's handbag. How could she have found anything? No time to waste. I shook out the contents: a bunch of keys, bulging billfold, hairbrush full of brown hair, sunglasses, frayed tissues, and, underneath, the time travel device.

I perused the user-friendly menu. The software version was dated twenty-seven years in the future. On the back of the device was the familiar logo of Angel IT.

I slipped it into my pocket and headed towards the door.

"Where are you going?" Iris asked, tears sliding down her cheeks

"To the office. If I can duplicate the time travel software, TLC's cash flow problems will be history. With my programming skills and Travis' marketing talent, we'll be back on top."

"What about us?"

We needed time to get to know each other. Maybe she'd had good reason to shoot her first husband.

I blew Iris a kiss.

One Last Gamble
by Shawn Cook

The pools of shadow that surrounded Kepler grew deeper, wider, as if they were a living, multiplying entity. He forced away a shudder, a tingle of panic tickling his nerve endings, and continued to dig through the debris. He pushed aside broken concrete and shattered bone, dug farther down past coils of rotten wire and plastic that would outlast the human race. His hands scrabbled through shards of melted glass that cut through his gloves and summoned forth droplets of blood.

Kepler's fingertips met the resistance he'd longed to find. He traced his fingers across the square lid and began to work faster. The Continuity Box was battered but whole, as he'd known it would be. Outside the ruined science lab came the sporadic gunfire that signaled an end to this expedition. He was placing the box into a stained duffle bag when he heard the echo of running footfalls.

"C'mon, Doc!" The voice echoed across the ruined lab, its owner coming closer until he materialized from the dark like a battlefield apparition. "We gotta go!"

"Coming, Sergeant." Kepler replied with an almost childlike glee. "It was here, Sergeant. I told you it would be!"

Sergeant Marconi wrapped his large right hand around the older man's thin arm and hoisted him to his feet. "Great, Doc, just great." His voice was a growl, but not menacing or unkind. "Now, let's get the hell out of here before more bogies show up, huh?"

Outside the cavernous ruins, the sound of gunfire picked up in intensity, and Marconi squeezed his hand reflexively. Kepler gasped slightly at the pressure.

"Sorry, Doc." Marconi spoke in a gravel-filled whisper and loosening his grip but didn't let go.

"It's okay, Sergeant. No harm, no foul." Kepler said with a slight grin, patting the younger man's hand. "Let's head home, yes?"

In the night, a chorus of deep, burbling growls could be heard in the distance.

"Doc, that's the best idea I've heard all day." Placing a finger to his earpiece Marconi spoke in a clear authoritative voice. "Troops! Disengage and haul ass back to the bunker. The Doc and I will meet you there."

* * *

Kepler's hands shook as he turned the numerical lock that held the lid in place, missing the combination on the first two attempts. He tried to fool himself, reassure his ego that it was the cold and damp that made his hands disobey. But when one hits the downside of fifty the body grows a will of its own. Compound that with the problem of near starvation, exhaustion, and constant fear...

The locks clicked, hissed once, and slid aside while the lid eased open on two thin hydraulic cylinders. A faint pulsing glow emanated from within, accompanied by an almost sub-audible buzz that Kepler could feel vibrate in his chest. From across the room Marconi shifted uncomfortably.

"Is it working, Doc?"

"Yes, Sergeant. The Continuity Box is operating just fine. Now, we just have to wait for Mr. Faraday to make a connection."

Marconi sighed. "That's assuming he survived."

Kepler straightened and placed his gaze on the weathered sergeant. "I assure you, sir, that your man made the journey."

"Positive about that? How do we know—"

"Doc!" The voice that emanated from the Continuity Box was crystal clear. *"Doc, can you hear me? This is Faraday."*

"Holy," Marconi said quietly. "It worked."

Kepler made a shushing motion with his hands. "Yes, yes. I told you so."

"Doc, you ain't gonna believe this but... I'm here! It took me a while to get my bearings, and stop puking my shoelaces up, but I've made it. The rifle came through without a scratch, but I'm going to tear it down and give it a good once over. I've not only confirmed the date but the location. I'm right where you said I would be, Mississippi. I think I... landed?... a few miles outside of some place called Natch— Natch—Nachos— NatCHEZ. Yeah, Natchez."

Both the doctor and the sergeant could hear a ruffling of paper in the background before Faraday continued.

"Okay, they apparently don't have a newspaper in this place, so I swiped some food and a diary from a farmhouse. It looks like, from the last entry, that the year is 1840, and it's the sixth of June. I arrived a day early, which is fine by me. Your little experiment left me a bit on the weak side right now. I'm going to make camp not too far from where I landed. Got to get prepped, I'll check in tomorrow. "

Kepler stepped away from the box and grinned a Cheshire cat smile. Before either man could speak, Faraday's voice once more leapt into the room. *"And tell Sarge not to worry. I got this."*

A long silence filled the room, the two men lost in thought. Marconi spoke first. "Is there any way to speed this up? A fast forward button or something? Or do we have to wait for the transmission to get here?"

Kepler laughed. "It doesn't work that way. What you

have just heard was in real-time. That box is a direct link between Faraday and us. Think of it as a one way radio; we can receive but not transmit. He, on the other hand, can transmit but not receive."

Marconi cleared his throat. "Doc," he began. "Are you sure this will work?"

Kepler fixed him with tired eyes. "Is your man as good a shot as you believe him to be?"

Marconi laughed. "Frank Faraday is a screwball and a half-assed soldier—but he is, without a doubt, the best shot I've ever seen in my life."

Kepler's eyes crinkled at the edges as he smiled. "As long as the screwball can hit the mark, it'll work."

"Let's say it does." Marconi said softly. "Does that mean all this misery will go away? Things will go back to the way they were before those bastards crawled out of the ground ten years ago?"

"Unfortunately, Sergeant, no." Kepler took a seat upon a rusted folding chair. "What will happen, what we surmise will happen, is that the creatures will cease to exist in the here and now. We'll know they were there, that they caused the death of billions and the destruction of our world. But they will be gone from the here and now the second his shot hits home."

"How can you be so sure?" Marconi said, taking a seat on the cold floor.

Kepler sighed and pulled a crumpled pack of cigarettes from a shirt pocket. He lit two and passed one to Marconi. As smoke hazed the air above their heads, he spoke. "Let's say that we plotted to assassinate Hitler in, oh, 1934. Reality would not allow this to happen. Frank's gun would misfire, or he'd only wound but not kill his target. At any rate he wouldn't be able to significantly alter the course of our timeline because Hitler would already be ingrained into our reality. You see, Hitler is and always will be, a part of our timeline because he was born from events that originated in our time continuum. Reality will not allow that to happen."

"Now, the beast that Faraday is going to kill, that

creature is different. It's not of our world, nor our dimension. If we kill it in the past, before it spawns and floods the world with its young, we'll erase them all from the here and now. But the intervening years will remain unchanged; those years are a part of our timeline."

"How do you know it's not of our dimension? It could just be an alien or something."

"Signs. Clues as to its origin," Kepler said but elaborated no further. "Now, Sergeant Marconi, I suggest that we get comfortable. Waiting for Faraday to call will be as arduous a task as facing those creatures on the surface."

They spoke little, as Kepler eventually nodded into a fitful slumber.

* * *

Marconi grew anxious. He wanted to fidget with the humming machine but was afraid he'd destroy what Kepler had worked so hard to create; that he'd ruin mankind's last chance at survival. Instead, he patrolled the bunker and checked upon the remaining men under his command.

Their living quarters were once part of an underground utility complex that fed power, water, and air to a small government office building. Now it was little more than a series of fortified rooms connected by crumbling concrete hallways. Fallback positions were set up at every t-intersection, heavy machine gun nests and debris blockades manned by no less than twenty soldiers. It wasn't much, but it was safer than the ruined world above.

Eventually, he stood a shift in the radio room, scanned the frequencies and listened to other areas of the nation as they fought and died. He left the room when the report of Chicago's ultimate destruction came across the airwaves.

Marconi was chewing methodically upon an energy bar in the makeshift cafeteria when a harried young soldier burst through the door.

"Sarge! Hawking is gone and Harvey is dead."

Marconi leapt to his feet. "What?"

The young soldier nodded and fingered the trigger guard on his rifle. "I was taking some MRE's to the guard post when I found what was left of Hawking. Something had crammed his body into a ventilation duct."

"Christ." Marconi said. "Tell the men to pull back here to the main rooms and go into lock down. Nothing gets in, no one goes out. I've got to check on the Doc."

* * *

Kepler was asleep on the floor when Marconi found him; started violently when the younger man shook him awake. "Doc! They're inside! How much longer?"

Kepler's eyes darted around the room, lingered on the heavy steel door that connected to the main hall. "Should we close that?"

"In a minute. Doc, how long?"

"Doc Kepler? This is Faraday. It's starting."

Kepler looked at Marconi with fearful eyes. "We just have to hold out for a few more minutes, Sergeant."

Marconi nodded, squeezed Kepler's shoulder. "Lock the door behind me and stay out of sight."

"Good luck, Mr. Marconi."

The gruff sergeant smiled a faint, wistful smile before stepping into the hallway. "See you around, Doc."

Kepler closed the door and rammed the lock home.

"Doc, something strange is happening. The clouds... the sky is boiling and the wind has picked up. I have a clear view to the emergence site. It's starting to rain."

Of course, Kepler thought. The transference through time and space is having a metrological effect.

"Uh, Doc? It's getting really freaky around here. The lightning is... What in God's name is that sound? Everything is... the sky is green..."

Kepler was vaguely aware of the beginnings of gunfire from within the bunker complex. He heard screams, human and otherwise as the battle raged.

"It's here!" Faraday exclaimed. *"Oh God, it's here!"*

"Steady, boy." Kepler said to the empty room. "Steady."

"The wind is... My God, look at that thing. It's huge. I can smell ozone burning..."

175

Kepler could hear slaughter just outside the door. He focused on the Continuity Box before him as Marconi's screams of agony were silenced abruptly.

He jumped as heavy blows rained down upon the door at his back.

"Okay... okay..." Faraday continued. *"I'm aiming for the..."*

"The eye, Faraday." Kepler spoke quietly, as the door to the room began to buckle and give way. "Hit the eye and the bullet will travel through the membrane and into the beast's skull."

"...the eye. It's... it hasn't noticed me yet. It seems disoriented."

"Shoot, boy. Shoot!" Kepler urged. "Quick! Quick!"

The steel door crumpled and fell with a metallic resonance. Kepler began to shake as the creatures entered the room. He could hear their claws clicking across the concrete, could smell their fetid breath cloud the air. Tears raced down his cheeks as they approached slowly, their growls vibrating in the marrow of his bones.

"Taking the shot."

Kepler heard the crack of the weapon through time and space, traced its trajectory with his mind's eye. The shriek of pain that violated the speakers and filled the air was a sound not found in the natural world.

The growls behind him ceased abruptly.

Kepler let loose a shaking lungful of air he hadn't realized he'd been holding.

"Oh, God! I missed! Doc, I missed! I'm so sorry!"

Kepler's eyes went wide as he turned in his chair, only to fall beneath tooth and talon. His screams were matched seconds later as Faraday was pulled to pieces at the other end of time.

What Would You Ask Yourself?
By Karl G. Rich

The early morning clouds hovered low and grey over the church steeple. The bare fingers of the maple trees waved and quivered in the swirling breeze. The misty drizzle froze on contact with the concrete steps of the church and melted under the black, boot heel of a lone congregant. The dark-skinned man pulled his bowler hat down over his close cropped hair, rearranged his black satin coat, and tightened his blood red tie. He glanced at the crucifix hanging above the double wooden doors, winked and smiled. "Okay, Trece, time to go to work."

Incense smoke hung in the air and its cloying sweetness coated Trece's throat as he removed his hat. The temperature in the church was cooler than outside, but the cloistering effect seemed oppressive. He genuflected, but didn't drop all the way to one knee, and scooted in front of an old woman sitting on the main aisle in the last pew. "Pardon me, young lady." He settled his backside on the even cooler, hard wooden seat.

She glared at Trece, sniffed, and clutched her purse to

177

her chest. "Couldn't you wait for the end of Mass?"

Trece shrugged and picked up a worn and dog-eared missal from the rack. She slid away from him, opened her Bible, and began to read aloud, "Yea, though I walk through the valley…"

At the altar the priest held his arms up with palms out. "The Mass is ended. May the blessing of the Lord be with you." The priest gathered his flock and recessed down the main aisle.

Trece waited until the handful of faithful left the church before approaching the priest. "Pardon me, Father Malvida, I'm Trece de Jesus. Do you have a minute?"

The priest pulled his vestments over his head. His swarthy face had big pores; his coal-black hair had a touch of grey, and his garlic breath articulated volumes for his ethnicity. When he spoke he had an accent that had most of its roots erased by time. "Trece? Like Dick Tracy?"

Trece smiled, held his hand to his chest and splayed his fingers. "Yes and no. May we speak? For a moment?"

"Do you seek to repent your sins, my son, and ask forgiveness," Father Malvida asked with a patrician's tone as he hung up his vestments and closed the door to the sacristy.

Trece's Adam's apple bobbed once and he gazed at the floor while clasping his hands together. "No, Father. Even though I'm an egregious sinner, I seek no forgiveness or repentance."

"Very well, follow me." Father Malvida entered his inner sanctum and led the dark man to his office. The Baroque styling of his space conflicted with the modern desk the priest placed himself behind, but only after indicating the oversized, stuffed chair Trece should sit upon. "How may I help you?"

Trece took a shallow breath and coughed. He removed a white handkerchief from his pocket and wiped his paled lips. Red stain sprinkled the cloth. "I am approaching the end of my life, and I want to know if I'm doing the right thing."

Outside the window of Father Malvida's office, the setting sun glowed red and a black cloud covered the horizon.

Father Malvida steepled his fingers and tapped them

on his lips. "Most men consider their lives at the end. Man is the only animal to consider their mortality. Have you made amends?"

"Yes, Father, my affairs are in order and I have made peace with my enemies and my loved ones."

"Very good. So, what can I do for you?" Father Malvida leaned back in his chair and glanced out the window.

"I'm worried about the end," Trece paused, "about what will happen." Sweat beaded on the dark man's brow, and he wiped it away with the sleeve of his coat. "I'm not sure if it will go well for me."

"It's in God's hands, my son. If you've done your best, pray for mercy."

"Pardon me, Father, I believe you misunderstand." Trece blew out a long breath and puffed out his cheeks. He glanced up and stopped. "I'm worried about the last few minutes of my life. Will I take it like a man or leave this mortal shell crying like a baby for my mother."

Father Malvida smiled, but only one side of his mouth curled as one eyebrow shot up, and he nodded at Trece.

"What about you, Father, have you ever wondered about the end of your life? I'm sure you know where you are going, but what about those last few minutes?"

The priest stood and approached a side table with decanters of liquor arranged in a row on top. He poured a measure for himself and returned. "Yes, don't we all?" He took a sip, swirled it in his mouth and swallowed. "What will it be like to take your last breath?" He gazed at the ceiling.

"If you could ask yourself, in those last few minutes of life, if you would do it all over again, would you?"

Father Malvida's eyebrows drew together and he frowned. "Well, I suppose... yes, if it was possible..."

Trece reached out with his left hand. A beam of red light leapt from his fingertips and engulfed the priest. "All right then, off you go."

* * *

It was a cold, sterile room with white painted walls and no decorations. There was one door in and a window with beige curtains that swept back and forth as if they had just been shut. An analog clock above the door read 11:55. The EKG machine marched off the patient's heart beat and the art-line read his blood pressure, 140/95. Dr. Jones made a note on his clipboard. God, I hate this job, he thought. He hiked up his scrub pants and smoothed his white coat. *Why do I always get to pull this duty?*

"How's it going, doc?" asked a sallow-skinned, wispy-white haired man on the gurney. He attempted to tug at the gown that slipped down off his shoulder, but the restraints kept him from completely covering up. IV lines snaked out from under his sleeve and connected to a saline/drug infuser next to his bed. The room smelled of isopropyl alcohol and Muzak lilted over a commercial speaker.

"Don't worry, Mr. Malvida, this won't take long," replied Dr. Jones as he picked up three vials, loaded three fat bodied syringes from them, and started to install them in the infuser. One syringe held sodium thiopental to put Mr. Malvida asleep. "This won't take long, at all," the doctor muttered under his breath as he flicked and gazed at the syringe to check for trapped air. *God forbid an air bubble might hurt or harm someone about to die. Thank you—stupid-ass lawyers and bleeding-heart liberals.*

The second syringe held succinylcholine to paralyze Mr. Malvida. "The sooner I'm done here, the sooner I can get back to bed," said Dr Jones.

The third syringe contained potassium chloride to stop the condemned man's heart. The plungers in the syringes would be depressed automatically by a group of anonymous executioners in another room. *I do all the work, and they get to push the button. A monkey could push the button.* Dr. Jones peeked over at Mr. Malvida, pushed his horn-rimmed glasses back up the bridge of his nose, and breathed noisily out his nostrils. *One of these days, I'm going to push the button.*

"Whoa!" Mr. Malvida wiped at the brown encrusted corners of his mouth and scooted back on the gurney. "Who are *you*? You're not the warden."

"I'm Doctor Jones, I'm—"

Mr. Malvida glanced at the other man in the room. "Not you, doc, *him*." The man bound to the gurney pointed with his chin. "The guy in the habit."

Dr. Jones searched the room visually. *There's no one here,* he thought. He looked at the curtained window. *Except for the twenty people seated outside the window waiting for...* "Perhaps, I have given you too much sedative." He reached up, adjusted the IV, and made another note on his clipboard.

"Oh, it's me. How appropriate..." Mr. Malvida relaxed against the bed and ran a palsied hand across his hospital gown to flatten the wrinkles. "Where are we? Why, this is a correctional facility. Any minute now, Dr. Death, there, will execute me."

Dr. Jones clicked his pen and secured it in a pocket. "Now, now, Mr. Malvida, the *State* is executing you for your crimes, not me." *I'm just the lucky one to set it up.*

Mr. Malvida nodded as he stared with rheumy eyes off at the far corner of the room. "I killed people, that's why."

The doctor slammed his fist on the top of the infuser. "You didn't just kill people. You tortured, raped, murdered and ate your victims. You are the most prolific, mass murderer since John Wayne Gacey, but without the clown suit. God, no wonder people hate clowns." Dr. Jones closed his eyes and shivered. The local papers weren't allowed to print the pictures, but Mr. Malvida's case file was available at the prison. The post mortem autopsy pictures had been the worst Dr. Jones had ever seen in his ten years of working for the prison.

"I have a brain virus." Mr. Malvida shrugged. "It's not my fault. I couldn't help myself."

"Uh-huh, that's what you claimed, and the courts didn't buy it, either." Dr. Jones went to the door, opened it, and looked back at the prisoner. He nodded his head back and said, "Hang on a second." He peered outside, waved at someone and then closed the door. "It's not time for your last words."

"And that is why I'm here. I'd get it fixed if I could." Mr. Malvida took a deep breath. "Any day now, Doctor, I don't want to keep my maker waiting, now do I?"

"You're not going to meet your maker, Mr. Malvida!" A young man in a black shirt and pants answered, walking through the door. "Except for a brief view of the pearly gates, you are destined for Hell."

The young man pulled out a pocket-sized Bible, flipped through the pages, and began reading aloud, "Psalm twenty three, The Lord is my shepherd, I lack nothing."

"Oh, Lord, they've sent me a Baptist." The condemned man held up a hand. "No offense, pastor, but I've had just about enough religion in my life."

The pastor closed his book without finishing and stared at Mr. Malvida. "In my opinion, you haven't had enough." The pastor clutched the bible to his chest. "May God have mercy on your soul." He spun on his heel and left.

"Please, don't leave me." Mr. Malvida reached out to the door.

"I think it's a little late for begging for forgiveness," said Dr. Jones as he walked over to the curtained window and rapped on it with his knuckles. The clock above the door read 11:59.

"Not him, you idiot. Me!" Mr. Malvida pointed at the retreating pastor with his middle finger.

Returning to Mr. Malvida's bedside, Dr. Jones felt a cold, pins-and-needles sensation reach through his clinic coat and brush the hairs on his arm. "Do you think it is wise," he asked as he chaffed both arms, "to insult the man who is about to execute you?"

Mr. Malvida extended his arm as far as the restraints allowed him, and curled his fingers as if shaking another person's hand. A red flash leapt from his palm and disappeared.

"What the hell was that?" Dr. Jones' eyebrows rose as he gasped.

The door opened and the warden stepped into the room. "Mr. Malvida, it has been deemed by the state that you are to be executed for your crimes against humanity. Do you have any last words?"

The prisoner merely shook his head.

"Dr. Jones, when you are ready, please buzz the executioners in the next room." The warden left.

The doctor waited until the door clicked shut. He picked up a syringe of Narcan. "This should bring you down." He injected it into Mr. Malvida's IV. "And wipe that smile off your face."

Mr. Malvida's eyes went wide as he clutched the rails of the gurney, and said, "On the other hand, you may not want to stay and see your future demise."

The doctor picked up a pair of hemostats and clipped it to the IV line coming out of the sodium thiopental, blocking its delivery. He whispered into Mr. Malvida's ear, "You're going to suffer a little bit of discomfort." Dr. Jones went to the wall and pressed a doorbell button. Through the wall he heard a buzzer.

The curtains swung open. Visitors and witnesses slid forward on their seats.

"Wait!" Mr. Malvida's eyes went wider. "You're supposed to knock me out first." His hands clenched against the restraints as the infuser attempted to depress the plunger on the first syringe and failed.

"I hope your victims are standing here in this room, watching you." Dr. Jones drew near, placed a hand on the prisoner's forehead and stared into his eyes. "I hope they are watching you suffer like you made them suffer."

The second plunger depressed in the infuser. Mr. Malvida's eyes closed. "I know you can hear me, I only gave you enough succs to paralyze your voluntary muscles."

The clock ticked to 12:00.

"The next medicine will stop your heart," said Dr. Jones. "I diluted it so it will work slower and hopefully, not too painlessly.

Mr. Malvida shook, convulsed and went limp. The EKG looked like a seismometer during an 8.5 earthquake as the art-line declined to zero/zero.

* * *

Father Malvida gasped. "What, in the name of all

that's holy, happened?" When he could focus, he stared at Trece de Jesus sitting across from him. Father Malvida glanced at the half full tumbler on his desk and picked it up. The amber liquid slopped out as he raised it to his lips and drained the glass.

"What did you see? Did you meet yourself in the future?" Trece frowned and leaned forward. "What did you learn?"

"I had a brain virus. They are going to execute me. I was there. I saw it. How could I have possibly done such horrible things?" Father Malvida opened a desk drawer and rummaged inside as sweat beaded his forehead.

"You didn't have a virus when you *left*." Trece's lips parted as his breathing slowed. "Now, your fate is set."

Father Malvida pulled a revolver from the drawer.

Trece gripped the arms of his chair, and his knuckles turned white. "What are you doing," he asked.

The priest checked the cylinder and pulled out two used shell casings. "How did you know what I'd see?" He placed the gun on his desk and withdrew a box of shells from the same drawer.

"We know everything." Trece stuttered and went cross-eyed as he tried to keep his chin up and stare down at the gun, fearing what the mad priest might do to him.

Father Malvida rolled two bullets in his hand like he was going to shoot craps. "You knew? And you sent me? And now I'm infected!" He picked up the gun, slammed the shells into the empty chambers and closed the cylinder. The click punctuated his statement. "I can stop myself, I know I can."

"We don't want you to stop." He held out his hand to the priest. "Now, don't be rash. If you murder me, think of your parishioners, and the doubts they'll have."

The priest cocked the hammer. "Who said anything about murder?" He stared at the dark man as the barrel of the gun wavered. Slowly, he brought the muzzle up under his chin.

"Wait! If you kill yourself now, you'll never know if you can beat this thing." Trece waved his hand and slid back in his chair.

"I'm in God's hands now. Whatever He wanted has come by His choice."

"Possibly, but Satan wants to know the future. That's why *he* sent you." Trece held his hand out, palm forward.

Father Malvida pointed the weapon and pulled the trigger.

The City at the End of Time
by Jeffery Scott Sims

In the olden days, the great sorcerer, Jacob Bleek—who would know all things in heaven and earth that ever had been or ever would be, who would conquer knowledge for his eternal glory and private satisfaction—made a mighty magic in the secret lower chamber of his shunned, old house. There he gazed through steaming mist and roiling vapors into a unique crystal, an uneven, geometrically-confusing mass of rare element wrought by his own hands, and peering through the crystal he beheld a far marvel.

There, at a distance infinite in space and time, he saw a bleak, blasted, lifeless plain of broken rock, beyond which low mountains aged by eternity rose, shadowed in perpetual gloom. In the inky sky there burned a staggering number of stars, thousands of them, of various colors and hues, each as bright as the *Star of the Dog* that he knew from the commonplace winter constellations. In the center of the plain loomed the Black Tower, a mighty edifice of iron, with a single sheer shaft rising up to a vast domed chamber residing atop the spire. Ugly it was, harsh and painful to the eye, yet intriguing and alluring to a man such as Bleek, for no doorway graced its structural perfection of unity, no openings of any kind save that in the bulging cap which crowned it, where a single square window emitted a pale, weakly yellow, baleful light, a mysterious radiance thrown out into the world by the unknowable forces within.

Bleek was thrilled to see this much, for he guessed—nay, he deduced from his arcane studies—the Black Tower to exist beyond the wearisome sweep of time and matter. Rather, it stood at the center of all things, within and apart; raised not by the hand of man nor any other material entity, but by the great powers that controlled all existence; the Old Gods, the original and the eternal, as personified by Their boundless master, Xenophor, "He Who Creates and Destroys," who lords over the universe and is the universe, the cosmic totality of all. The Black Tower was Their citadel, encapsulated inside the attainable realms of being, and there Jacob Bleek would go, and experience wonders.

Never taking his eyes from the crystal of vision, he made the proper obeisance, uttered the secret words, offered all that he could afford and more that he could not; damned himself a dozen times over, pausing only to laugh as he did so, then concluded the rites with imperious demand. As he did so, the foul mist swirled afresh, and the image in the crystal faded from view as the grim stone chamber disappeared around him. He found himself in a terrifying, mind-stealing void, but he didn't tarry there. Presently, he came to full awareness, finding hard ground beneath his feet, and shattered rocks about him on a level surface. Dense gloom was all around, and the majestic sight of the Black Tower rose before him.

He had come to the appointed place; very well, but what should it signify? He did not approach the tower, choosing instead to circle it distantly, in order to confirm what he assumed—that no doorway existed at its base.

There was no reason to approach, then. One did not stride up and knock at gates which did not exist. Therefore, he lifted his gaze, staring into that solitary window so far above, a

Jeffery Scott Sims

window which, he noted with strange pleasure, beckoned still from whatever direction he observed the structure. He saw nothing within that window—no faces or mock-faces peered down at him—saw nothing at all save the sickly, feeble glare that trickled over that unreachable sill. Upon that he focused, and though nothing changed to his eyes, a whisper crept into his mind. Within the deepest recesses of his mortal brain came a voice without words, a speech of impressions and hints and indications more true and intelligible than any common utterance of the tongue. It spoke to him, seeking to draw him in, dangling ultimate insights like priceless baubles should he agree to enter... as *They* would have him do so. He had only to bow down and agree, and it would be done; he would be translated into the tower, there ever to reside, there ever to know as They knew...

...But Jacob Bleek refused, for he knew it would mean more than the death of him. He denied, pushing away that final prize, yet he did so with sacred reverence, and having done so asked for a lesser boon.

The strange light from the tower winked out. Bleek waited pensively in the grim darkness, then saw a new source of illumination gathering before him. An eerie greenish radiance developed, oozing up from the harsh ground, coagulating into a scintillating ball of cold, silent fire. A shape appeared within it, a suggestion of willowy form—human form—the image of a young and lovely woman with golden tresses cascading past her ivory throat, and bright eyes like diamond stars, and silky dress of antique or oddly foreign style. The green glow faded but did not die, instead radiating softly and steadily from the beautiful vision.

In a voice like rare music, she said, "Jacob Bleek, mage extraordinaire of your world and time, the Great Ones have heard you, and They grant thy request. Fain would They take thee unto Themselves, but this thou would put aside, so the lesser shall be given as it pleases thee. All thoughts are known to Them. Thou would penetrate the wall of eons, gaze upon the final, the ultimate glories of your kind and your cosmos. Come, then, with me as thy appointed guide, and behold marvels of the final days. Is this as thou would wish?"

He said it was, and she cried a mighty word that no mortal could ever speak. In an instant, the scene around Jacob Bleek changed--the tower, the terrain, and the woman all disappeared, and he gazed down from an aerial vantage upon another place, a dark orb mysterious to him, from which one discrete, circular source of light gleamed. He realized that he hovered in the outer spaces above a dark world, one lit by no sun, in a vast, cold universe devoid of stars. In every direction, his disembodied presence observed total blackness, save from a single round spot far below his invisible self.

The musical voice of the woman spoke from nowhere into his ear. "This is the culmination at the end of time. Let us stride amidst that glory."

Darkness obscured his vision. After a moment, marked by no sense of falling or motion, he stood in the heart of an incredible vista. A realm of pure artifice confronted him. Above him, stretching to distant horizons, hung the interior of a mighty metallic dome, well lit by curious lamps hanging from a stupendously vast ceiling, lamps that never flickered, only burned with unwinking white light. Bleek deduced that he stood within the solitary light he had seen from the void. Impressive—for how could the sweat of human labor ever have raised that roof?—yet what lay inside left him breathless with awe. The amazing dome shielded, from the ravages of eternal night, a titanic city of dazzling light and frenetic activity.

"Is it not wondrous, Jacob Bleek?" asked the woman at his side. He had not noticed her until she spoke. She took him by the hand. "Are not the fruits of the ages magnificent beyond thy most astounding dreams? Thus is the eventuality of thy kind, thy people, men and minds like thy own, fashioning and delving to the brink of ultimate attainment. Observe, investigate, and be happy with thy legacy, for thus is the destiny of all for which thou hast striven. I leave thee to it, but I shall not wander far. When thou hold my hand again, then may thou return to thy own time and place." And with those words she was gone.

Bleek didn't mind her absence. He had come to the scene of mankind's triumph, the city at the end of time, a deathless metropolis which held at bay (perhaps forever, he mused joyously) the implacable forces of entropy which would have annihilated a more feeble race. It thrilled him that his folk should have achieved this; that studied brilliance and the lust for knowledge should combine, in accordance with his fondest fantasies, to defy even the remorseless cruelties of blind fate that ever operated to sweep away accomplishment and life. Bleek's descendants had followed his chosen philosophy, to never admit defeat before the innate hostility of the universe. They had struggled without pause, without flagging, until they conquered the forces of death and decay which had plagued man since the dawn of time.

And what an accomplishment they achieved, a marvel without peer through all the ages!

The city moved and flashed and beamed with vibrant life. Across the artificial sky, strange gleaming machines buzzed and swooped like insects, darted like lightning, cruised imperiously like stately ships. Around the unending array of spires, minarets, soaring spikes of metal and glass swept encircling balconies and ledges, sky-flung roadways on which cruised or raced weird conveyances, metal carts without horses that drove faster than eagles could fly; others like trains of wagons joined together, inching quietly and surely up and down the planes without any hint of propulsion. He had never beheld a landscape so alive, yet one without any evidence of what made it work. His keen eyes sought the masters of these mechanisms, but where were they? Bleek could only suppose that the drivers of these rolling and flying carriages were housed within the metal bodies, gauging their courses through unseen windows.

He stood in the center of a square plaza, its quarter mile surface an unbroken, unlined mass of firm metal that shimmered like fine steel. It resembled a public square, but no denizens were about at the moment. Strange buildings—low, rectangular edifices of windowless metal—brooded around the deserted perimeter. They were buildings without doors or windows, but held many lights that flashed on and off at intervals, creating patterns which meant nothing to him. Narrow lanes passed between the structures. Beyond rose the stupendous towers of the city, rank after rank fading into distance. It was a big place, this city, and he would see it all, converse with its wise men, mingle with its blessed inhabitants. Such stories they could tell him!

Bleek set forth, choosing a direction at random, making for a particular dagger of gold that knifed the air, glittering prettily between two solemn towers of gray metal. Toward this he strode because it amused him, because he must begin somewhere, and the gold spire pleased his eye. He entered the relatively shaded passageway leading that way, with the odd buildings at each side. No one emerged to greet him or ask his business, nor were there any portals for them to do so. Were these ubiquitous structures artifactual? It might be that they, in some manner currently beyond his ken, performed service to the wonders about him. In the past, he had speculated about such possibilities.

Before him, his quick ears detected an amalgamation of sounds which quickened his pace, for he desired to meet those who produced the noise. He chuckled when he pondered the difficulties of introducing himself, explaining his presence. Yet, these people must be all wise; they would know, they would understand.

The passage opened onto a smaller square, this one strung with metallic wires drawn tautly overhead, strands of coppery hue along which hummed pulses of red light. Through the air among the wires unusual rays of intensely blue light danced and flared back and forth, emitting at times a sound like the crackling of electricity, at periodic occasions a powerful droning which oppressed the ear. These were the sounds he had heard. He brightened when a metal carriage whined into view from an enclosed passage, advancing gracefully on several metallic rollers. It moved purposefully to a spot beneath a humming strand, and a skinny, segmented metal arm rose from a hatch to fiddle with the wire. The points of contact twinkled blue and white. Then the squat conveyance began rolling away into another tunnel. Bleek leaped forth, striving to attract the attention of the occupant or occupants, to no avail. The thing vanished around the corner without heeding him in any way.

He consoled himself by concluding that these people, so accustomed to marvels in their daily life, would not be overly intrigued by his obscure appearance in their midst. They were used to stranger wonders. He left the open space, threading his way along a corridor framed by larger slab-sided structures, emerged onto a shelf overlooking a metal gorge hundreds of rods across. At his feet the path ended abruptly at a yawning brink, from which he could look down into shadowy depths, where moving lights glistened and throbbing sounds welled. He threw himself at the edge of the gulf, for it dropped without slope at least a mile, and he imagined more. So this city plunged down in subterranean majesty as its towers rose, level upon level. Bleek could hazard no guess as to its full extent.

From the lower murk ascended a series of transparent, glassy bubbles, large shimmering orbs that caught and reflected the multi-colored lights. What they were he did not know, but within one of them he spied a definite human figure. At last, he was to be acknowledged! A closer view dashed his hopes; it was the woman, beckoning to him and laughing. As she drifted by she called to him, saying, "Thou seem forlorn and lonely in the midst of the great city. Continue thy delving, that thou may learn more and know all. The revelations to come are many and instructive." She passed beyond the rim of the gulf, lost to sight, laughing again.

It struck Bleek that he should find the inhabitants within the towers that rose like the spires of fairy castles. There they could live in splendor, and there he would meet with them, learn their ways, and gain their thoughts on the past and present, for all secrets must be open to them. He recalled the golden spire, which he had lost in the maze, moved through another passage in what ought to be the requisite direction, glimpsed it and its framing towers looming above a wall of blank, humming buildings. A broad avenue of sorts spread before his path and led him immediately to his destination. Sure enough, a round, open doorway gaped at the base of the spire. He strode to it, peeked inside, and found the interior well lighted. Entering, he found no one there, but the place more resembled living quarters than anything he had seen so far. There were chambers connected by a central hall—rooms approached by doors that opened as if by magic—all constructed of metal and glass and other elements he could not identify. There were counters filled with lights, knobs, and levers. Such ornamentation crowded the walls as well. In one room he actually found something like a chair, in which he sat before an array of esoteric devices. He tinkered with the mechanisms and got results. An empty portion of the wall suddenly flared into life, revealed to him an image of the city as seen from a point near the top of the sky dome. It made for an excellent map. Bleek experimented with the ornate controls, causing the image to expand, shrink, and change. It was fantastic! This marvelous instrument allowed him to search distant regions for signs of his fellow men. He undertook this goal, devoting considerable time to the task... without success. Eventually, he gave up the attempt, and chose to ascend into the upper reaches of the spire.

This proved a simple matter, though he sought in vain for a staircase. In time he discovered a tiny, drab chamber which upon entering immediately began carrying him upward. Bleek was amazed by this moving room. There were no controls on the walls, which mystified him, until he spoke to himself aloud and discovered that the odd conveyance responded to speech. His specific words meant nothing to the machine, but trial and error determined which basic vocal sounds made it start, stop, and proceed up or down. For a while it was a shaky ride.

He got off at certain floors to examine the desolate contents. Many of the chambers were clearly dwellings, but all were vacant, impossibly clean, none containing a single item nor any evidence noting current or recent occupancy. He could not understand, cursed his ignorance, and moved on with his exploration. In the end, Bleek bowed to the transport device, which seemed to have some intent of its own, and let it carry him to the highest level at the slender peak.

He stepped out onto an isolated balcony that was disconnected from the spire's encircling ramp, and gazed out over the busy vista of lights and machines. He peered down, clutching the railing, observed the woman standing on an out-jutting ledge directly below. She cried, "Where are thy people, Jacob Bleek? Do they hide from you? Have they mastered concealment in addition to aught else? 'Tis a pity, for much they could tell. Over eons without number they dreamed of taming death, of extending themselves, individually and racially, in perpetuity. Against all odds they labored, in the waning days of time, to fabricate this city which should endure as they, so long as the universe should last.

"Out there, in the cold, dark beyond, all has returned to the void from which it sprang. The stars have burned out, their ashes blown away by the breath of the Old Ones; the planets, all save this, have crumbled to dust; even light and time falter, grow sluggish, expire.

"Yet, the city still lives; perhaps it shall do so though a thousand eternities die. Is it not magnificent? Is not the soul a paltry price, to gain in return the pure knowledge of this? The Black Tower stands invitingly, but thou would rather hear thy truths from the mighty among men. Go to them, Jacob Bleek. Seek them, for all time is thine. No need for thee to sleep, or drink, or eat; go, search, investigate until no hiding place remains. Then call for me. My hand is warm."

Bleek searched. He looked everywhere, through mystic lifetimes, without finding what he sought. Every room, every burg finally opened to him, yet never did he behold the masters of the city. He learned the ways of the moving vehicles, forced them to halt, broke into them, found artifice, amazing contrivance, but that only. He learned how records could be revealed and read, studied them, learned only of mechanical cleverness. He descended into weird regions beneath the city, delving leagues below the surface, and eventually uncovered the mighty storehouses of energy, drawn from the earth's core, which powered the city and gave it life. It was a faux life, though, a life of preconceived motion and mindless effort, a life granted to machines that had been erected in a long forgotten age to serve the builders, the masters of the city who'd dreamed of eternity.

And they were gone. The life man had breathed into his machines had eluded him. The city lived, but the masters had departed forever, suffering the fate of all men before them. Neither their knowledge, their charms, nor their ceaseless determination could hold at bay the murderous forces of cosmic death. They had failed, as had all the great and glorious minds who grasped at forever and sought to break it to their will. Vast knowledge had availed them naught—in the end, they too died like dogs, the city lingering as their splendid tomb.

Bleek quailed at this realization, and sobbed piteously to himself, for he sought no less than had they, and with lesser means. If the city, that sterile mausoleum, be their culmination—the conclusion of their story, of every tale that had ever been written—then what scope of success remained to him? Was not he, the questing man of a forgotten past, merely a meaningless footnote in the ancient war against nothingness? One more who had striven, fated to face doom?

As Bleek sat in despair, the lovely vision of the woman came serenely to him. "Time it is that thou came home," said she. "Those who sent me know of thee, Jacob Bleek, and would take thee unto Themselves. Encompassed within Them is entirety, the all of all. Journey with me to the Black Tower, where all thy care, worry, and useless struggle fade as doth thy dregs of flesh and mind. Accept the oneness of imperishable oblivion."

"No," Bleek replied fervently. They might soothe the pain in his soul, but They could never satisfy the longings of his mind. That he could never accept. "Send me back where I belong. Now!"

The beautiful woman sneered and spat out a grotesque word, after which she vanished, and in another instant the city blinked out of view. Bleek felt himself falling, tumbling head over heels, roughly buffeted by angry forces, and then he found himself standing in his familiarly grim chamber of magic, with smoking retorts on the oaken table and a grinning skull staring from the mantle.

The odyssey was over. Bleek had seen the despicable future, learned much, and imagined more. All in all, it had been an edifying journey, one providing a great deal of wisdom and food for subtle speculation. So, that was the time to come as the Gods conceived it? Very well. He knew now the tribulations he must confront. Though the Great Ones—though Xenophor Himself—strove against him, he would face the ordeal, overcome all opposition. If only the Gods could decree the future, then he would make himself like Them, and with Their power remake the universe to suit his own demands. This outcome he would pen in the book of destiny.

PARADOX LOST
by Diane Arrelle

Filmore Petri sat on the bar stool and absently chewed at his fingernail. "Damn it," he muttered. "How could Dad have done this to me?"

On the stool next to him, a young executive type was drinking wine in the seat where a regular guy had been perched just a few minutes ago.

"Life's a bitch, you know?" Filmore said conversationally.

"You don't say," the wine sipper answered coldly, a look of disdain crossing his face as he rose to leave.

"Yo buddy, where you going?" Filmore called to the retreating young man, then glancing around quickly, snatched the bill next to the abandoned wine glass, stuffed it in his shirt pocket and returned to his drink. He studied the watered liquor in the foggy glass, shrugged, and downed it with a satisfying slurp.

Hand raised to signal for another, an invisible cloud of heavy perfume attacked his nose. He sniffed in the cloying fragrance, momentarily intoxicated with the scent of woman, and glanced over to the recently vacated seat, delighted to see a feminine back facing him.

"Hey sweetheart, how's it going?" he asked, sitting straighter and sucking in his belly.

The woman turned and with a toss of yellow hair flashed a grateful smile. "Fine honey, just fine. How're things with you?"

Ugh, used goods, he thought as he studied the more than middle-aged broad with stiff bleached hair and a face buried under tons of make-up. *Oh well, an ear's an ear*, he decided, letting his belly sag back over his belt.

"Terrible. Let me tell you about rotten luck," Filmore said.

Her hand on his thigh, she said, "Look, honey, if I'm going to have to listen to a tale of woe you'd better buy me a drink. Name's Mona."

"Sure Mona, order away," Filmore sighed and moved his leg away from her touch.

"Bartender," she signaled, waving a red clawed hand fettered with goldtone bangles. "A strawberry daiquiri."

Filmore groaned, "Hey, wait a second, Babe. Make it cheaper."

Mona eyed him, shrugged and said, "Change that to a white wine." Looking back at Filmore, she added, "Well? Let's hear your story already."

"My illustrious father, Franklin Petri, kicked off last week—" Filmore started.

"Hey, I heard of him!" Mona interrupted. "He's that famous but eccentric millionaire inventor who died."

"Word for word out of the headlines, Baby," Filmore snapped." Obviously, you read on the check-out lines. Anyway, he croaked, and left everything to—"

"Yeah, I remember," Mona interrupted again. "He left 15 million bucks to his only son. Hey, that means you're worth megabucks, Honey!" she purred and put her hand back on his thigh, only higher up.

"Lady, quit interrupting!" Filmore bellowed, his blood

pressure surging. The noise level in the bar abruptly dropped, so he said in a softer tone, "Look, shut up and I'll tell you about it. My father had two sons. But the old man hated the fact that I had the balls to stand up to him, so he disowned me and left everything to my younger brother, Fitzgerald."

She removed her hand without his help and pursed her lips into a pouty, crimson frown.

Filmore didn't even notice, he was too much on a roll. "You see, I'm not quite as smart as Fitzy, and Dad was ashamed of having what he considered a dummy, you know. To top that off, I had a string of bad luck." He started talking faster, "I like to play the ponies. Well, last year I got wind of a winner. The sucker couldn't lose, only it did. I didn't have the money to cover the bet so I borrowed one of Dad's inventions—you know the one, the extended wear, totally bio-degradable diapers made from recycled newspaper. Anyway, I stole it, sold it, and used that money. And do you know what that son of a bitch did?"

Mona yawned into her hand.

"He had me arrested! For a lousy crap holder! My own father put me in jail!"

"Come on Honey, get on with it," Mona mumbled.

Bearing the weight of the world on his shoulders like that Greek guy he could never remember, Filmore savored his troubles. "Yeah, then there was the time I got caught with the coke. But I guess the worst was when that stupid broad claimed that I... Hey Mona, where ya going?"

"To the can, Honey. Self pity tends to make me puke," Mona yelled back with a jangling wave.

"Dumb Tramp!" Filmore snarled and discovered an elderly gentleman taking Mona's seat. The man smiled through a walrus mustache and said politely, "How do you do?"

"Terrible!" Filmore barked, and turned away.

"I say, I couldn't help but hear your sad tale, my good man," Walrus said. "Fascinating story."

Filmore turned and studied the old guy, taking in the dated tweed suit, the wild white hair, and thick glasses. "Do I have

Diane Arrelle

to buy you a drink too?"

"Well it is customary to be cordial when dumping on a stranger," Walrus replied.

"Why not, I've got enough left for a few more drinks," Filmore sighed.

"The name is Ernest.   It sounds to me like you are a misunderstood soul."

"Yeah, that's it. I'm misunderstood," Filmore said with relish. "Dear, old, dad always hated me. The old putz was just too much of a perfectionist to accept human failings in anyone, ya know. God, he used to drive me crazy with his favorite saying; *If at first you don't succeed, make it perfect the next time.*"

Filmore ordered another round. "I can't remember how many times he'd said to me; *Son, you're a bad apple, my only failure. I really wish you'd never been born or had died before we'd ever learned what a pathetic disappointment you were. Would have been so much easier to bear. Tragedy is just so much easier on the soul than genetic catastrophe.*"

"Tsk, tsk," Ernest muttered.

"Yeah!" Filmore was basking in the inner glow of his sorrow. "Fitzgerald took pity on me and is going to give me a small allowance. An allowance! Damn it, I'm 32 years old and that creep is doling out my allowance!"

"Shocking!" Ernest agreed and ordered another drink.

Filmore flinched slightly, but decided he was too much on a roll to worry about a few more bucks. "I wish that bastard had never been born!"

"Or he could have died as an infant and made you stand out more as the surviving son," Ernest added. "Why, even your mistakes would have been forgiven, the poor child with emotional guilt issues because he'd survived."

"That would have been wonderful, Ernie. I've always hated Fitzy. The little jerk came along and made me look bad. That's what he did, you know." Filmore hesitated for a moment, glanced around in drunken caution, his every movement exaggerated, and said in a loud, conspiratorial whisper, "In fact, I tried to kill him, pushed him out of a tree

200

when we were kids. Dumb luck, he landed in a bush and only got scratched up. Sad thing was that I fell after him and broke my freakin' arm."

Ernest shook his head, "Not fair at all!"

"Last year I paid a guy to knock him off, but the creep took my money and ran. Last time I'll ever pay for anything in advance."

"I sympathize completely," Ernest said. "Filmore, I think we can help each other. You see, I'm a scientist and—"

"Whoa, Buddy," Filmore snapped and sat up out of his drunken slouch. "I may not be a genius like dear, old Dad, but I sure ain't dumb. I'm not parting with what little bread I do get backing any harebrained inventions. Sorry, but you baited the wrong hook, Ernie."

With an offended expression, Ernest sat erect, put down his drink. "My good man," Ernest said haughtily, "I see that you are not even going to listen to an intelligent suggestion. I'm certainly not in need of your meager funds! Good day, Sir."

Filmore grabbed at Ernest's sleeve with an unsteady hand. "Hey wait, Ernie. Sorry, I'm a little loaded, ya know. Look, have another drink and tell me what you were thinking."

"Well," Ernest said with hesitation, "all right. As I mentioned, I'm somewhat of an inventor." Ernest paused dramatically then whispered, "And I've discovered time travel!"

Filmore sat there, trying to comprehend the concept. "Wow! Time travel. That sounds like something Dad should have invented. I bet he's rolling in the grave!" he muttered, reaching for his glass and knocking it over. Cold liquid dripping onto his leg, he muttered with wide-eyed drunken awe, "Time travel!"

"Yes, exciting isn't it. So far I've sent objects and some animals; all survived the trip admirably. And now I'd like to send a human back in time," Ernest explained.

"Cool!" Filmore said. "Who ya gonna get."

He studied Filmore earnestly, "My friend, how would you like to be famous? How would you like to prove to that family of yours that you don't need them? Will never need them?"

Ernest paused dramatically before continuing. "How would you like to literally get away with murder!"

Perking up, Filmore asked, "Who?"

"Why, your brother, of course. All you would have to do is go back 27 years and poison him as an infant. History would be changed and you would grow up an only child," Ernest said furtively. "Why, Filmore, you would be a rich man when you returned to the present."

"Wow!" Filmore said and tried to drink from his empty glass. "Wow!"

"You see, we would both come out ahead," Ernest concluded. "And famous!"

"When can we do it?" Filmore asked like an excited child.

"Right now."

Jumping up, Filmore slammed his money on the bar and yelled, "Hey, Mike, keep the change."

Staggering against Ernest, they went outside. The cold air did nothing to clear the fog from Filmore's brain as they walked ten blocks to a dilapidated garage.

They entered and Ernest handed Filmore a thick metal belt with a switch where the buckle should have been. "This is my time machine."

Filmore struggled with clumsy hands to put the belt around his waist. "Uh, Ernie, how about a quick hop to the future? Say, a few short hops to a couple of Super Bowls and Kentucky Derbies. I could make a killing, *a killing* next year! I'd not only be super rich, but I'd actually be a winner. Those bookies would finally show me some respect."

Ernest sighed. "Filmore, you don't need to do that. After you return from your own past, you will return a very rich man.

"But, the respect! I want to see the respect from everyone who though I was a total screw-up."

Ernest sighed again, louder. "Filmore, you will have changed your own history. You'll return here an only child, raised in the loving home of your now smaller and doting family. No one will ever think of you as a failure again. Now, here is what you will do. You'll go back to when your brother was just two weeks old. You take this syringe of poison and inject him. He dies, you throw this switch and you come back to the present a rich man."

"Sounds good," Filmore agreed. "But what if they do an autopsy?"

Putting the belt around Filmore's waist, Ernest answered, "It's an unknown poison I just invented, and what do you care? After all, you'll be back in the present, anyway."

"Yeah!" Filmore said. "Hey wait, what happens if I see myself?"

Chuckling, Ernest replied, "Why, Filmore, you'll cause a paradox and one of you will explode."

Filmore started to undo the belt. "Forget it!"

"No, no, wait," Ernest said stifling his laughter. "I was only making a joke. Nothing terrible will happen. If you meet, you'll have a new childhood memory of meeting a stranger the tragic night your brother died."

Before Filmore had time to ask any more questions, Ernest threw the switch.

Just like that, in the blink of an eye, Filmore found himself in a familiar bedroom. There was no gut retching feeling of movement, no swirling colored lights, no shrill ear shattering sound. One moment he was in the lab, the next he was in his old bedroom, the one he had slept and played in for years until his brother came along and forced him out.

He smiled at the steamship wallpaper and the white crib and dresser. "Who says you can't go home again?" Filmore muttered as he walked over to the crib and looked down.

Staring at the tiny, pink baby, he smiled with wicked glee. "Hey, Fitzy, now you're gonna pay for all the hell you've put me through."

The baby stared through him with all the innocence of infancy and cooed.

He jabbed the syringe roughly into the baby's leg,

while covering its face with a blanket. He listened to the muffled screams, absently scratching at an itch on his thigh.

"Hey, Fitz, I want to watch you die," he said conversationally as he removed the blanket and scooped up the baby. I want to see one of my plans for you actually work."

He rocked the baby gently until the cries ceased, then laid the infant back in the crib.

The baby whimpered softly.

Filmore wanted to enjoy the show but couldn't. Cramps and dizziness wracked at him. Wrapping his arms around his gut, he whined, "Damn cheap booze. That's the last time I'll ever get drunk."

"You are so right, my boy," a voice said from behind him. "The very last time."

Filmore spun around and fell to his knees, staring incredulously at Ernest.

"Why, Filmore, you're as white as a ghost! Feeling under the weather?" Earnest said with a hearty laugh.

"What's...What's going on?" Filmore stammered.

Ernest peeled away heavy latex make-up and took off his face.

"Dad!" Filmore gasped in horror. "You're dead!"

Chuckling, Franklin said, "And so are you, my boy. So are you."

Struggling to get up Filmore collapsed. "How?"

"I'll make this quick, son. Fitz and I invented this machine before I died. I hopped into my future, your present, to set this up. After we're finished here, I'll do a hop back to my present and then I can die a happy man in about two months my time."

"Why?" Filmore whimpered. "Why did you go to all this trouble to kill Fitzy? I thought you loved him."

Heaving a huge exaggerated sigh, Franklin squatted next to his son. "Filmore you really are stupid, you know. That dying baby isn't Fitzgerald, it's you."

Filmore sobbed as the words sunk in and he realized that he had just committed suicide.

"I could never kill a fly, let alone my own child," Franklin mused. "But I always felt that you were capable of just about any sin, including murder. I must say, your zeal in this has made my decision to get rid of you much easier to bear. Still, I feel bad for your mother. She must have cried horribly to lose her baby, but you know, things happen."

Franklin stood and added, "Well, I have to be going, son. I can't stand to watch that baby suffer."

Filmore tried to cry out but was too weak. He realized that any one of the next few breaths would be his last... that when the baby died he'd cease to exist.

Franklin started to touch the switch on his belt, then stopped long enough to add, "It's ironic Filmore, but do you realize that in committing this murder, you have finally done something that lived up to my expectations!"

Extinction
by Steven Gepp

The large feet crashed across the barren ground, leaving in their wake enormous footprints embedded in the dirt. Slowly but surely, the mammoth beast lurched its way across the plain of dust, wandering from one coniferous forest to the next, across the path cut centuries before by the lava that had flowed from a distant mountain. Still active, the volcano occasionally rumbled to let the world know it was there, but that meant nothing to the huge beast that made its way forward. Sated after a recent kill, it was now guided by a second instinct, one which over-rode everything else in its primitive brain—the sex drive.

Somewhere in its male mind, the five-ton beast knew that it had to go forward to the next part of the forest in order to find a mate. The bellowing sounds it had heard on the wind indicated that there was another of its kind in a receptive mood somewhere within the forest. And its instincts told it very strongly that it was important that this female be found. Almost more than instinct, it was survival. Even its under-developed brain understood that it was survival.

When it had been younger, there seemed to have been many more of its kind. But the numbers had dwindled to such a degree that there was virtually no competition for the food that roamed through the forests and across the vast plains of grass and flowers that marked the valleys around the watering holes and rivers. But even food was becoming more and more scarce as time went on. The creature could only vaguely comprehend that something was happening to its world that was destroying everything about it.

He paused and gazed at the cloudy sky. A lone winged creature sailed on the warm air currents, occasionally squawking to nothing in particular. A pang of hunger gripped its stomach, but that small creature was too far away to be anything but a dream. The monster grunted to himself and continued to lumber forward, towards the other part of the forest and the sounds that had activated his sex-drive. The stony ground beneath his feet gave way a little and he stumbled, his useless forelimbs flailing pathetically. But the sturdy and muscular legs supporting his enormous weight managed to keep him upright. He shook his huge head and growled at himself and the ground before continuing on his slow, laborious, energy-conserving fashion.

He reached the edge of the forest and sniffed instinctively at the air. His pause was a long one and the eyes took in every detail of their surroundings. An odor came to him from close by within the forest, and the huge beast could not decide if it was prey or a competitor... or the object of his desire.

He took a cautious step forward, onto the softer ground cover between the trees before him, then paused again. There was more than one aroma on the wind, confusing his olfactory senses, and he growled intuitively. A low rumbling sound, it vibrated down through his three-toed feet and into the ground itself. A brief crashing sound came from behind a nearby tree as a small creature—almost a miniature of the monster standing there, though with longer fore-limbs and a slightly different gait—sprinted away as fast as it could. It had taken heed of the warning given to everything nearby, and had fled before being discovered. The larger beast watched it go, a scowl on his scaly mouth, his enormous teeth glinting in the sun. The creature was too fast to be captured, he knew, but at least a potential rival was now gone. He allowed himself a low roar of satisfaction and took a few more tentative steps into the greenery. The smaller trees here on the edge of this forest barely came up to his chest, and once more his eyes scanned the surrounding vegetation for any sign of another living creature.

The only things he could see were the plants. That stirred something deep within his primal mind. That was not right. There were none of the feathered creatures or winged reptiles that customarily followed him, hoping to scavenge something from his own hunting. Even the annoying insects were barely present. There was something disturbing here, hidden from view, but there. His every instinct told him that danger was lurking here somewhere. But that other instinct, still stirring within him, was also pushing him on. He growled indecisively and took another step forward.

Once more he stopped and sniffed at the air. He recognized a few of the odors—there was another creature somewhere up ahead. Briefly he turned and stared behind himself, across the lava flow at the part of the forest he had recently left. Then he shook his head and once more slowly made his way forward into the depth of the vegetation. Feeling his way with his toes digging into the soft earth and smelling the wind all the while, he made his way forward. Once again, instinct took over, and he raised his head and let out a long, low roar. A mating call, not anything taught by his mother, but something that only that primeval part of his mind could tell him to do—something that had worked for him many times in the past. When he had first reached sexual maturity, it had been a regular occurrence, but as the years wore on and numbers of his own kind had decreased, it had grown more and more infrequent. Now, it became the over-riding instinct, even overcoming his desire to stay within his own part of the forest and hunt and eat.

But he found that instinct disappearing, fading from

the forefront of his mind. Something else was taking over his mind. He stopped and raised his head again. It wafted through the air and came to his over-worked nostrils. It was a smell he knew straight away. A perfume to his confused mind. This day was not one he was comfortable with, and his vigilance had so far meant that he was still alive. But that smell was suddenly making all of his caution move to the background of his mental processes. It was one that made his saliva glands start to work of their own accord and his eyes automatically began to search for its source.

The aroma of a fresh kill. The blood was still flowing. Most of it was still intact.

And that explained a little of the strangeness of his surroundings. It was most likely the female of his kind that had made the kill, and the other creatures of the forest had fled in terror at the sounds, sights, and smells of the battle that had resulted in this death... and this potential food. It did not matter what had made this kill, he knew he could deal with anything that stood in his way. For more years than most he had been fighting and surviving in his world; the scars that riddled his body and the long line of vanquished foes were a testament to that. Even the faster, smaller meat-eaters that dwelt within these forests, even the female of his own breed would not survive if they tried to prevent him from getting what he knew he could get.

But with that in mind, his approach slowed and became cautious. He tried the air once more. It was there, a definite fragrance beneath that of the dead creature he was tracking. There was something else in the vicinity, something close. And that meant a potential rival. Once more the snarl curled the reptilian lips and the head dropped down as it made its way forward, towards the source of all of these conflicting aromas.

The smells grew stronger. The meat smell was the overriding one, filling the air and driving away all the other plant-eaters. They knew that the scent of blood would bring predators, and they made sure that they were nowhere near it, to prevent becoming more of the same. But even the flying reptiles that scavenged the carcasses were not flying around, making themselves known with their noisy crying and diving to snatch a mouthful of meat here and there, risking their own lives to feed themselves. And years of hard-earned experience told the huge beast approaching the scene from the security of the trees that that could mean only one thing—the killer was still present, or, at the very least, another predator was gorging itself on the corpse.

That second smell—growing as strong as the first the closer he came, telling his instincts that it was right near the first smell—was also indicative of that. But the approaching monster was confused. He knew most of the smells of his world, knew what animals to avoid, what to attack, when a female was approachable, when she was just another rival for food and territory, what animals were not worth pursuing for their speed, taste, or size, what animals were an easy kill. His many years of life had taught him all of these things. But the smell that came with the decaying flesh was not one he could recognize. It was too new and too different from anything else he had experienced. And with that unfamiliarity came extreme care. He knew he was ruler of his domain, but even he could not risk a confrontation with the unknown that seemed to be now stalking his world. No matter how much that carcass lying just out of reach seemed to beckon him onwards, his growing fear was keeping him back. This was not something he was used to experiencing.

A small, feathered creature flew past his nose and he automatically snapped at it. His reflexes were still quick enough that he managed to swallow it whole. He barely felt it or even realized he had eaten it, being so preoccupied with what was happening somewhere in front of him. Two conflicting instincts fighting within his simple mind, and he was rooted to the spot. A movement in the trees beside him caught his eye, and he whipped his enormous head in that direction and sniffed at the air. He opened and closed his mouth, tasting the breeze now, revealing the dagger-like teeth, rotted pieces of meat from his own latest kill still hanging down like the vines in a tree. The smells and tastes were starting to encircle him, and he did not like that feeling.

He lifted his head and let out a mighty roar, the cry that would send rivals fleeing and panic the huge herds to separate the weak and the elderly and the very young from the rest as they all madly attempted to escape his terrifying jaws. And, indeed, from many directions, the sounds of small animals retreating in abject terror from his presence came to him. But they were only small animals. The larger ones—the hunter or scavenger out there, others like it—none of them could be heard attempting escape. His experience did not tell him what to do in this situation, but his intuition told him to get the food and then escape, himself.

He breathed in deeply, creating a grumbling sound that echoed in the deserted forest, before crashing forward towards the source of the smell of rotted meat. Through the thick trees and bushes he ploughed, using his head and sheer bulk to force his way onwards. Nothing stood in his way until, finally, he entered a clearing around a wide part of the river that ran through this part of the forest. There, half submerged in the water, was the carcass. It was indeed a fresh kill; the huge gash in its side was still letting steam out from within the punctured organs, the blood was flowing freely down its scaly hide and into the water, where the river was running a sickly red. Small fish tried to nibble at the skin that was beneath the surface of the water, but there was nothing else even near this animal. Cautiously, the monster sniffed at the meat, then looked around. There was something out there, but it was keeping its distance. And finally instinct took over completely as he bowed his heavy head and sank his teeth into the exposed flesh at the side of the dead animal lying before him. He tore off a hunk of meat and swallowed it whole, then lifted his head to the sun and bellowed a roar of victory, his mouth and teeth stained red, his useless arms dripping with the blood flowing down the strong jaws, his own hide stained by the bodily fluids of the dead reptile he had come across.

Another bite, another roar, this one even louder. The trees themselves seemed to bow to the power of that cry, and what few animals were left in the area seemed to take flight.

He cast a quick glance at the plant life that surrounded him, making sure there were no others coming near to him, then once more buried his head in the side of the dead animal. Now the only smell in his nose was fresh, tantalizing blood, and all he was thinking about was eating his fill. And he did not notice the two smaller creatures emerge from behind a nearby tree.

A third roar to let the world know that he was still there. But it would be the last sound that the ruler of his world would ever manage. With head thrown back in triumph, a red dot appeared on the back of his neck, at the base of the spine. A dull buzz sounded in the air as the red dot became a solid red line, and the smell of burning flesh briefly flared. The huge body suddenly lost all of its strength and toppled forwards. The primitive mind could not comprehend why no muscles below the neck were responding to any mental directives, why the automatic impulses that powered parts of its body were no longer functioning.

And the eyes closed as the Tyrant King was finally vanquished...

***

"Good kill." The first man walked over to the tyrannosaur and kicked it with his booted foot. Not even a flicker. "Very good kill."

"This one's a big one," the other man muttered, joining his companion. In his hand he held a long, thick-barreled weapon that looked vaguely like an old Mauser rifle.

"Damn right." The first man knelt down and touched the hole in the back of the neck where the laser had entered before burning away the entire nervous system of the prehistoric monster.

"So, how do we get it back?" The second man was clearly nervous about the whole thing.

"In the bigger crate we brought with us are some of the same bands we're wearing. We just have to attach enough of them to this creature so that its coordinates can be picked up with ours and, zap, it's back in our time and you've got your trophy." The first man sounded almost bored, but after years of these hunting expeditions it was losing all of the luster it had once had. When the government had first allowed time travel to be used for rich men and women to go into the past to hunt extinct animals, it had been fun and daring, something no human in the history of the world had ever done. But now...

"Good." the second man said, though his voice seemed distant, vague, not filled with the joy of someone who had just managed to bag their very own Tyrannosaurus Rex.

"What's wrong?" the first man growled.

"I don't know," was the muted response. "What if, I mean, what if we're changing history here by wiping these things out."

"Look, the government only allows a certain number of dinos to be killed from any one time—or megafauna from later on. As it is, we're in the Comet Zone. In less than a hundred years a comet is going to smash into this planet, killing them all off anyway. The fact that we're hunting them into extinction in this time period first is irrelevant. They'll be dead soon anyway."

"But what if they keep taking the time back further and further?" the man whispered. "Won't that mean my trophy may not exist because this one may never have been born?"

And the other man smiled. "Look, pal, I leave the questions like that to the chronophysicists and just get on with bringing rich guys like you back here to hunt. Okay?"

"Okay..."

Their speech was cut off by a sudden disturbance. The roar was long and loud, and made the very earth tremble with its power. The two men turned in horror to face the beast as it crashed into their clearing, attracted by the scent of fresh blood. The man with the gun tried to lift the weapon, but he was trembling so much he only succeeded in dropping it into the water beside the dead animals already there. The other unslung his own high-powered conventional rifle and aimed it, but the deafening explosion meant nothing and the gaping hip wound the projectile opened went totally unnoticed as the huge mouthful of dagger-like death lunged forward. The human flesh was torn to ribbons by the female who had attracted the male tyrannosaur there in the first place.

***

Tens of millions of years later, a series of curious objects swirled into being at the chrono-laboratory. Some were instantly recognizable—two crates, one marked 'Supplies' and the other marked 'Weapons/Tech,' as well as a 'Nerve-Burner' rifle fitted with a homing device. Two things weren't as easy to identify.

It was an autopsy two days later that positively identified the partially digested remains, mixed with fresh stomach acid and several unknown meat sources, as those of millionaire politician Gregory Warner and professional chronohunter Shaun Mayer.

There's an App for That
by Chris Allinotte

Ricky tightened the topmost nut one last quarter turn. If the time machine wasn't perfect *now*, it never would be. The machine had started to rattle when he flipped the switch to power it up a few minutes ago. With this final adjustment, he was ready... almost.

While the physics and quantum mechanics of bending space-time to his will were undoubtedly the trickiest part of the problem, they at least had been *finite;* there had been a definite end to the process, and it had come when he'd sent his hamster, Nico, forward in time by five minutes. He'd adjusted the containment beam and lased the time marker strapped to his pet for precisely thirty seconds while the computer did its calculations. On precisely the thirty-first second, a beam of green light shot out from the apparatus in the middle of the room and bathed Nico in crackling energy. With the smallest of squeaks, Nico had vanished. Five minutes later, he reappeared. His fur had been standing on end, and he became manic for awhile, darting from his exercise wheel to his water bottle three times in quick succession, but otherwise, he seemed unharmed. That had been two weeks ago—before he'd gotten himself tangled up in a logistical mess.

Ricky had wanted to continue the success of Nico's temporal voyage with his own time jump. It was reckless, but after five years of work, and no apparent ill effects to Nico, he was tired of waiting. *Now we'll get to see if this thing is worth the years I put into it.* First, he'd removed the quarter-sized sensor from Nico's belly, receiving a nip on his finger in the process. Rodents were so *touchy.* Next, he fastened the sensor to his own chest and was about to engage the beam when he had his first doubt. It wasn't about the trip itself. That much he'd settled. For years he'd been obsessed with Woodstock. His uncle Charlie had stoked this passion with years of tales that had only gotten more detailed, and much dirtier, as Ricky had grown.

"Sure kid," his uncle had growled, "We were all there for peace. Down with Nukes, the whole thing. But don't let *anyone* tell you it wasn't about getting laid too. Smokin' grass and getting some trim. *That* was Woodstock." Ricky had been enthralled. He'd read everything he could get his hands on about the festival, talked to as many people as he could that had been there, watched the movie—he was ready.

His finger was on the button when he suddenly had the thought that would ruin his day.

It was a simple thought: *I can't go dressed like this.*

That, however, led him down a winding road of problems that he had to think about before he could even attempt to go back to 1969. Not only would he have to make sure he was dressed appropriately, he had to make sure that wherever he appeared, it wouldn't be overly crowded, so he had to go to the library and research the history of the real estate around Bethel, New York, to find an appropriate place to make the jump. Getting back wasn't a problem—the sensor crystal would act as a beacon to the time machine. It would either bring him back after a pre-set length of time, or he could activate it earlier. As of now, he hadn't built in any way to override the return beam and let a traveler stay longer.

The more he thought about the trip itself though, the

more problems seemed to crop up. He couldn't spend any money, as the dates would be all wrong; he'd have to try to find currency from the period. That was also a problem, as he wasn't sure that his clothing would make the trip. Because it was touching his skin, the sensor would be fine, but what else? It was all well and good to think about stealing what he needed, as *The Terminator* made it seem, but Ricky wasn't sneaky *or* confrontational.

How should he speak? Where should he go? Who was the president? As his set of notes got longer and longer, he finally decided that what he needed was a portable guidebook that he could bring with him, to give him all the information he would need about the time he was visiting, at the touch of a button. And where else did one turn these days for information but one's cell phone? With one final, loving caress, Ricky shut down the Time Jumper and sat down at his notebook. He began to program "The Time Jumpers Almanac".

When it was complete, he'd included the whole of *Wikipedia, the Encyclopedia Britannica*, and all the maps of North America he could find, going back as far as he could find. He coded page after page of dialects and idioms, customs, fashions, and—most importantly, what technology was available at any given time. These things would serve to help him blend in, and may even keep him alive, if it came to it. He didn't want to find himself arrested for treason just because he accidentally mentioned details of World War II in 1918 (not that *he* would, but he was convinced more and more that he was programming for the ages now).

That led to more questions. How accurate was the information he was putting in, anyway? Obviously Wikipedia had its limitations, but even "true" historical accounts were biased. How could he, in seeking to inform voyagers to the past, ensure that they would be prepared?

And that was when he knew what he had to do.

Ricky uploaded the applications in their present, half-finished state to his phone, uncovered the Time Jumper, and strapped the sensor to himself. There was only one way to tell what had really happened in the past, and that was to live it himself. He would write the most accurate account of history on record, because he would go there. It would be scary, and it would be dangerous—especially because he didn't have all the information he needed to blend in.

With his finger on the button to set his first destination, Ricky had to smile. What he was doing was also a stroke of genius. In writing the perfect traveler's companion to time travel, he was also going to become the undisputed master. There would be no refuting his results when he brought back photos and evidence from ages past.

He did a final check of his gear—the time sensor, the phone (with extra battery and solar charger). These were taped against his skin. It didn't make any sense to bring anything else with him, because he wasn't sure anything else would go. As it was, he'd made a new sleeve for his phone out of the same material as the sensor—just in case.

Keying in his first destination, Ricky pressed the button, and the green light came on.

TIME TRAVELER'S COMPANION (excerpt)
Year: 1969
Location: Bethel, New York
Major Event: Woodstock Music Festival

Culture Notes:
Dress
Casual – very casual. Blue jeans and a plain white or solid color shirt are okay. The longer your hair is, the better. If you have short hair, be sure to accessorize with beaded necklaces. Wear the clothes for a week without bathing before you go.
Idioms
Intersperse your sentences with the following idioms: "man," "you know what I'm saying?" "peace."
Helpful Preparation
Watch: Woodstock, (Dir. Michael Wadleigh)
Listen to: Get Together (Youngbloods), Are You Experienced (Hendrix)

Ricky's Notes

*When they say "do not take the brown acid." Do **NOT** take the brown acid. I was tripping so hard the time sensor thought I was in distress and sent the signal to jump me home.*

Bring your own birth control. It's way harder to find than you'd think, and you're going to want it. My uncle Charlie was right on this one. I haven't sorted out all the paradoxical ramifications of interacting with the past, but to be on the safe side, just assume that making babies in the past is a bad thing.

The message indicator on Ricky's phone was flashing, although he'd returned from 1969 within minutes of his departure—it was part of the machine's design, and meant to ensure the relative comfort and safety of the traveler. After all, Ricky reasoned, nobody wanted to come home to find that his apartment had been cleared out and someone else moved in while he was away. No—the reason his phone was flashing was that he'd gone immediately to the computer to start typing up his Woodstock notes.

He'd made sure to take lots of pictures, though he'd learned quickly to be extremely stealthy—the better to avoid awkward questions. As the party had gone on though, he'd gotten a little more reckless and ultimately, he'd wound up with the best shot of the bunch—himself on-stage with Crosby, Stills, Nash & Young. He'd convinced the roadie that took the shot that the device was a light meter for his film project. It was an insane thing to have done, but what the hell good was traveling in time if you couldn't have some *fun?*

Dialing up his answering service, Ricky heard his brother Joey's voice asking him where the hell he'd been. This couldn't have been about the Woodstock jump, he had to remind himself. Ricky had been out of touch with everyone since he'd gotten closer and closer to making time jumping a reality. He resigned himself to calling Joey back later and making dinner plans. It wouldn't do to get so caught up in the past that he forgot to live his own present life.

Then he started planning his next jump. On a whim, he punched in the Late Cretaceous period, entering it as "-65,000,000". He looked at Nico, winked, and hit the button.

TIME TRAVELER'S COMPANION (excerpt)
Year: -65,000,000
Location: New York (approx.)
Major Event: Late Cretaceous Period
Culture Notes
Dress:
Light. It's hot. If possible, stay close to areas of higher elevation to escape the increased humidity.
Idioms:
N/A

Helpful Preparation
Do Cardio. A lot of cardio. Scratch that, it needs to be more specific – running. Practice running as fast as you can.

Ricky's Notes
Okay, I had to look it up, because I hadn't even heard of a "Dryptosaurus" before I went back. Holy shit*. The thing is like a cross between a Velociraptor and a T-Rex, and it's covered in purple feathers. Picture a Great White Shark, after it's eaten a flock of parrots. Dryptosaurs look like that. That's about the point where I hit the sensor to come home.*
Long story shor—don't go looking for dinosaurs. Your time jumper will end up bringing home a pair of bloody feet with a sensor attached.

Also, I got bitten by a mosquito the size of my head. I put some peroxide on it. Hope it'll be okay.

Ricky's heart was still pounding when he materialized in his living room. He went to the kitchen of his apartment and poured a stiff glass of scotch. His arm was throbbing where the monster insect had jabbed him. First things first, he thought, and downed the drink. After that, he went into the bathroom and tended to his arm. Not wanting to take chances, he took a razor blade and cut the bite open. It hurt like hell, but the alternative of having eons-old monster saliva coursing through his veins wasn't an alternative at all. He poured hydrogen peroxide right into the incision, and it foamed immediately, creating a foul smelling yellow froth that dripped into the sink. Repeating the ministrations until the bubbles were clear, Ricky bound his arm up with some bandages and went to record his notes.

Unfortunately, there wasn't going to be much he could add to the stock books of knowledge. He'd managed one clear photo of a two legged meat-eating dinosaur before it had smelled something new and appetizing and come after him— so there was that much at least. The rest of his notes could be summed up in four words—*don't mess with dinosaurs*.

* * *

As the weeks rolled by, Ricky found his motivations changing. He was finding he was no longer concerned with making his entries as lengthy and accurate as possible. Instead, he confined his writings to "Ricky's Notes." *That* was the stuff they couldn't find out in the books and websites. Let other people do some of their own work on the periods before they went back—if, that was, anyone else ever got the chance to go back. He was having too much fun jumping to worry about completing the discovery process. The information app had become an excuse for him to keep putting off sharing his results with the scientific community at large. And if someone else figured out the problem in the meantime? If someone else learned the secrets of bending and jumping through time? That was fine too. They wouldn't have his "Ricky-pedia," and they wouldn't have his experience.

He jumped, and jumped, and jumped again.

TIME TRAVELER'S COMPANION (excerpt)
Year: 1692
Location: Salem, Mass.
Major Event: Witch trials

Ricky's Notes:
Be polite. Study the lingo. Under no circumstances should you ask ANYONE if they'd like to see you "pull a coin out of their ear."

TIME TRAVELER'S COMPANION (excerpt)
Year: 1969
Location: New York
Major Event: Moon Landing on TV
Ricky's Notes:
Be polite. Don't show your phone to anyone. Everyone's so keyed up about technology that if they even get a glimpse of it you'll be explaining yourself for days. The best thing to do in this situation is to try and get to a bathroom and jump home.

THE TIME TRAVELER'S COMPANION (excerpt)
Year: 3199
Location: New York
Major Event: ???
Ricky's Notes:
Oh my God. What have I done?
If I'd known when I started this – if anyone had known... oh God, how could we?

I'm so sorry.
Time travel is... it's a horrible idea.

Ricky finished the last entry, and re-read it twice. He smiled, but it was a bitter, lifeless thing. Why had he even bothered writing in the log, when nobody was going to read it anyway?

He went to the closet, returned with a baseball bat, and smashed the Time Jumper into nothingness.

Before that final jump, Ricky's biggest challenge had been keeping good notes, and staying alive long enough to record them. Now, all he had to worry about was living with what he'd seen, and what he'd done—what *others* had done with his machine. He took the pieces of the machine's processor and burned them in a garbage can outside.

Hopefully, it would be enough. Time, it seemed, would tell.

Is the Caller There?
by Jon Wesick

First Worldline November 2006

"Stretch yourself," the director had said. "Play against type."

Max Gerund had followed Italo Verlucci's advice and look where it had gotten him! He tore open a copy of *Variety* and read Ibor Zyzco's review.

> *Jungle Jim a Real Howler*
>
> *I dread each new film by Italo Verlucci, but this has to be his all-time worst. In this disaster of a movie Max Gerund plays Jim Smedley, a stuttering scientist at the Xerxes Primate Research Center. After a lab accident exposes him to radioactive chimpanzee blood, he develops super strength, the ability to climb anything, and an irrepressible appetite for sex with both genders.*

"That's bonobo blood, you moron," Max muttered and rested a hand on the bulge under his waistband. He skipped a few paragraphs.

Max Gerund delivered a passable if somewhat wooden performance as Captain Ulysses Reilly in the long-running TV series, Space Quest*. He's gained a lot of weight since the series ended. The thought of him as an action hero would be laughable, if it weren't so pathetic. If his performance in the gay love scenes is any indication of his future movie career, he'd better get used to doing late night, bail bond commercials. Although to be fair, no actor could prevent being turned into a monkey by Verlucci's ridiculous script.*

Max crumpled the magazine and tossed it at the trashcan. A nice lunch at Cipriano's would take his mind off his troubles, but he had to lose the sixty pounds he'd gained for that awful movie. He should have known better than to trust a director who'd made his name by showing Kimbery Hu's privates in a slasher flick. Max lifted the garbage bag out of the trashcan, sealed it with a twist tie, and carried it outside. The empty bottles of Space Quest Ginseng Cola inside rattled as he dragged it down the driveway and deposited it on the curb next to his tilting mailbox. He consumed a lot of the stuff after he quit drinking. Good thing he got it free with his endorsement.

"Good morning." His neighbor Purvis Henson set down his hedge shears, waved, and adjusted the ear buds from his Ipod. He wore a red, USS Midway baseball cap and appeared to be in his sixties.

Purvis and his wife Mabel were the salt of the earth. Max couldn't say the same for his other neighbors, who only seemed to come out at night in a limousine with blackened windows and an *I'm-for-DeMolay* sticker on the rear bumper. Max looked at his strange neighbors' mailbox. De Saint-Marie. What kind of name was that? Probably related to DeMolay. As far back as Max could remember, the couple had never placed any garbage on the curb. He went back inside.

Time for some damage control! He turned on the radio and turned to the public station. It was time for *Film Talk*. The show was already in progress. Max had taken the cordless phone out of the cradle and dialed when he heard the announcement on the radio.

"Today's show is a repeat broadcast from April 2004. Please do not call in."

He was about to hang up when someone answered.

"Is the caller there? You're on *Film Talk*," the announcer said over the phone. His voice echoed over the radio a few seconds later.

"Hello?" Max paused.

"You're on *Film Talk*. Turn off your radio."

Max turned down the volume. There must have been some mistake with the announcement. "Yes, this is Max Gerund. I'd like to say a few words about Italo Verlucci."

"Welcome aboard, Captain Reilly." The announcer mimicked the Eastern European accent of the Starship Garamendi's second in command.

"At ease, Mr. Blini." Max carried the cordless phone to the picture window. He craned his neck to look between the mansions for a view of the Malibu coastline. Even though it had been two years, he slipped easily into the role of the starship commander.

"It's a real honor to have you on today's show, Max," the announcer said. "You wanted to talk about Verlucci's movies?"

"That's right. I just want to say that you shouldn't blame the actor when one of Verlucci's movies goes belly up. He's the biggest moron in Hollywood and basically wouldn't have his job if he hadn't granted sexual favors to a certain studio head."

"Wow! That's tough criticism, but that's the kind of straight shooting we like here on *Film Talk*. Say Max, you mind if I ask you a question?"

"Go right ahead."

"With only two shows left before the Space Quest finale, things look bleak for the Confederation. The Lizard Men of Gorlon lured the Terran armada into the Alpha sector leaving Earth defenseless against the Tremulon death star.

How will Captain Reilly escape the narcotic clutches of the Corwellian witch Izmeldadon in time to save the day?"

Max looked at the blue LED numbers on the radio's face. Was this some kind of joke? The series had ended over two years earlier. Better choose a safe response.

"Well, you'll have to watch the episode and see."

"Max Gerund, ladies and gentlemen. He's a real stickler for Space Fleet security. Duty, fidelity, and honor, Captain."

"Duty, fidelity, and honor." Max held his right fist over his heart and pressed the disconnect button on the phone.

Second Worldline November 2006

"Mr. Gerund, this is Sylvia at the realtor's office. A nice couple from Nebraska's interested in your home. Would it be okay to show it in an hour?"

"All right." Max hung up.

A little more notice would have been good, but with his pending bankruptcy he couldn't be picky. If only his weird neighbors wouldn't chase the potential buyers away by playing their industrial, theremin music! Max's transition from TV to movies hadn't gone as well as planned. In the two years since Space Quest ended, he'd only had one cameo appearance.

Max went to the wet bar and mixed himself a Screaming Orgasm. It was only 11:00 AM, but he'd been under a lot of stress lately and could use a little something to help him relax. He turned on the radio and sat in front of the big picture window. He'd better enjoy the view while he still could. The morning's episode of *Film Talk* was a repeat. He was about to turn the radio off when he heard a familiar voice, his voice. The charlatan was ridiculing Italo Verlucci. Why hadn't anyone told him about this? No wonder Max's film career had been stillborn! The director must have heard the show two years earlier.

The impersonator was convincing. Max would give him that. How convincing would he be in a lawsuit? Max needed to call his lawyer but first he'd give the radio station a piece of his mind. He didn't have the number, but they'd probably transfer him from the call-in number. He picked up the phone and dialed.

"You're on *Film Talk*," the announcer said over the phone. His voice echoed over the radio a few seconds later.

"Hello?" Max paused. What the hell was going on? The show was taped two years earlier.

"Turn off your radio."

Max turned the radio off. "This is the real Max Gerund. The earlier caller is a fake. I have nothing but respect for Italo Verlucci. If you continue perpetrating this hoax, I'll see you in court!" Max stabbed the phone's disconnect button with his index finger.

Third Worldline April 2004

Max Gerund was already half an hour late. He parked his Corvette, set the brake, and rushed into the studio. His pulse pounded his temples like a jackhammer. He swore he'd never drink Screaming Orgasms again. Two men in a zebra suit waited by the door. Extras dressed as blue-skinned Theradons and finned Sharkmen from Sigma Eridani V loitered in the hallway. Max ducked into his dressing room, washed down a handful of Ibuprofen, and changed into his gold Space Command jumpsuit. There was only one free chair in the makeup room and Max took it.

"How are you today, Mr. Zorax?" he asked the woman in a furry costume to his left.

"How the hell do you think I am getting up at 4:00 AM to put on this freaking gorilla suit?" Penelope Austin, his sweating costar, asked.

A makeup artist placed a tissue around Max's collar and began brushing powder on his face. The procedure took less than a half-hour, a benefit of being a humanoid. When the makeup artist was done, Max paused to admire himself in the lighted mirror before heading into the hall. That's right. They were shooting the love scene with Izmeldadon, today. Max pictured the busty brunette who played the Corwellian witch and popped a breath mint. Ah, the perks of being a starship captain! Before he could get to the set, a blonde woman ambushed him with a microphone in front of a TV camera. He'd completely forgotten about the *Entertainment This Month* interview.

"I'm speaking with Max Gerund on the set of *Space Quest*." She pointed a microphone at Max's face. "Max, will you have something exciting for your viewers in the final episodes?"

"Well." Max squinted in the bright lights. God, his hangover was killing him. "With the writing team of Dick Slaughter and Evan White you can expect a dynamite conclusion."

"Some critics have charged that *Space Quest* is nothing but a low-budget copy of *Star Trek*. How do you respond?" The reporter pointed her microphone at Max's face.

"We're character driven." Max projected his thoughtful expression, the one he used when Captain Reilly mused on the moral lesson learned after an hour of interstellar sex and violence. "Don't get me wrong. *Star Trek* was a great show for its time, but with an all-alien crew *Space Quest* focused on how beings from other cultures get along and ultimately triumph."

"Do you think your comments yesterday on *Film Talk* will affect the chances of there being a *Space Quest* movie?"

"Comments? I didn't make any comments."

* * *

A phone call to the radio station led to a phone call to Stephanie Kim, a private detective who'd helped Max beat a false paternity claim. They met a week later in her office in Korea Town. The walls of the small conference room were bare except for a travel poster with a man and woman in traditional Korean dress.

"Thanks for coming over." Stephanie motioned Max to a seat. Her girlish looks had caused several adversaries to underestimate her at their peril. "Would you like some barley tea?"

"No thanks." Max hated the stuff. He sat at the table where a computer with a microphone had been set up. "What's this for?"

"We'll get to that in a minute." Stephanie sat beside him. "The radio station gave me a tape of the show. Unfortunately, they don't keep caller-ID records." She used the mouse to start a program. "Would you read the phrases on the screen, please?"

"This is Max Gerund. This is the real Max Gerund. Italo Verlucci. I'll see you in court." While Max read a series of squiggles appeared on the monitor.

Stephanie used the mouse to drag these over some saved waveforms. They were identical.

"This software says your voice is identical to the one that made the calls." She swiveled her chair to face him.

"That can't be," Max said. "There must be some kind of mistake."

"Only if you have an identical twin."

"I swear to you, Stephanie. I didn't make those calls."

"It's not my job to check up on you, Max. But if I were you, I wouldn't take this to court."

Third Worldline November 2006

"How dare that critic! Max crumpled the offending issue of *Variety* and tossed it at the trashcan. It bounced off the rim and onto the floor. Time for some damage control! He called the radio station and got the assistant.

"This is *Film Talk*. What's your name and where are you from?"

"Max Gerund from Malibu."

"Please make sure your radio's off and hold until we put you on the air." The assistant switched to a live feed of the radio show. A familiar voice was talking, Max's voice. It was a recording of the show with the impersonators from two years earlier.

"Next we seem to have yet another Max Gerund on the line," the announcer said. "Hello, you're on *Film Talk*."

Max put his hand over the speaker. It was just like *Space Quest* episode thirty-six, when the Time Lords of Nehru opened a portal into the past. He had to be very careful not to set up a causal loop.

"Is the caller there?"

Max pushed the disconnect button on the phone. A man with a lesser ego would have doubted his sanity, but his years of playing Captain Reilly gave Max the confidence to believe in his own conceits even when they conflicted with the entire body of scientific knowledge. What could be causing this gateway into the past via the radio? The Time Lords in episode thirty-six had harnessed the tremendous energy of black holes to create wormholes through spacetime, but other episodes of *Space Quest* had dealt with time travel, too. For instance, in episode forty-three a poorly shielded tachyon beam sent Captain Reilly back to Nazi-occupied Poland. Maybe someone nearby was sending faster-than-light communications, possibly with an entangled quantum state device. But who? Max had a pretty good idea. He picked up the phone and began making calls.

* * *

If Max were actually a starship captain, he would have teleported an away team directly into his strange neighbors' living room. As a B-list actor he had to settle for standing on the Saint-Maries' front porch and ringing the doorbell. Despite the fact that his Space Command jumpsuit now bulged at the middle, saving Earth from an alien invasion would be the crowning achievement of his show-business career.

"So why did you drag me away from my tennis lesson to get dressed up in this stupid costume once again?" asked Penelope Austin who scratched under the collar of her moth-eaten Mr. Zorax outfit.

"Yeah," seconded Dale Hunter whose makeup gave the illusion that he was covered in red, chitinous plates.

"Audition for a *Space Quest* movie," Max said. "The producers are pretty eccentric, so just follow my lead."

"*Allo.*" A thin woman with a face as pale as copying paper answered the door. Her black, stretch slacks and long-sleeved turtleneck covered everything but her face and hands.

"I'm Captain Ulysses Reilly of the Starship Garamendi and this is my away team, Mr. Zorax and Mr. Blini. May we come in?"

"If you wish." The woman stepped aside.

Max noted her European accent, possibly French. The away team followed her into a cavernous living room, their zip-up boots echoing on the hardwood floor. Cloths covered all the furniture as if it were in storage. A man with a shock of white hair emerged from the back room. Like the woman, he was pale and dressed entirely in black.

"Étienne, this is Captain Reilly of the Starship Garamendi," she said.

"Ah, Captain, at last we meet." Étienne did not offer to shake hands, preferring to keep his arms crossed over his chest. His European accent carried a whiff of condescension.

"I'll be brief." Max assumed the ramrod-straight posture of command. "We detected stray tachyon emissions from orbit and traced their source to this location. I don't need to remind you that the Krylon Protocol forbids meddling with class-one civilizations, such as Earth's, and authorizes the use of force to stop such interference. You will cease and desist your activities immediately, sir! Mr. Blini, what is Garamendi's weapons' status?"

Dale pushed a few buttons on his digital watch. "Photon beams online and a full load of antimatter torpedoes, sir!"

"Well, we wouldn't want to cause an intergalactic incident," Étienne said. "Would you care for an absinthe?"

"Regretfully, no. I must get back to the bridge. Mr. Zorax, Mr. Blini, this way!" Max led his away team out the door.

After they were gone Étienne's wife asked, "What do you suppose that was all about?"

* * *

In the house opposite Max's, Mabel and Purvis Henson huddled over an alien keyboard and typed a message into the quantum communication device.

> *Lord Ligator Maximus of Kargon*
>> *Your humble servants Laetril and Osimax wish*

to report their completion of advance reconnaissance of Sol's third planet commonly referred to as Earth. We conclude that our glorious invasion fleet will meet little resistance from the Confederation, as the Starship Garamendi appears to have been "cancelled" due to poor "ratings." Its captain, Ulysses Reilly, has been inactive for two planetary orbits. We're pleased to report the way is clear for the subjugation of humanity. All hail the Baloryx

Application of the Novikov Self-Consistency Conjecture to the Daily Commute of One David Jensen
by Lauren A. Forry

He would've preferred crawling.

Crawling. Inching. Scooting.

Yet the only movement which existed was that of fellow commuters giving in and switching off their engines.

Not David.

No, David Jensen had traveled I-78 every day for a good year and a half with no major problems, and David Jensen was absolutely certain traffic would move again as long as he kept his Civic running. David was also aware that the salary he earned as a Junior Ad Sales Exec barely supported the area's $4.05 per gallon price tag and that his daily commute now cost $48.62 per day. The sobering realization that he spent $243.10 a week on fuel made him finally turn off his car like everyone else.

Without air conditioning, the lack of a breeze coupled with a black vinyl interior transformed his pleasant Honda into a small pocket of hell. The hairs on his arms and legs collected the sweat forming underneath his brown, polyester suit. The beads on his forehead glued his carefully combed bangs to his skin, revealing the true depth of his prematurely receding hairline. A sorry specimen, David Jensen could no longer look at himself. He flipped up the mirrored visor and removed his jacket, exchanging minor heat relief for the smell of his armpits.

Something to drink would have improved his situation. In his cup holder sat the stained paper cup containing remnants of lukewarm Wawa coffee, the preponderance of which had surged onto his pants when that asshole Range Rover cut him off. The heat lifted a rancid smell from the cup, turning his stomach and making dehydration the preferred option.

Concluding that his actions had absolutely no impact on when the highway would clear, David opened his door and joined the masses outside who lingered in the tight spaces between cars. Some commuters stood on their hoods or roofs, desperate for a glimpse of the assumed carnage, Googling for news bulletins on their phones. Others climbed up the grassy knolls on either side of the two-lane highway to take pictures with their iPhones or record the bumper to bumper cars for a YouTube upload. David stood by his little black car and hoped traffic would start moving before the sweat stains on his dress shirt became permanent, and passed the time by watching grainy TEDTalks on his four-year-old Blackberry Storm. Discussion of wormhole theory kept him well occupied until the phone battery died in the middle of the lecture. David shook the phone. This, of course, did nothing. What could have helped was if he'd remembered to charge it. That simple thing he hadn't remembered, but everything else from last night he couldn't forget. He tossed the phone onto the driver's seat. Something bumped his foot.

A dented, plastic water bottle lay on the pavement, dripping in its own deliciously cold sweat.

David scanned the area—the people on the sloping roadside, the idiots standing on their cars. He even braved a glance at the lone cross-country trucker leaning outside his cab, hocking a fat loogie onto the steaming pavement. Using deductive reasoning acquired from watching too many crime shows, David concluded that since no one else was claiming this beautiful, glistening bottle of ice cold water on the summer's hottest day so far, it was his.

Free water.

This was the most excitement he'd felt since that night five years ago when he, Mike, and Lee decided to see who could throw an empty beer can into the next door parking garage.

Cool condensation seeped into his palm, snaking down his arm as he flipped up the cap and pressed the spout to his chapped lips. One drop reached his mouth and seared his tongue, choking him. David retched, coughed, flipped up the mirrored visor then paused.

He looked to his right then to his left then behind him.

He was in his car. His suit jacket was on. Yet, he clearly remembered removing said jacket and stepping out of said car. Perhaps that was another day, another traffic jam. But David had traveled this route for a year and a half with no major incidents.

David Jensen decided he drank too much last night.

He joined the masses outside and found the TEDTalk Lee recommended. As the professor mentioned relativistic time dilation, the phone died. David shook it then tossed it onto the driver's seat as a bottle bumped into his foot.

David decided today was going to be a very odd day.

Since no one, not even the spit-happy trucker, was rushing to claim the glorious, ice cold bottle, David took it, flipped open the cap, took a long sip... and switched off the engine. Without air conditioning, the lack of a breeze coupled with the black vinyl interior transformed the pleasant Honda into a small pocket of... what the hell was going on?

How was he back in the car and where did the bottle come from? David Jensen never bought bottled water. At the gas station, he chose only the cup of stale coffee, the majority of which was now all over his pants.

Lee.

Lee could've left it in the car last night. Lee was

always leaving things in the car—socks, CDs, his daughter—and yesterday, David did drive him home after he got wasted and a phone call to Monica resulted in a screaming match where she said she wasn't loading the baby in the car at 12:30am just to pick up the poor girl's drunken-ass father.

Lee was in the car. The bottle must have been his.

David raised the water to his lips. A whole mouthful went in, a whole mouthful went down... and Sarah's coffee smelled delicious—a hint of almonds, like cyanide.

"Do you want me to get anything for dinner?" David asked, as she poured herself a cup. Her short, blonde hair bobbed stiffly as she turned. He remembered when it used to swish—long, supple strands that slid through his fingers.

"What's wrong with leftovers?" she replied, voice as clipped as her hair. He watched as she sipped from her mug and knew that they'd had this conversation before.

"Nothing. Whatever we've got is fine," he said and went into the bathroom, setting the bottle on the counter.

Yes, they'd had this conversation several times before. Why Sarah obsessed so much over leftovers he couldn't remember, but this particular conversation, on this particular Thursday, had happened before.

Hadn't it?

When he emerged from the bathroom, Sarah was gone. There was coffee left in the pot, but as he searched the cabinets the only clean travel mug he could find was the photo-mug he gave her on their second anniversary. The picture collage of them at Hershey Park, with their faces covered in chocolate and happiness, was stuffed in the back of the cupboard, a thin layer of dust coating their frozen smiles. David decided to forego Sarah's coffee and instead get a cup when he stopped for gas, but then he started feeling nauseous. Maybe Sarah brought that stomach virus home from the hospital. He shouldn't go to work if he was sick.

He changed into his sweats, lay on the couch with his brother's hand-me-down iPad, and watched the TEDTalk Lee recommended. As the professor droned on about the twin paradox, David reached for his water bottle. He flipped back the cap, took a hefty swig... and dodged the book Sarah chucked at his head.

"This is you being home at eleven?" she said. "It's one in the goddamn morning!" Her fingers clutched the hips of her Mickey Mouse pajamas. David stared, disgusted that a woman in her early thirties would wear Mickey Mouse pajamas. It was like sleeping next to a child. He set the bottle on the counter.

"I had to drive Lee home," he said.

"Oh, so you had to wait until Lee got completely off his face and then offer to drive him, instead of leaving early and letting someone else scrape him off the bar?"

"I was being nice," he said.

"Well, you are a nice guy, David, aren't you? How is it you're nice to everyone but me?" Once the tears started, she disappeared into the bedroom.

David stared at the imprint her slippered feet left on the carpet. Usually when they had this argument, he had no idea what she was crying about. This time he noticed the book she threw was the first edition HG Wells he'd bought for her birthday and that there was a half-empty cup of coffee on the living room table, even though she never had caffeine after six. He noticed how she wasn't being sarcastic when she called him a "nice guy."

David removed his coat, draped it over the kitchen table, and grabbed the water bottle. It was three-quarters full, but he knew tomorrow would be hot and took it to the sink for a refill. Their argument had left his mouth dry, though, and he couldn't resist a drink. Just a small sip. He flipped open the cap and downed a good third of it... while Lee stood to the side, egging him on.

"Aw, c'mon, you pussy." Lee smacked him on the back. "My grandma drinks faster."

"Then why don't you call her," David said.

Lee laughed, his face turning red from the effort. The bar was almost empty now, the lights bright to encourage stragglers to leave. The barman had already shut off the juke box. If Monica refused to pick up her husband, and David already knew she would, he'd have to take Lee home.

Lee wasn't even his friend, he was Mike's, but since David was Mike's friend, too, they often ended up hanging out together. But Mike moved to New York and David hadn't seen him in three years. According to Facebook, he'd just married some girl David had never heard of.

After Lee fell off his barstool, David forced his BlackBerry into Lee's hands and made him call his wife.

"Screw you, Monica! One thing. I ask you to do one damn thing and you... Don't bring Ally into this! Monica! Monica, I'm sorry. Don't hang up, baby, please. I'll be good, just... Bitch." He dropped the phone. "Hey Dave, hey bro, can I get a ride?"

"Sure. I've just gotta..." David nodded to the restroom. "You know."

"Yeah, yeah. Sure thing, man. No prob. Always the same shit with her, you know?" Lee grabbed David's beer and downed the last inch.

"Same shit," David repeated. "Yeah, I get that a lot. Lately." He took his water bottle and crossed to the men's room. The slick bottle slipped from his hand and dropped to the floor, bursting open at the cap. David scrambled for it, scooping it off the floor and closing the top before any more damage could be done... while Sarah leaned over the counter, laughing.

"If you need any help, Emeril, let me know," she said as David wiped the spilt coriander off the floor.

"I was going for more of a Naked Chef, thing," he smiled, his hands covered in herbs.

"Think you have too many clothes on for that." She tied back her long hair.

"Well, that's easy to fix."

"Nope. You're supposed to be cooking us dinner, and I don't want any unsavory ingredients in my chicken, thank you very much."

"Guess I should dump this, then?" He nodded to the dirtied coriander.

"Please do. I'm going to finish unpacking the

bedroom. Want me to leave your suitcase in the closet, or do you need me to unpack your clothes for you?"

"I think I can handle that, thanks. I'll call you when this is ready." He nodded to the pan.

"If it's ever ready," she shouted back as she walked away. David stared at the two raw chicken breasts in the pan.

He knew the apartment was too far from his new job, but it was close enough for Sarah to bike to hers and that was important to her—to them. It was a nice apartment. Two bedrooms. One and a half bath. Decent kitchen. It was just the sort of upgrade she was looking for—*they* were looking for. Already he loved it. Loved her. The commute wouldn't be so bad. His office was straight across I-78 in New Jersey. Only a two hour commute. Each way. Every day. Five days a week. The traffic would be fine during morning rush hour. The long days wouldn't strain their relationship.

He flipped the chicken over thinking how it was a shame the offer from TD Bank came too late. It would've been a better job, a fifteen minute commute. He dumped the vegetables in the pot and kept the water at a boil, remembering he needed to call Mike with his new address. He adjusted his laptop so he could better see the crappy YouTube rip of a BBC Stephen Hawking biopic. The video kept freezing and buffering as cooking oil threatened to leap onto his keyboard. David sighed. There should be a better way to watch stuff like this, he thought, something easier to carry, with a touchscreen, about the size of a notepad.

The image froze as an increasingly disabled Hawking proved the Steady State theory wrong. David stared at the image then rewound the video. It played for a moment then stopped. David rewound it further. It played then stopped, waiting for him to reverse it again. The chicken started to burn. The smoke detector sounded.

Beep. Beep. Beep.

"David?" Sarah called.

Beep. Beep. Beep.

"Did you set the place on fire already?"

Beep. Beep. Beep.

"Are going to get that? Open a window!"

Beep. Beep. Beep.

David grabbed the water bottle, flipped back the cap, and chugged. He drank as fast as he could, letting it burn his mouth, his tongue, his throat, not stopping until... the pretty blonde girl with the long hair set a glass of milk on his tray.

"They meant it when they said the chili was spicy," she said, sitting across from him. David, eyes watering, reached for the glass.

"I didn't see the sign," he gasped.

"I can tell from the way you scarfed it down. Better drink up if you ever want to use that tongue again."

David swallowed the cold, blessed milk as she pulled Tupperware from her messenger bag and filled it with food from her tray.

"What are you doing?" he asked, wiping a dribble from his chin.

"Dining hall food may not be the greatest, but at least it's free. And all you can eat." She scraped some brown rice off her plate. "I'm going to get my money's worth from this place. Plus, I love leftovers. There's just, I don't know, something homey about them." She clamped the lid down tight. "What're you reading?" She nodded to the magazine at his elbow—an old copy of Scientific American open to an article on the latest chronology protection conjecture. But it wasn't old. It was this month's issue.

"Nothing. I'm David." He held out his hand.

"Sarah."

He forgot how smooth her skin could be.

"You know, milk's much better for spicy burns." She pointed to his empty bottle. "Water just makes it worse."

"Not always," he smiled. Usually he was so nervous around girls, but he and Sarah left the dining hall together and sat at the café for hours drinking coffee, David talking about his business classes, Sarah worrying about switching into the nursing program. David told her she would make a great nurse and that for no reason whatsoever should she remain in accountancy. They left hours later and went to her room to double-check David's tongue was indeed in proper working order.

From then on, David never had to worry about disappointing Sarah or saying the wrong thing or behaving the wrong way. He never had to worry whether he would pass his economics class or if he'd land that job with TD Bank. He never had to worry about driving on I-78, either, but his boss explained how important this client was and how much he needed David to sort out the problem.

It was hot, one of the worst days in all of July. He found a battered water bottle in the back of the fridge, behind the Hershey Park photo-mug which held Sarah's iced coffee. The Range Rover's air conditioning broke the night before, so he drove with the windows down. Between the wind and NPR on the radio, it was difficult to hear Mike's call.

"What?" he shouted into his iPhone. "Mike, speak up. I can't hear you... I'm driving... Driving!" He checked his mirrors then came alongside a slow moving Honda Civic. The car looked familiar, but the driver was utterly unrecognizable with his unfashionable brown suit and prematurely receding hairline. David sped past, then cut over to bypass a tractor trailer lumbering in the passing lane. The Civic honked. The driver spilled coffee all over his pants. David didn't see it, but he knew.

"Yeah, seven... Seven! Sarah and I will meet you there." He tossed the phone onto the passenger's seat and turned NPR up. The wind howled through the windows. An astrophysicist was speaking about closed timelike curve and the Novikov self-consistency conjecture—the impossibility of paradoxes. David flipped on his turn signal and shifted into the left lane, misjudging the distance between cars. He caught the front bumper of a large Ford Escort and lost control of the Range Rover.

Tires screeched. The smell of burnt rubber filled the car as the Rover spun to the left, blocking both lanes. A pick-up hit David's door and the force flipped the Rover onto its side. His car skidded across the pavement and slowed to a stop.

David remained very still.

His water bottle landed in the small space between the passenger's seat and the cup holder. Blood trickled down the side of his head as his fingers grazed the side of the plastic bottle. David could reach the bottle easily, but he couldn't move his arm...

Uninjured commuters raced to his side, telling him the ambulance was on its way.

...or his hand...

Everything was going to be all right.

...or his legs.

Tires screeched and the smell of burnt rubber enveloped him as an ambulance pulled up beside the accident. The medics assessed his injuries and began stabilizing him, causing the water bottle to fall from the car and roll away somewhere down the highway—still full, still cold. David lost consciousness.

From then on, David never had to worry about disappointing Sarah or saying the wrong thing or behaving the wrong way because she felt sorry for him. She would do whatever he asked, fetch him whatever he wanted, smile when he knew she'd rather cry.

He measured time in reruns of Maury. The unpleasant hospital room served as his personal black hole, all hopes for a future collapsing in on themselves as physiotherapy failed and his body remained frozen. His mind drifted towards its own dark singularity, where any desires he may have held were torn apart by the infinite depression expanding within his soul.

The day they transferred him to a permanent care home, Sarah wrapped him in a jacket and checked to make sure his catheter was still in place. Then she, too, vanished. A nameless nurse wheeled him to a nondescript ambulance. As David was hoisted above the ground, he watched people staring, but was unable to shout for them to stop or even turn his head in shame. So, he closed his eyes and fell into the darkness.

He would've preferred crawling.

Author Biographies

<u>Author Biographies:</u>

<u>Chris Allinotte</u>

Chris Allinotte lives in Winnipeg with his wife and two sons.

In 2008, his story *The Dirt on Ronnie Wilkins* won first place in the Toronto Star Short Story Contest.

Chris is the author of the short story collection *Gathering Darkness,* and the creator and editor of the *Eight Days of Madness,* and *Nine Days of Madness* anthologies. He is currently working on his first novel.

<u>Diane Arrelle</u>

Diane Arrelle, the pen name of South Jersey writer Dina Leacock, has been writing for more than 20 years, has sold over 150 short stories, and has had two books published, *Just A Drop In The Cup*, a collection of short-short stories and *Elements Of The Short Story, How to Write a Selling Story*. She was one of the founding members as well as the second president of the Garden State Horror Writers and is also a past president of the Philadelphia Writers' Conference. When not writing, she is a director of a municipal senior citizen center. She is married with one son in college in England, and she lives with her other son, her husband and her cat at home on the edge of the Pine Barrens in Southern New Jersey (home of the Jersey Devil). You can visit her at dinaleacock.com

Barbara Austin

Barbara Austin writes suspense novels and short stories. She grew up in Houston and studied at The University of Texas, but has spent most of her adult life in The Netherlands and the UK. She is a long-time member of two fiction critique groups in Amsterdam. A recent story was published in The Amsterdam Quarterly. She's looking for an agent for her suspense novel The Wool Comber's House and is working on a new novel.

(Foto: Adrienne Korzilius)

Carolyn M. Chang

Carolyn is passionate about writing science fiction and fantasy stories and helping fellow aspiring writers (www.stuckonmystory.com). She has had a story written in collaboration with Leslie Lee published in Aurora Wolf Literary Journal's Novus Creatura: An Anthology of Never-Before Seen Monstrosities. She lives in Amsterdam, Netherlands with her husband and two children where she also leads a local SF&F writing group.

Shawn Cook

Shawn Cook lives in Martinsville, Indiana, with his wife and children. His short stories have appeared in several anthologies, including Pill Hill Press' *Patented DNA & Haunted*. He's still new to this, so cut him a break.

Arthur M. Doweyko

As a scientist, Arthur has authored 100+ publications, and shares the 2008 Thomas Alva Edison Patent Award for the discovery of Sprycel, a new anti-cancer drug. He writes hard science fiction, fantasy, and horror. His unpublished novel, *Algorithm*, which is a story about DNA and the purpose of humanity, garnered a 2010 Royal Palm Literary Award (RPLA) and is represented by the Literary Counsel Agency, NY. He has published a number of short stories, many of which were finalists in the 2011-2012 RPLA competitions. P'sall Senji was awarded an Honorable Mention in the L. Ron Hubbard Writers of the Future Contest (2012).

Harry and Harry garnered first place in the 2012 Preditors and Editors Readers Poll for SF/F short stories.

He is currently working on a new novel, *Angela's Apple*, wherein a guardian angel that is not an angel falls in love with a human, and together they uncover the greatest conspiracy ever to face mankind.

He lives in Florida with his wife Lidia, happily wandering the beaches when not jousting with aliens.

www.ArthurMDoweyko.com

Lauren A. Forry

Lauren A. Forry is a sci-fi and horror writer originally from Bucks County, PA. She holds an MA/MFA in Creative Writing from Kingston University, London and a BA from New York University. She is currently writing a series of historical horror novels which explore the sociological changes in the UK over the past half century. The first, 'Mr. Brownawell's Collection', was awarded Kingston University's Faber and Faber Creative Writing MA prize.

Steven Gepp

Steven Gepp is an Australian who is married with two children, has two university degrees, and a résumé that looks like a list of every job you could ever have without really trying, including stints as a performance acrobat and professional wrestler. He has been writing for 25 years with a list of short stories in more than 20 anthologies. He also has a novella *Relick* available. Further, he writes for insidepulse.com. A dull life.

A. C. Hall

A.C. Hall lives in Fort Worth, Texas, and spends almost all of his time writing. He's the News Director of a local newspaper by day, and a creative writer by night, with several novels available for purchase. You can find his books by searching amazon.com or by searching for him on goodreads.com. On the rare occasion he isn't writing, A.C. likes to hang out with his nephews, watch television, read, and listen to music.

James Hartley

James Hartley is a former computer programmer. Originally from northern New Jersey, he now lives in sunny central Florida. He has published five fantasy novels, "The Ghost of Grover's Ridge," "Magic Is Faster Than Light," "Teen Angel," "Cop with a Wand," and "Magic to the Rescue," and has two more, "This Wand for Hire" and "Fortunatus" due out soon. He has had short stories published as e-books, the collections "Five from the Future" and "Worlds Away and Worlds Aweird," in anthologies, and in various e-zines and print magazines. He is currently working on a new novel, "Magic versus the Empire." He is a member of IWOFA and the Dark Fiction Guild. His website is http://teenangel.netfirms.com.

Martin T. Ingham

Martin T. Ingham is the author of various Science Fiction & Fantasy works, including *West of the Warlock*, *The Guns of Mars*, and *The Rogue Investigations*.

When he isn't writing, Martin likes to dabble in numismatics, horology, and antique auto restoration, among other hobbies. He currently resides in his hometown of Robbinston, Maine, with his wife, Jenna, and their four children, Sylvia, Wyatt, Kathryn, and Lois.

Learn more about Martin's works at his website:
http://www.martiningham.com

Paul Lamb

Paul Lamb lives in Kansas City but sneaks off to his little cabin in the Ozarks whenever he can. His stories have appeared in BartlebySnopes, Danse Macabre, Little Patuxent Review, Crossed Genres, Midwest Literary Magazine, Platte Valley Review, and others. He rarely strays far from his laptop.

Tony Laplume

Tony Laplume is the author of *The Cloak of Shrouded Men* and the short story collection *Monorama*. He earned a Bachelor's Degree in English from the University of Maine in 2003, and has worked on student papers the *Academic Advocate* and *Maine Campus*, literary journals

Hemlock and *Dead Letter Quarterly*, and written for websites *Paperback Reader*, *Lower Decks*, and *Examiner*. He's previously had a short story published in the anthology *Villainy*. He lives in Colorado Springs. You can write him at bandido@gmail.com.

Bruno Lombardi

Bruno Lombardi was born in Montreal in 1968. He has had a rather distressing tendency to be a weirdness magnet for much of his adult life. If your friend's cousin's brother-in-law tells you a story and swears it's true and that it 'happened to someone he knows,' it was probably Bruno.

His hobbies include attempting to dissuade the cults that form around him, managing the betting pool on the next Weird Thing, and being a slave to his two cats, Mynx and Sphinx. He currently lives in Ottawa and works as a civil servant for the Canadian government. Rumours that he secretly runs the Canadian government from his nuclear bunker with an android called 'Stephen Harper' as a front have never been substantiated and *are* merely rumours. Honestly.

He has also met lots of people off the internet and has yet to be murdered by any of them. His cats, on the other hand, have other ideas.

Bruno recently had a novel, *"Snake Oil,"* published by Daverana Enterprises. Ask for it by name.

Robert MacAnthony

Robert MacAnthony is an editor and Intellectual Property Attorney. Despite his affiliation with the legal profession, claims that he was not born but rather spawned during a primeval ceremony to Nyarlathotep remain unproven. He enjoys reading, writing, playing basketball, and RPGs (tabletop and computer). Favorite authors include Mervyn Peake, Guy Gavriel Kay, and H. P. Lovecraft.

His short story, *Temsy*, won first place during Martin T. Ingham's Exceptional Summer Shootout writing contest in 2012.

Karl G. Rich

"I was born and raised in Florida. At the age of twenty I moved to Traverse City, Michigan to attend the Great Lakes Maritime Academy. As a lifelong sailor, I envisioned working as a pilot and later, a ship's captain on the freighters that work our inland waterways. Is there anyone around that remembers the recession of the late 70's? At least half of the fleet had been mothballed by then—dream dashed. Fast forward thirty+ years, five granddaughters and a successful, rural Ohio, business later, and I have been writing about Great Lakes sailing lore for six years. My first writing was as rough as a barnacle-laden hull of a salty, just ask Edmund Wells (a good friend and co-contributor to The Temporal Element). I sharpen my teeth and humor on short stories while I polish and revise my first book, *The Mad King of Beaver Island*."

Jeffery Scott Sims

Jeffery Scott Sims is an author devoted to fantastic literature, living in Arizona, which forms the background for many of his tales. His recent publications include a novel, *The Journey of Jacob Bleek*, and the short stories *"A Critique of Vorchek's _Holobiologia," "The Witch's Cave," "A Little Peril In Brisbett," "In the Box," "In a Tight Place,"* and *"The Wheel of Dargalon."*

Edmund Wells

Edmund Wells was born on a damp Thursday on the Isle of Wight, England. He spent his formative years locked in a wine cellar arguing with crusty Irish philosophers. Using only his wits and a sharpened potato, he escaped by ferry to America, where he was captured by actuaries and forced to work in insurance.

During his rare moments of freedom, Edmund enjoys writing science fiction and fantasy, imitating Belgians, and the occasional philosophical limerick. He maintains a shrine to Monty Python in his basement, where he likes to sacrifice coconuts and is working on a plan to steal Terry Pratchett.

After much begging, Edmund's story "The Light of Venus" was granted first place in Golden Visions Summer 2011 writing contest, while a modest bribe secured "Neptune Rising" third place in the Winter 2012 edition. Due to a computer error, his 'weird west' fantasy "Oasis" won first place in Fantasy Faction's 2013 Anthology. He is presently working on a novel involving Australian robots.

Jon Wesick

Host of the Gelato Poetry Series, instigator of the San Diego Poetry Un-Slam, and an editor of the *San Diego Poetry Annual,* Jon Wesick has published more than sixty short stories in journals such as *The Berkeley Fiction Review, Space and Time, Zahir, Tales of the Talisman, Blazing Adventures,* and *Metal Scratches.* He has also published over two hundred fifty poems. Jon has a Ph.D. in physics and is a longtime student of Buddhism and the martial arts. One of his poems won second place in the 2007 African American Writers and Artists contest.

William R. D. Wood

William R. D. Wood lives in Virginia's Shenandoah Valley in an old farmhouse turned backwards to the road. His profound love of horror and science fiction routinely leads him to destroy the world, whether by alien artifact, zombie apocalypse, or teddy bear. http://writebrane.blogspot.com

Also Available from Martinus Publishing

MARTIN T. INGHAM'S
WEST OF THE WARLOCK SERIES:
TWO VOLUMES—ONE CAPTIVATING SAGA

A dwarven gunslinger, a warlock sheriff, an independent elvish widow, and a scandalous elvish barkeeper, along with a whole host of Wild West characters set the stage for thrilling Fantasy Western adventures.

Available in both Print & Kindle formats.

www.ingramcontent.com/pod-product-compliance
Lightning Source LLC
Chambersburg PA
CBHW072215170626
46813CB00003B/942